BEYOND
THE GATE

BEYOND
THE GATE

DANIEL T. ADAMS

*To: Ray
Thank you for redemption
sharing stories of
with the world.
Enjoy your journey...
... Beyond The Gate!*

ISBN: 1466357126
ISBN-13: 978-1466357129

1
Clyde

I awoke with a startle and a cold sweat as the red digits from my alarm clock cast a foreboding reminder of the early hour. The witching hour, as some refer to it. I overlooked however, the fact of the time…*three forty-seven AM*…and rather focused on the *color* of the numeric display; the color that emitted a slight glow over my nightstand and its contents. It was the color of my anger – the hue of hysteria – and with the night's dream still freshly lingering in my mind, it was the color (not the time) that triggered my rage.

It was red. *Always RED!*

It had been over a year since the accident and yet any reminder of my life and the success that had been ripped away from me because of that fateful day, still brought the emotions swelling inside of me like a pack of wolves. The potency of my anger remained, and as the cold morning air sequestered its presence in my bedroom with a slight chill, the *RED* took the foreground of my mind. I suddenly hated the alarm clock. I despised it with its red digital face that jeered at me in the darkness of the room.

Make it stop, my eyes cried out! *Make it stop laughing at me!*

Without a second thought, as the *RED* turned dark – turned *BLACK* almost – I snatched up the clock and hurled it across the room. A loud CRACK rang out in the stillness of that October morning, killing the clock with its incredulous *RED* eyes.

From somewhere in the mess of sheets and blankets where he lay every night down by my feet, I could see my dog's head jump up with a

"I'm sure it *has* been around the block a time or two. But it's new for *me*. I bought it in a yard sale recently." I slid the money and the check even closer towards the elderly woman and added, "Keep the change."

"Thank you, ma'am."

Judi flashed one of her Taker-like smiles at me and scooped the money into the pouch of her apron. After all, she only cared about getting her money; the talk about the book was probably nothing more than idle chatter.

"I've read that one you know," Judi stated. "It scared the wits out of me. Make sure you read it with plenty of daylight and a strong *man-friend* of yours close by."

The laughter that I heard rising from my mouth in response to her comment was the laugh of a Taker. I had learned how to emulate their way of life although I despised it – how to play in their world so-to-speak – and so melding myself into Judi's diner conversation was not a difficult task by any means.

"You know, rumor has it that he lives up there in Bridgeton somewhere. He's supposedly a local boy although I aint ever seen hide nor hair of him."

"Who? The author?" I asked.

The nicotine-stained teeth and rancid breath of the old lady had managed to grab my attention, although her information was not news to me in the slightest. Knowing that Clyde had left Florida and moved back to his hometown of Bridgeton was like saying that snow was cold. It was so plainly obvious that I found the old waitress' comment to be insulting. What I didn't know however – the information that I had been trying to dig up for the last few days – was *where* in Bridgeton he had settled down in. Bridgeton was not a large town when it came to population, but the land was wide and the mountains steep, therefore making it difficult for me to find good old Clyde on my own. What I needed was some helpful information – a finger to point me in the right direction. As it turned out, I had needed the help of a cold-blooded Taker.

"Waiting tables in this dive might not be all glitz and glamour, but it sure does come in handy if one wants to keep up in the local gossip wheels. For instance, about three weeks ago, I overheard a couple of suits in here talking about some high-and-mighty writer fellow who decided to move into some house that was supposed to be off limits. The land was said to have been cursed or something. I can't remember now. All I know is that the people of Bridgeton, and even here in Canyon Pulse, were not too particularly keen with his decision to move in to that property."

"And that was him? Clyde Baker?" I asked, hoping to get the old biddy to spill it all.

"I'd bet my bottom dollar on it."

Judi turned around to face the man who was still pretending to read the morning paper, the pitcher of ice water in her hand sloshing about as she moved. "What do you think there, Pete? That writer fellow in Bridgeton, do you know if his name is Clyde Baker?"

Pete lowered the paper and looked first at me, then up to Judi. He was dressed in a pale green button-up shirt with the kind of brown tie that looked as if it had been purchased from a nineteen-eighties catalogue. The hair on his head was cut short and running that inevitable race against time, receding back down his scalp. His face was bulky and his tired eyes stared at us through golden-rimmed glasses. There was a slight crumb of jellied-toast clung to the corner of his mouth, but I didn't bother myself to tell him. If we had been sitting in a diner in New York City, I would have said that he looked like a helpless blue-collar worker, but in a place like Canyon Pulse or Bridgeton, Pete was donning the look of the elite.

"Are you running your mouth again, Judi? Since when is gabbing the gums part of your job description?"

The old woman placed her free hand on her hip and riled up some of her certified, New York attitude.

"About the same time that getting booted out of my restaurant became part of yours. I'm not one of your employees at the Chamber of Commerce, so I don't plan on being sassed by you. Sound fair enough?"

Judi cracked a small grin and hovered towards Pete's table with the pitcher of water in hand. The middle-aged man ignored the vocal waitress for the most part and continued to stare me down with a perverse glaze of calculating discernment. There was something about his dark eyes that I didn't like; something that made me want to jab the butter knife into the balding man's throat.

"Any more water, sugar?" Judi asked of Pete.

"Just another cup of Joe should be all. And none of that decaf crap you tried to serve me last week. I've got a headache worth of work today, so I'm gonna need the real deal."

"No, the house is fine. My small corner of utopia." But then I paused for a moment, wondering how much I should actually explain to Slater, if anything at all. Say too much and my friendly agent in the South gives an ear full to the local Sheriff. Say too little and he reads the lie between the lines like one of my stories.

"Is it the dream?" he asked. "Is it still keeping you up at night? It is, isn't it?"

I cringed at the thought, knowing full well the dream that he was talking about; the nightmare that had plagued my mind almost every night since the accident. I had told Slater about the dream early on in my recovery, and how that each reoccurrence was a continual opportunity for me to relive that night of the accident. That much he knew. However, there were *some* facts about that September night one year ago that I hadn't divulged to anyone, and probably never would. Why should I? All thirty years of my life had been shrouded with cover-ups and secrets. What did it hurt to add a few more to the list?

"Right you are," I agreed. Lying. The dream was the scapegoat I had needed in order to avoid talking about the old man that Spock and I had seen out on the property. "But the dream will pass soon enough, Slater. Of that, I have no doubts."

"Do you ever get a glimpse of him in your dream? The driver of that car?"

"No," I said plainly.

"Maybe that's why you're still having that dream then. Even though you don't remember seeing the driver's face, you might have stored it away in your mind and your subconscious is trying to pull it out of you by making you relive that night over-and-over again. It might be your mind's way of looking for closure on the accident."

Under normal circumstances, I would have thought that Slater had a point. But the truth was: I *had* seen the face of the driver who had run me down that night. Moreover, I knew the driver personally, I just didn't think that naming the assailant would bear weight on anything.

"Perhaps. But it doesn't really matter though, does it? The car already did it's damage, what good would it do to rehash any of the details? Why don't we just drop it."

"Why don't I put a call into Dr. Sedgewick – get him to fill another of those prescriptions for you?"

24

"Not needed, Slater." But he didn't hear me.

"He can have it ready for you at that Rite Aid in town in about twenty minutes. I'm sure Karla wouldn't mind making an extra run out your way later on." His kindness was admirable, but it still couldn't subdue the growing anger that was swimming around in my head.

"I'm fine. Really. Like I said, it will pass in it's time. A season for everything, right?"

There was a brief pause on the other end of the line – Slater's way of accepting defeat. I took that moment to rub away the pain hatching just below my temples. The RED was always accompanied by pain; just another reason for me to despise it.

"Is there anything I *can* do for you? Anything at all?" he asked, his words searching for some kind of silver lining the way one might seek out a light switch in a dark, unfamiliar room. And that is exactly what I had become since the accident. Unfamiliar. Not just to Slater, but to myself as well. Slater had tried to keep me near – in Florida – but he had lost that battle. He had tried to keep me writing. Strike two. Now, his words seemed to suggest that he was just trying to keep *me*. Keep me afloat. Keep me happy. Keep me *alive,* perhaps?

"I've got everything I need Slater, thank you. Spock and I will live to see another day. But you might want to let me know why it is you're *really* calling this morning. The pleasantries are fine and all, but don't you think we've passed all that by now?"

Another brief pause arose from his end of the line. Then he spoke up, saying: "You might call them pleasantries Clyde, but I call them necessities – preparations for a soon-to-come famine you might say."

"I don't follow."

"Of course you don't Clyde. How would you? You don't dance in the circles any longer. You don't even acknowledge that there's a dance to be danced. And I get it. I *really* do, and not just because it's my job either. I genuinely get it, my friend. I'm on the hook and you've got the reel. You know what I'm saying?"

"A fishing analogy? Now that's a shock coming from a Florida boy." The sarcasm was blatant, but it always was whenever the RED was gaining strength. I didn't want to lash out at Slater but...but he was causing this, wasn't he?

"You were a Florida boy yourself not so long ago don't forget," he replied. "And also a damn fine writer if I may add. I know you don't want to hear that Clyde but I've gotta say it, friendship be damned."

Slater was still speaking as the fissure of anger in my head erupted, consuming me in a sea of RED. I was unable to even comprehend his final thoughts, nor control myself as his words seemed to take the form of a hammer that was now pounding at my skull. *Whack. Whack! WHACK!*

"You call this a friendship?" I hollered, the sound of my voice penetrating the morning silence. "If this was any kind of a friendship you would have known when to shut your mouth! Why do you always have to bring up the past? You just can't let it go, can you? You have to keep pushing the issue on me like a snake. That's what you are Slater," I spoke his name with an extra *hiss* to emphasize my point, "you're a snake just like the rest of them! Do you honestly think you can call me with a two-cent smile and some Howdy Doody banter about my condition and try to sell that to me as concern?"

As I spoke, I could feel my control ebbing away from my grasp and washing into the oblivion that I called the RED. Slater remained silent (either that, or he had disconnected the call, which was my hope) while Spock stared in bewilderment as the swell of emotions in the room awoke him from his nap.

"You have no concern for me! Only for yourself and for those dollar-grubbing publishers!"

"Now just you hold on one second there, Mr. Baker! What gives you the right to judge my intentions all high-and-mighty like? Have I not taken care of every one of your last complaints and concerns, making sure that you not only got settled in, but that you would not have to worry about a thing? And not to mention when you went and pissed away all the people in your life that gave a damn about you – your fans especially – how I overlooked all the crap that you were slinging – and still are! And..."

But then Slater paused, using that moment to take a deep breath. Whether it was for his benefit or mine, I was not sure. When he spoke again, the defensive aggression had surprisingly left his heavy, Southern drawl and had been replaced with a searching, almost pleading tone. The change had helped to stifle my anger, but not enough.

"And who do you think is going toe-to-toe with the publishers on a daily basis for you, Clyde?"

Spock engaged my eyes with his in that instant as if...(no, that was crazy to believe or even think, but yet the idea lingered in my head)...as if Spock had heard the words I had been thinking and moreover, that he had *felt* the RED cloak my anger had wrapped them in. It was a nonsensical thought, something that I might have written about in one of my old...

I allowed that thought to trail away as well, into the RED abyss that somehow was receding while my eyes remained locked with my dog's.

I had felt the urge to lash out at Slater again, with hopes to sever the relationship once and for all, but only managed a few small words with a flat and calmer delivery than before. "But it's always business, isn't it?"

"Well, it is the all mighty dollar that makes the world go round, sadly enough. But who says that you can't mix business with pleasure?"

With my eyes still transfixed upon those of my blonde friend who remained as still as the cold, morning air that was creeping into the house, I replied, "I wish it were that easy. But let's face it, if you didn't need me to write, would you still be calling?"

For a moment I was taken back by how flat and almost lifeless my voice sounded. The anger was gone for the time being; burned out like a fire only to leave a slight depression as its ashy residue. And if I could hear it, I was certain that both Slater and Spock could as well.

"Why don't we just take things one day at a time," he said, ignoring my question in the blatant side-stepping fashion that had made him such a great agent for me in the past. But in that moment, I didn't care that he was now using that method against me. "Here's what we'll do, Clyde. As far as the writing goes, I'll put a pin in that for the time being. The publishers will fight and protest something fierce, but they're just gonna have to understand that if they want that promised third book from Clyde Baker, they're just gonna have to give you the time you need to recover. They haven't started clamoring on about a breach of contract yet, but that's because they know as well as we do that all I have to do is put one call in to my press contacts and have a humanitarian hay day against them. They don't need that coal hanging over their heads, so we should have as much time as you need. So we'll just hold that as our trump card for the time being."

I knew that what he was saying was true, but only to an extent. There was going to be a day when the publishers would require me to live up to the three-book deal I had signed on for. The day was closer than Slater was letting on to, but I didn't bother correcting him.

"In the meantime, you just get yourself settled in and rest up. We'll deal with everything else when you're good and ready."

I rubbed at my head again with my free hand. Although the anger had dulled, the headache it left was still as lively as ever.

"I'd better get tending to some things around the office here, so I'll let you go." Slater said without allowing time for a response. "And one other thing, Clyde. If you have any more of those strange nights as you call them – anything at all that's gonna keep you from resting up, you let me know right away. Okay?"

I was ready to tell him that I would be fine, that the strange nights were done and over with. But as I stared even deeper into Spock's brown eyes, a slight tint of blue starting to glaze over them as it had the night before, I suddenly knew that the strange nights were about to get even stranger.

* * * * * * * *

After ending the phone call with Slater, the desire to do anything but lay down – anything at all – had completely and utterly rendered pointless in my mind.

I wheeled my chair over to the couch and, because I had forgotten my cane in the bedroom, transferred myself onto the sofa with a great surge of pain in both my legs and lower back. I plopped down like an over-stuffed duffel bag full of wet laundry; the increasing weight of my body forcing out the odor of old sweat from the cushions, most likely woven into the fabric during my year-long recovery process. And it was a process that would span well beyond a year at that, although I would soon discover that the healing to take place would be far greater than that of what had already occurred.

I looked up at the clock that hung over the fireplace and loathed it's very face. Ever since the accident I had come to refer to that blasted time-telling contraption as a *death meter*. I had once used the clock to live by, work by, and even to play by, but now I used it to die by. Each fractional movement of the clock's hands no longer kept me in the flowing stream of life and life's endless possibilities, but rather chipped away at the remainder of my forlorn existence. The irony of it all, I had come to realize after breaking the original clock during one of my bouts with the RED, was that although a clock counts time forward with the rotation of each gear and cog, it is simply sucking dry the batteries within it, counting *them* down to their demise. So as I looked upon the face of the clock and saw that it was just after nine o'clock in the morning, I realized that I was nothing more than time's battery. I was having my life siphoned out of me by the very gears and cogs of living that were trying to propel me forward.

With the gray light of that October morning seeping into the family room where Spock and I lay, I desired to do nothing more than sleep. Sleeping the day away seemed like a good idea to me at the time. And if I so chose to sleep a week away as well (And why not? What else was there to do?), then perhaps I would do just that. Maybe even longer. After all, I did have quite a few of my Oxycontin tablets left. It wouldn't be hard to crush up a handful of them and down it all with a bottle of ice-cold Poland Springs from the fridge. I had written about a similar scenario in one of my books – had it been in *The Town Kids* or *A Day Like This*; I couldn't recall – so I wasn't apt to be a stranger to the ritual. Besides, it would be sure to grant me a rest that would end my pain once and for all – or so I thought at the time.

But that was when my eyes moved on from the clock and rested upon my yellow lab who was still lying peacefully next to the fire. He was no longer resting with his belly to the heat. Instead, having flipped over onto his opposite side, his back with all of its short, blonde hair was now receiving the warming comfort from the flames. *Toasting both sides of the bread*, I thought. But it was not my final thought, before drifting off into the land of dreams; or in my case since the accident, the land of pain and hauntings.

My second to last thought was how much weight poor Spock had put on in the last year. I guess that was his burden to bear for practically having an invalid as a master. I hated what I had become, or what the supposed loving God of my childhood beliefs had *allowed* me to become, but Spock had been by my side through it all – including the RED. His affection and devotion was admirable to say the least. He had been down right loving, and to watch him suffer on my behalf was well-beyond by my agent to tend to things around the house as well as to make sure that the pantry and cupboards were freshly stocked. And now I feared that I was going to need her to help me save Spock.

Karla remained quiet in the corner, watching me as I repositioned myself back onto the couch with a constant grimace. The thought of asking her for help made THE RED swells within me more potent than that of the pain I was in. Spock was my only concern though, and my wheelchair was going to do nothing but slow me down from helping him.

"I need my cane. Now! It's in the bedroom!"

"Maybe you should just take a moment to rest," Karla reluctantly offered. Her lack of compliance erupted the tumult of my mind. My brow furrowed as I cast an exasperated glare in her direction.

"I don't need a damn babysitter! Just get the cane! Spock is in trouble and he needs me! He needs me now!"

I wasn't able to blockade the emotions any longer and so they began to seep through in streams of tears. My face was hot with anger and red with pain, and although I despised myself for breaking down in front of Karla, I could hold back no longer.

"He needs me to help him!" I declared as the images of THE FACELESS ONE striking the fatal blow to my dog kept playing in my mind like some kind of hellish, horror movie. "Spock is in danger and you're not helping me! Why won't you help me?"

With a surge of helplessness chocking at my ability to reason like weeds to a flower, I had failed to notice that the back door had been left open and that my dog had just trotted back inside.

Spock gazed around the room with his playful, brown eyes, digesting the scene in the family room with as much confusion as Karla. But the difference was that when he came over to console me, I welcomed him with a thankful and tearful embrace that filled my heart with an unspeakable joy. He returned the loving warmth with a swing in his tail and a gentle lick on my nose.

As always, the sight of Spock's brown eyes – although a hint of blue shone through – sent the rage ebbing back into my mind's pool of forgetfulness. Karla however watched on with concern and an ounce of fright.

* * * * * * * *

"What were you doing here in the first place?" The question was straight forward and abrasive, but it was an answer I needed to know. Karla at least owed me that much.

The post-dream ordeal was over with now that Spock's safety had been incurred, but the foolishness of my over-reaction still hung melodramatically in the air. How was I supposed to have known where the dream world ended and the real world began? They had both felt genuine enough; perhaps one intertwining with the other like some sort of surreal tapestry? Besides, ever since my accident, the line between reality and fiction had become as blurry as the bottom row of an eye chart. I was beginning to think that even the Walking Man had been nothing more than an illusion as well. *Who was to know anymore?*

Karla was still standing near the foyer, although the anxiety of wanting to bolt out the front door had faded from her face. Instead, she had the look of a nervous student who had to stand before the principal and give an account for her conduct. It was evident in the way she fidgeted while she spoke.

"I received a call from your agent, Mr. Slater earlier this morning. He said that he was worried about you and that it would give him peace of mind to know you were okay. He feels that the transition might have been..." She hesitated, choosing her words as carefully as a man in a minefield. I prodded her on with my stare. "He just said that he thought the transition might have been too much, too soon. That's all."

I rolled my eyes at the thought, suddenly thankful that I had not said anything to Slater about the Walking Man.

Spock nestled his head into my thigh. I tickled him on the back of his neck, staying silent as Karla spoke. Although most of the dream's details were already fading from my mind, there was still an unease churning through my body like a low voltage current.

"So at his request, I stopped by to check in. I tried knocking, but after not getting any response, I was just ready to leave. That was when I heard you screaming and shouting though, as if you were in a fight for your life. I'm not gonna lie, it freaked me out a

The large woman released another rumbling of hot breath and then answered, "We don't know for sure. But all we do know is that as long as the house is being lived in, strange things start happening. People turn up dead, or missing, or both. So we've just been insisting that house stay empty."

"Empty?" Karla asked.

"Yes, ma'am. As vacant as a virgin; pardon the expression. It's just better for the town that way."

Karla's eyes turned up to me. I shook my head.

"I'm sorry, but, I've been there almost a month now and nobody has died or up and disappeared, now have they?" I was about to turn away and end the conversation abruptly, but a sudden image flashed through my mind. It was an image of the Walking Man strolling out on the property in the early, foggy hours. I could see the details of his straw hat and the tree branch that he used as a walking stick. His face however remained a mystery because he had never turned and looked in my direction. Was he somehow a part of the nonsense that Edna was speaking of?

Don't be stupid, Clyde.

"You just wait and see, son. You'll find out soon enough, you and this pretty girl of yours."

Spock began to whimper and moan, impatiently trying to move down the sidewalk even against the restraint from the leash. All three of us looked down at my dog as he tried pulling forward.

"He might have to go to the bathroom, Karla. Would you mind walking him over there just in case?"

Karla was reluctant at first, as I knew she would be. She wanted to hear more about the house and the supposed cursed land that it sat on, but orders were still orders, and so she smiled, thanked Edna, and took Spock down the sidewalk to an empty patch of grass.

"About the property," I said after making sure that Karla was far enough away from earshot, "I know that there's hundreds of acres out behind my house, but are there any other homes out that way? Any reason for people to be out on the property?"

Edna was a bit stunned by the question.

"Homes? What on earth are you talking about?"

"It's nothing. I was just wondering." I said, suddenly sorry for having asked anything at all. In the distance, I could hear Spock begin a low series of growls, but I regrettably ignored it.

"Why? Did you see something? It's that house. I'm telling you..."

"I didn't see anything," I interrupted. "There's just a lot of land out there and seeing as to my condition, I'm not able to really explore any of it. So I was just wondering what was out there. That's all."

Edna eyed me carefully. She wasn't buying into what I was saying because her mind was too preoccupied with the nonsensical idea of the land being cursed. But before she could carry on with her persistent interrogation, Karla's screaming voice pierced the calm of the morning.

"Spock! Come back!"

I turned around only to see Karla standing in the patch of grass I had sent her to with a look of horror playing across her petite face. She was screaming and panicked, and it was evident as to why. Spock had broken free of her grasp and was running across the street in a blind fury. His blue leash flopped behind him like an untied shoelace, but slowed him down none.

My eyes widened at the sight of a farming truck as it sped around the bend in the road, heading straight towards my helpless dog. Karla was screaming for Spock to return, but with no luck. I tried to call him back to us as well, but the words were momentarily frozen in my throat as I watched the truck nearing my dog.

A sudden flashback of that night in Florida coursed through my mind. I could once again see the headlights of Mindy's car holding me in place. I could feel the drenching rain as it poked at my face. I could see the haunting eyes of Mindy as she screamed in torment while behind the wheel.

The sudden blare of the truck's car horn snapped me out of the past and hurled me back into the danger of the present. Spock was oblivious to the oncoming truck, dashing forward towards Sal's Pizzeria without a concern for anything else. Karla was still screaming, standing at the curb of the road watching the scene unfold before her.

The sound of screeching tires sliced through my ears as the truck swerved to its right in attempt to avoid barreling into Spock. Karla shrieked as the truck whirred past Spock's hind legs, missing them by mere inches. A cloud of dust and gravel kicked into the air and shrouded the entire moment with horror. Spock darted across the street in the last possible moment as the rear tires finally hugged the pavement and straightened out. The driver once again laid on the horn as it sped forward through town and out of sight.

With the truck gone, Karla immediately leapt into the street and began to chase down my dog. Her screams for him to stop were useless as Spock sprinted down the sidewalk, passed the Post Office, and towards the dumpster behind the pizzeria. My legs finally kicked into gear, propelling me into the chase regardless of the pain.

The sounds of the near collision with the truck had begun pulling the local shop owners and patrons out onto the sidewalk to see the confusion that had taken place. Karla and I were both still screaming. The local townspeople – including Edna – were cursing at us for not having control over my dog. I ignored the insults and pursued Spock although he was nearly one hundred yards ahead of me.

Before my barking, blonde friend could round the corner of the pizzeria, one of the cooks – who had been watching the scenario unfold – grabbed Spock's dancing leash. He dug his heel into the ground and tugged back on Spock's collar.

Karla shrieked with delight as she neared the courageous pizza cook. My unraveled heart turned right side up as Spock's joyride through town ended. Karla regained control of the leash from the strong, Italian man while showering him with praises of gratitude. The cook however did not seem too pleased with the event that had transpired.

"What the hell do you think you're doing letting your dog run wild like that?"

"I apologize," I said as I finally caught up with Karla. Although Spock's chase of the unknown had ended, his eyes were still dead set on the dumpster next to the pizza joint. A series of consistent BARKS and low-pitched WOOFS flowed from my dog as if he were at home hunting the rabbit that lived out back in the woodpile.

"I'm terribly sorry. I don't know what got into him." I apologized again. "Spock! Stop!" I took over the leash from Karla and yanked back with a solid tug. The first jolt from the leash did nothing. The second, quieted him down.

"Get him the hell out of here before he causes someone to get hurt! Is it not enough for you to curse this town by moving into that damn house? Now you've gotta let this mut run free?"

The frustrated pizza cook with the angry eyes, whispered some kind of Italian curse under his breath and then marched back inside his establishment.

I turned around and watched as the growing crowd on the sidewalks began to whisper and murmur amongst themselves. Most of their faces shot scolding looks in my direction; their eyes were piercing me like daggers from hell. Despite the distance between us, I could still feel their anger boiling over like a pot of water. It was a feeling I had become accustom to in my life, and it made THE RED begin to flare up in my mind.

Turning to Karla, I could see the tears forming in her eyes. She continued her non-stop apologies and explanations despite the shell-shocked demeanor that I bore.

"Coming down here was a big mistake," I said as I yanked again on Spock's leash. With little fight, Spock followed the pull of his harness as I hobbled towards the municipal parking lot.

"Clyde I'm so sorry," she said through a pleading tone. "I don't know how he got loose. One moment he was sniffing around and calm, and then next, he takes off running. I couldn't stop him."

Despite the anger that was bubbling within me, I knew full well that I couldn't put the blame on Karla – even if I wanted to. Maybe she had made a mistake by not watching Spock more carefully, but then again, she had defended my honor just a few minutes prior. I didn't want to be so forgiving – forgiveness is for the weak, that much I learned from my Shadow Life – but in that frantic moment as my nerves came down and my sense of thought returned, I realized one amazing fact. For a year, Spock had been the only person in my life who had been able to help control the balance of THE RED within me. But somehow – for whatever reason that even I couldn't see – Karla possessed the exact same ability. Looking into her tear-stained eyes managed to help ease the frenzying attitude within. One glance at the young – and yes, attractive – woman, helped to calm the raging storm in my mind.

10
Mindy

That was close. *Too close*.

It was one thing for Clyde to have seen me across the street. I had hoped for *that*. But it was not time for us to reunite again. It wouldn't have been right. Not like that. It was way too soon and yet that stupid dog of his almost ruined everything.

After making my appearance, I quickly ducked behind the far wall of the Post Office and slunk into the morning shadows. The look on Clyde's face when we locked eyes in that instant was surreal. It had been everything I had hoped for, and beyond. The intoxication of the moment was so inviting that I almost lost control of myself. I had to fight the urge to run towards him, battling my will against the will of time. The timing had to be right; it had to be perfect. As they say, time heals all wounds. So before any restoration could take place, I needed to reassure myself that Clyde's wounds were indeed healed. I had to know that he was ready for me again. Ready for us.

I waited for Clyde to turn his back to me before quickly shuffling into the back lot of the old antique shop. From there I crossed over one of the few side streets in town and into the municipal parking area. The rush of adrenaline that pulsed through my veins was rousing to say the least – better than any wine or drug could have made me feel. And I had enjoyed my fair share of the latter. But nothing could have lowered me from the high that I was experiencing as I rounded the corner of the local pizza joint – nothing except for the barking of that stupid dog of his.

I was in perfect position to watch Clyde and his new bimbo without being seen as they made their way west. Unfortunately, his blonde-haired mutt almost ruined everything. I was partially hidden behind the far corner of the building where the patio fence and the back wall formed a tight, right angle. I had been watching Clyde – studying his every movement as he spoke with the fat grandma from the deli – but never expected Spock to pinpoint my whereabouts.

Upon seeing the three of them heading in my direction, I jumped back around the far wall and ducked behind the dumpster out back of the pizzeria. That dog of his was going to ruin everything. It was not supposed to go down this way. We weren't supposed to meet like this.

I reached my hand into my purse and drew out the knife that had just claimed the lives of two Takers from Canyon Pulse – Pete and his nagging wife Tabitha. Spock was going to get in the way and I was ready to shut him up.

Death to the Takers.

I readied myself for the initial attack. It was going to have to be quick and silent, but the moment never came. Spock's barking grew louder and closer, but eventually died down at Clyde's command.

Clyde was nearby! I could hear his voice. I could almost see him even from behind the wall – from behind the dumpster. But nobody came any closer. There was a brief moment of dialogue between Clyde, his tramp of a girlfriend, and some unknown Italian voice and then everything fell silent. A moment later, they were gone completely.

As I watched the three of them pull out of the municipal parking lot in that girl's white Ford Escort, I had to control the anger that was feeding on my mind.

"You'll forget all about her when you get home, Clyde." The thought came quickly, helping to reassure my troubled heart that had been longing for this very moment. I had made sure to leave my first message for him before following them into town. He would get home, and know for certain that I was back and ready for our lives to continue where we had left off.

"*We'll be together again, Clyde – we were always meant to be together.*" The thought was like liquid fire burning through my very core. "*It was designed that way from the beginning, and I won't let anything get in the way of that again. Not even your dog.*"

12
Mindy

After having watched Clyde's new bimbo pick up the mail for him, I knew it was just a matter of time before he would receive the first of the messages I intended to send. If all went well – if the Takers of the world hadn't buried their thievish hooks too deep into Clyde's psyche – than he would accept my message with the same joy as with which I wrote it. But one thing I learned at a very young age thanks to my heartless (thank God she's dead) mother, is that life is a series of give-and-takes: Life *gives* you piss, and you have to *take* it. So I would not be shocked if Clyde's initial response to my letter was somber and standoffish. In part, I expected it.

I sat parked in Pete's Subaru just half-a-mile away from the Sugar Hill Farms Estate. The distance put enough space in between the house and myself, allowing me to keep an eye on Clyde without being spotted. From the safety of the car, I was able to observe their comings and goings – especially that blonde, shorthaired hussy that he had been making time with. Regardless, I was in place to ensure the delivery of the message, and he had in fact received it.

Now I just had to wait.

As the afternoon ticked away, I felt my mind beginning to wander. I had waited a year to once again make contact with Clyde – to allow him every chance to right the wrongs he had inflicted upon me – but instead I found myself sitting in a cluttered and trash-filled Subaru, down the road from some monstrosity of a house, waiting for some stupid sign that the message had left its mark! The plan could be unraveling before my very eyes but I would never know it. The unknown was driving me mad! I had to get closer. If I had any hopes of my plan melding into bronzed perfection, I was going to have to get closer. It was imperative.

"What would you do, daddy?" I whispered aloud into the quiet of the car. I had loved my father. I was special to him; daddy's little girl. But he didn't answer me. He never did, not since the day that his love was stripped away from me by my mother – the biggest Taker I ever knew. The Queen of the Damned.

I did not expect a response from father, although a shudder of eerie familiarity crawled down my neck, causing gooseflesh to unfold over my body like a bed sheet. Adrenaline began to spill into my veins like a good drug. My heart quickened its step. Although Clyde was within the walls of his home, most likely reveling over the letter I had left for him, I found myself focusing more on the barn across from the house rather then the house itself. Madness unlike any other pricked at my vision with red-hot pokers as my eyes honed in on the old horse barn. I suddenly loved and hated the structure, finding the aura of it's form electrifying yet stained with the repugnant stench of THE RED. And suddenly, from the depths of my soul, I could hear the tiniest fraction of a voice. It was raspy and high-pitched, like something out of a movie or a video game, but the sound was so soft that I could not make out the words. Regardless, I submitted to the unknown voice – to the depravity that was calling for me – and suddenly the answer to my problems became clear: I had to get rid of the Subaru.

Not only was the black vehicle stolen, but the owner was a dead man and so was his fat, deceased wife. The cops would be looking for it, which meant that they would be looking for me. Eventually. I had to find a place to hide it, to keep it safe, and I knew just the place. The perfect location. In order to hide the stolen vehicle away beneath the radar of Clyde or that pestering dog of his, it would require the cover of night.

"I'll have to come back later," I reminded myself.

It was the last weekend of October and I knew that the sun would be setting in a few hours. If I could find a place until then, perhaps under the cover of the mountains, then I would be able to come back and stash the car in a place where no one would ever look – not even Clyde.

I turned over the Subaru's ignition and pulled onto the road, heading west. I would hide up in the mountains until dark. Then I time into a letter that was unsigned and that had arrived in an envelope containing no return address. He would most likely laugh it off seeing as though Mindy had been reported dead for almost a year now. So I didn't bother wasting my time.

Sheriff Eckhart was still meandering about on the other side of the fence line where I had once again seen the old man. Eckhart held his Maglite in hand while his eyes followed the beam of light. I had a feeling that his investigation was going to be swift and pointless – just another reason for Eckhart to dislike me, that was if he hadn't forgotten who I was. After all, he was getting up there in years (and by the looks of how tight his red, flannel shirt was on him, he seemed to be getting up there in the weight department as well). But the Sheriff and I had a history together – as well as everyone else in town that knew I was the spawn of a murdering, suicidal woman. So the likelihood that Sheriff Eckhart had forgotten me was slim.

After a brief minute of scoping things out, although he never traveled more than ten yards beyond the fence line, Eckhart waived me over to where he was standing. His back was turned to me and he was staring blankly into the fog that had engulfed the miles of outstretched acreage. As I approached him, trying to stay warm in the tattered remnants of my blue, plaid robe, I could immediately notice the look of impatience that was playing across his face.

"So he went that-a-way?" Eckhart asked through a tightly clenched toothpick hanging from one side of his mouth. The beam from the flashlight pointed straight ahead until it finally vanished into the thick blanket of fog. The tone in his voice suggested that the question was asked with frustration more so than with concern.

"Yeah," I replied. "I even tried calling out to that old man too, but he must not have heard me."

"So there's no doubt about it? He was definitely walking out onto the property rather than just parallel with the property line?"

My level of frustration was already peaked because it had taken the Sheriff almost a full hour to arrive after I had placed the call. But his ramble of questions was getting to be too much.

"I told you twice already. *Yes!* And it was the same tonight as it was last night. The same guy. The same path."

Eckhart ignored my petulance and asked: "How can you be sure it was the same person? With a fog like this, the eyes can be as trustworthy as a two dollar whore."

"Well I don't know Sheriff," I said, not caring if my frustration was over-the-top. "How many old men wearing overalls, a cowboy hat, and carrying a tree branch as a walking stick do you know of that like to trespass at four in the morning?"

Eckhart stared me down. Typically, a look of contempt like the one he was displaying would not have bothered me, but there was something about the way his gray eyes were recessed into his tanned, hefty face that gave him more than just an authoritative appearance. When he was out of uniform, like he was on that chilly morning, he could easily be mistaken for the dangerous, trucker type. He had a full head of white hair that was pulled back into a ponytail with a thick goatee to match. His arms were massive, as if he had stuffed his shirtsleeves with bowling balls, and were inked up from his days as an adolescent. Needless to say, he was the kind of man that most people would avoid, even on a crowded street, and yet I was trying to piss him off because frankly speaking, I thought him to be nothing more than a judgmental jerk.

"All I'm saying is that there could have been more than one persons that you saw. Aint that something to consider?"

I shook my head. "Not particularly, no. I don't care if there was one old man or a herd of them. The point is that *somebody* is out walking where they don't belong."

The overweight Sheriff grunted under his breath, flicked his gnawed-at toothpick into the surrounding brush, and began his retreat towards the patrol car.

"Unfortunately, there's not much we can do Mr. Baker." He spoke my name with contempt, letting the words rumble passed his meaty jowls.

"There might have been something you could have done Sheriff, if you had gotten here when I called an hour ago! I could've hobbled after the man and been more productive!"

Eckhart paused before entering his vehicle, resting his hands upon the roof of the car. The flashing patrol lights helped to over exaggerate the frustration in his eyes. I apparently had struck the nerve I was hoping to.

"You Hollywood-types are all the same. You print a couple of stories, make a few easy bucks, and then think you can walk on water." Leaving the driver side door ajar, Eckhart stepped towards me like a hungry and injured coyote. "I checked out what I could, and there's nothing. You gave me no description to work from other than some overalls and a hat, which for the most part is the standard attire in a farming community like Bridgeton. Or have you forgotten that already? There's no damage to the property, no signs of anyone, and to top it all off, it's almost five o'clock in the

I didn't care to hear anymore; in fact it was beyond torment because the Sheriff's accusation couldn't have been farther from the truth. No, I did not return to Bridgeton from school when I received word that my mother had committed suicide, and I had no regrets about my decision. My mother was a woman who faced many hardships in her life, the biggest of all being the man she had married, so I was understanding of the fact that she dwelled within a constant state of depression. The reason I refused to come home – the reason that made me smile ever so briefly upon receiving word of her untimely death – was because I knew the secret she had been keeping. Although I never said anything to my mother, I knew about the monstrous cover-up that she had created for my father, and he was the type of man that makes you cringe just thinking about him. I wanted nothing to do with either of my parents, and so I felt that attending her funeral and pretending to care would have been a bit over-the-top.

"Sheriff, where are you going with this?" I asked. Until that moment, Eckhart's eyes were transfixed upon the rolling fog ahead of him. But as my question touched his ears, he finally turned and gave me his attention.

"Son, I'm telling you this because there have been only three scenarios that I have had to grapple with in my time as Sheriff. Two of them were answered the day your mother spilled her own blood. But there's still one unanswered question that I need to resolve before I can comfortably and in good conscience, turn over the badge."

I watched as he turned to face the property again, as if it were both familiar and strange to him at the same time. What surprised me however, was the single finger that he used to point towards the foggy land.

"I'm just warning you Clyde, stay away from that property."

"Are you ever going to tell me what the big deal is about that land? What's out there, Sheriff? And why is everyone in this town so bent out of shape about me living here? I'm not doing any harm to anyone. So please, enlighten me. Tell me what on earth you are talking about." I exclaimed.

"What I'm talking about is a man who is in no condition whatsoever to be traveling around out there. No man, woman, or child is, if you ask me, but I'm just an old man with a bad ticker, so people don't tend to mind my opinions too often."

"Why are you telling me all of this?" I asked again. The entire conversation was grating to my nerves but the Sheriff knew something about the land that he wasn't telling me. Maybe he knows the Walking Man, I wondered, and so I repeated myself again: "What is out there?"

Echkart sucked in a deep breath of the cool morning air, then released it slowly.

"What I know is that the property out there can look inviting enough, but after...well, after a certain point, it can twist and turn and drop out from underneath you without a moment's notice. It can break your every bone and cut you up like a visit to a demented barber. That's what I *do* know."

"And what is it that you *don't* know?" I asked. "What is your opinion on all of it?"

"I'm not paid to make opinions, Mr. Baker," he said as he turned over the ignition of the patrol car. "But I can tell you this: I cannot think of one, solitary soul in this town who would be caught dead on that property there – not one who knows the history of this place at least. And judging by the fact that the man you've been seeing is elderly as you say, he should know more than his fair share. With that said, I'm gonna keep an eye on your place tomorrow night and see if this visitor of yours shows up again. If so, just stay inside and let me do my job. But in the name of everything that is good and holy, just stay off that property."

Without another word, Sheriff Eckhart backed down the driveway and was gone.

* * * * * * * *

It took only twenty minutes to replace my current wardrobe with something that was fresh and free of week-old sweat odors. Only five of those minutes however, were spent changing clothes and cleaning up. The other fifteen were spent trying to find the right thing to wear for such a cryptic occasion.

I had finally settled upon a pair of faded blue jeans, a black tee shirt and a khaki blazer. I quickly ran a brush through my tangled hair after opting not to wear a hat, and then returned to Karla who was sitting on the couch in the family room with Spock nestled up against her.

As I entered the room, Karla rose to her feet and smiled like a high-schooler whose prom date had just descended a flight of stairs.

"The prodigal returns," she said humorously. "And he cleans up too."

I snickered nervously, suddenly feeling adventurous and semi-normal again.

"So what is this all about?" I asked. "Yesterday, you just said that you had something you wanted to *show* me."

"I *do* have something to show you. But I never said that I could *bring* it to you. Contraire, I must bring *you* to *it*." She flashed another playful smile. "So if you're done with the twenty questions now, the three of us should be on our way."

"Three of us? It's okay for Spock to tag along?"

With that said, she reached down and scratched Spock behind both of his ears. His tail drummed happily against the sofa cushions as she did so.

"I wouldn't have it any other way."

The Friday, October afternoon was bright but quiet, much like the mood inside the car. Karla drove. I sat nervously with thoughts of Mindy hanging over my head like a storm cloud. And Spock rode in the back with his head out the window, taking in all of the traveling scents. It was cheerful, but quiet.

The first stop was at a local deli named The Mountain Cafe. It was only three miles from my house, at the place where Route 209 branches out towards the college town of Canyon Pulse. It was an establishment that I was not familiar with, which led me to believe that it was a fairly new place; no more than ten years old. Few things had changed in Bridgeton since I had left for college – few things ever did – but time always has a way of making the familiar seem vague and distant, which is exactly how I felt on that afternoon.

"I took the liberty of having a couple of sandwiches made for us. I hope that's okay," Karla said as she pulled into the gravel-laden parking lot of the deli. I assured her it was, and then remained in the car as she bounced into the deli with a perky skip in her step. A moment later she returned with a plastic bag filled with food and drinks.

"One stop down. One to go," she said as we backed away from the sandwich shop and pulled out onto the road. We were once again heading west.

As we climbed higher up the mountain, I took note of how much of the suburban, Bridgeton life was absent from this location. The only structures we had seen since leaving the deli was the old firehouse, which was used solely for housing the extra pump truck for the Bridgeton Fire Department. Other than that, the grease-stained structure and the junkyard full of beat up vehicles that was home to Darcy's Garage, was the only other form of life.

"Have you ever been up this way before?" she asked.

"Not that I can remember, no. My family and I lived on the other side of the river, so we never came this way. There was never a need to."

The road up ahead continued to climb the steep grade, cutting sharply in the opposite direction just beyond a posted speed sign of five miles per hour.

"I've definitely never been up here before, that's for sure. I would remember something like this," I said as I tightened my grip around the head of my cane. Karla giggled as the car glided safely around the switchback.

"You haven't seen anything yet. Just wait until we get where we're going." Her comment made me wonder more than ever as to where she was taking us. But I didn't have to wait long for the answer.

When Karla finally brought the car to a stop in a small parking area just a mile after the switchback, my mouth gaped open in awe. The area we were parked in was large enough, I guessed, to accommodate parking for only four or five full sized vehicles. There was already a blue pickup truck pulled into one of

I laughed as her eyes narrowed into a playful glare. She swatted at my arm, saying: "Keep that up and you're walking home."

"If it has to be that way, I guess Spock and I will have to walk." I retorted. "It might take us a while, but we'll manage I guess."

"I didn't say Spock would have to walk, just you. *Spock's* a good boy. He'd get to ride back with me."

At the sound of his name, Spock lifted his head from it's resting position on his front paws. That too, made both of us laugh again.

"Can I ask you something?" I said. She turned to face me. "Why did you want to bring me out here? It's not that I'm not enjoying myself, because I am. It's just that...well, how did you know that I had never been up here before? For all you know, I could have made thousands of trips up this way."

Karla tucked a loose stand of hair behind her ear as a soft breeze wisped by. I could tell that my question had tapped into a source of information that she held within, and I suddenly felt that she knew more about me than I realized.

"Women's intuition?" she offered. I shook my head, letting her know that I wasn't buying into it. She shrugged and then took a moment to wipe away any crumbs from the sandwich that might have collected on her white cotton, embroidered blouse that she wore beneath a faded denim jacket.

"Well, a couple of weeks before you moved in, I got a call from your agent. He told me about your situation and asked if I would be willing to look after things for you: do the shopping and cleaning, stuff like that. I usually work as a nanny, taking care of children – mostly with disabilities and such – and occasional elderly people who can't afford hospice and whose families don't want to be burdened by their so-called loved ones. But I needed the work and he was paying cash, so it was a win-win situation. The next day I got the email with all of the particulars and decided right then that if I was going to do the job right, I had better know more about you than just your medications and favorite foods. To truly help someone, it's important to know as much about that someone as possible. You know what I mean?"

I nodded in agreement.

"So that's when I went out and bought both of your books. I'll admit, I was expecting to struggle through them, but like I said yesterday, they were amazingly well-written. So to read through both of them in a week wasn't a difficult task at all."

Spock suddenly sat up, moving into a seated position. He too stared out at the view as if the glorious landscape below enthralled him with the same peaceful relaxation that still had hold of me. I reached over and rubbed at his neck, one of his favorite tickle spots.

"And did my books render worthless in your fact-finding mission?" I asked, figuring it to be a rhetorical question. Her answer surprised me.

"Actually, it was quite the opposite."

I issued her a puzzled look and then asked, "In what way? My books were nothing more than two-bit horror plots oozing with inconsequential paranoia. You even said that yourself, remember?"

"That's what I thought too, upon first glance. But one rule that I've always tried to live my life by – and pardon the pun – is to never judge a book by it's cover."

As she said that, my thoughts immediately jumped back to Darcy's Garage and the way that the heaps of rusted metal out front made his place look like a stockpile more so than a successful business. From there, I thought next about Spock who was staring aimlessly out over Bridgeton. I knew there was more to my dog than could be seen – no surprise to me there – although I was yet to know the depth of his true character. But when my thoughts turned lastly to Karla, I found myself struggling to pinpoint what about her was true and what was simply the cover to her life's book. She was a puzzle to me, like the one sitting in pieces on my kitchen table at home, and like the fragments of my life that remained unsolved since the accident.

"I'm not following here," I admitted.

An equivocal look splayed across her otherwise confident and cheerful face, and I could tell that she was debating on how to proceed. However, when she spoke again, her voice sounded confident and sure-footed.

"Like I said, at first there was nothing that jumped off the pages at me. It wasn't until one day, as I was in the middle of reading your first book 'The Town Kids' that I began to notice a pattern. A lot of it was speculation on my part, and I could be wrong entirely, but it's my guess and I'm sticking with it." She smiled innocently before going on.

"Anyway, I was on my way into town one day but got stopped at the tracks as a train passed through. It was early to late

"That's why I suspected that you had never been up here before Clyde," she said in a hushed tone. "Because I just figured that someone who would use up almost every inch of Bridgeton in their stories, would definitely have written about a place like this. And now that I can see the look on your face, I believe I was right. It's the most beautiful view ever, isn't it?"

"Not the *most* beautiful," I said, unaware of when I had begun to stare deep into her eyes. "But close."

As if she had heard none of the implication in my words – thank God for small favors – she asked, "So you agree then? This view is a masterpiece of beauty."

"Of course," I replied. Confused.

"Then that is why I brought you up here today, Clyde. Yesterday, and through your books even, you shared with me a place – that very place down there – where you saw no hope, no love, no beauty at all. But by changing your *perspective*, you were able to see things differently. You saw it in new light. When you're down there," she said, pointing into the valley, "your fears can be overwhelming. They can overtake you because they seem so much larger than life. But from up here...well...they don't seem that big at all."

I didn't say anything. I only sat and listened as she spoke. Her words were filled with a wisdom that was both genuine and truthful. And although I knew the truth with which she spoke, it was hard to swallow, especially coming from someone who honestly, I really didn't know.

"Again, I apologize if I'm being presumptuous and nosey. You just tell me to cool it, and I will. It's just that I can see the potential that you have – the potential for using your gift of words to help better people's lives, not validate their ideas that life is nothing more than a winless maze that we wander around in until we die. That's all."

I ran a hand through my hair, hoping to seek purchase of the right words to say in response, but they never came. Thanking her was too easy and I wasn't even at all sure that I felt like showing gratitude in accepting the idea of *my* potential. I had sworn off writing ever since the accident, ignoring the third book that – although had almost been finished – was never going to go any further despite the contract I had signed. That was why I had made the movers take *that* part of my life and stow it away in the barn: manuscripts, story notes, outlines, office furniture, and all.

The only other option that I saw was to respond by telling her to leave it alone – *or else*. I could feel THE RED already brewing within me, but I didn't want to go that route either. Karla seemed like the kind of person who always looked at life through innocent eyes, seeing only the good in things (probably because her life had been free of pain and suffering, I assumed). But she had shown me nothing but kindness since we had met, and whether she was getting paid to do so or not, I simply was enjoying having her around. So allowing my anger to get the best of me was not the way to approach a response.

"It's fine," I finally said. "I don't mind."

Following Spock's lead, Karla and I turned to stare down into the valley. Her words echoed in my head as I spotted the Canyon Pulse River and the blue, steel bridge that allowed Main Street to cross from one side to the next. The river snaked in and out of trees, buildings, and homes, splitting the town into almost two perfect halves. Although it was only late October – two days before Halloween – many of the trees in the valley were almost bare, making it easier to spot landmarks that I knew.

My eyes wandered from the bridge, following the road as best they could, until they happened upon a gray-shingled roof of a white two-story building. At first, I wasn't sure if it was my barn, but through the balding trees I was able to make out the three large storm windows. Knowing that my life's work was stored just beyond those windows, I turned my gaze away from the barn and focused on the property that lay beyond instead. Besides, with images of the Walking Man still lingering in the back of my mind, I was more interested in the property than the barn itself, especially if I was ever going to find out who the old man really was (no thanks to Sheriff Eckhart).

Looking at the two hundred acres from where I sat, gave me a better appreciation for it's grand scale. The barn suddenly looked like nothing more than a single, Monopoly Hotel piece on an empty playing board. Most of the land was covered in autumn's golden trees and therefore unable to see, but I was able to pinpoint the initial walking path where I had seen the old man walking two nights in a row. It ran parallel to my backyard and then emptied into a large clearing. Just on the outskirts of that open land, before the patch of colorful trees took over, I spotted something that made me sit bolt, upright in my chair – pain and all.

"What is that?" I asked, pointing towards the property although I knew she wouldn't see what I was aiming at.

"*You didn't love me,*" she had said. "*You loved that!*" And that was when she had pointed me back into the storm; although it was not the storm she had needed me to see. Alexis had been pointing me to THE FACELESS ONE – the character I had created from my fears of scarecrows as a child. It was a creation of my mind; a monster with devilish character that I had designed for my hopeful third book. The book was to have been titled: SEVER, and I had been close to unleashing it into the literary world, but the accident in Florida had halted my work with only a few chapters left until completion. So rather than allowing THE FACELESS ONE to drive fear into the hearts of readers, he was buried in a cardboard box alongside all of my other life's work, and stored away in the top level of the barn. So why then, had Alexis accused me of loving such a creation more than her, a creation that was now haunting my dreams? Was that why she had left me for another man? And why could I not shake the feeling – as absurd as it sounded – that THE FACELESS ONE was somehow wandering about on my property, beyond the gate and that stone wall?

Absurd?

I know.

But there was just a gnawing feeling about it in my gut that I couldn't shake free of, like a fly ensnared in a spider's web. The last time I had felt so strongly about something, I had been standing in the way of an oncoming car amidst the worst hurricane ever to hit Florida, knowing that the driver would end up destroying her life – or worse, somebody else's – if she didn't receive some much needed help. I could have just as easily let Mindy leave that night, but I never thought she would have actually run me over with her car. The insatiable feeling within told me to at least attempt an intervention for her. And so I had.

Revisiting that moment in my mind was painful, and the sound of rain tapping against the windowpane didn't do much in the way of easing the nagging torment. Instead, the rage I had always felt within – THE RED as I called it – resurfaced into the forefront of my heart and mind, climbing out from the depths of my soul and submerging my eyes with bitter, cold tears. I cried and I wept, choking back the agonizing moans for fear that hearing my own sobs in the darkness of night would be too unbearable. Too *real.*

"Why, God?" I angrily bellowed, the question rising up from what remained of my broken heart like a pillar of smoke from a war-torn city. "How can you call yourself a loving God, and yet let me suffer this way?"

Tears streamed down my cheeks like the rain against the house, soaking the collar of my shirt with the cold reminders of my past. But no answer came to help soften the blow of my reality; no voice with loving words to offer comfort despite my tragedy. I had only three thoughts to help relax my nerves and give me purpose for a new day: First, I needed to find out more about the Walking Man because he would probably have information about the gated, stonewall. For all I knew, he might possibly live beyond that gate, in which case I would have a series of questions for him to answer. Then there was Spock with all of his unfailing love. And lastly, there was the sweet, smiling face of a person that I barely knew, although I desired to know her much greater. It was the latter of those three thoughts that I clung to as I drifted off to sleep...

...the beautiful face of Karla Turner.

19
Deputy Henry Bowers

"And now we sit here and wait," I said to Kelly as I cutoff the engine and killed the lights, allowing the darkness outside to flood into the patrol car. Kelly was the hot blonde I had met three days ago in Snookie's Pub outside of the college. She was looking for an older guy and I was looking to get lucky, so we hit it off right from the start. Snookie's was a great place to don the badge because when it came to a man in uniform, the college girls were easier than one-plus-one.

"So why did you get stuck having to do this?" she asked. Surprisingly, coming from her, it was a good question. Eckhart was supposed to have manned the Clyde Baker stakeout himself, but he had supposedly come down with a cold earlier in the day. So rather than giving such a punk-out assignment to one of the donut-eating, desk jockeys that call themselves deputies, he ordered me to give up my Saturday night instead. Unlike the other nomads on the force, I actually had a life – and liked it. The truth was: Eckhart hated me, probably because I threatened his authority. But it wasn't my fault I was a better cop than he could have ever hoped to become. So rather than allowing me a chance to shine, he stuck me with a grade-A punk out mission. But I didn't feel like saying any of that to Kelly. To be quite honest, I didn't feel like talking at all. The steady-growing migraine in my temples seconded the motion for silence.

"I don't know," was all I said in return.

Kelly had willingly offered to tag along on the assignment with me, partially because she gets really clingy whenever she's hammered, and partially because she was hoping to have sex in a police car. I had only known her for three days, but I knew enough to know that she was all about finding the craziest scenarios for sex; the first night with her had been no exception to the rule. The second night however had been a colossal embarrassment. I had told her that I was too tired, but it was the only reasoning I could concoct to hide the fact of my sudden onset of impotence. She had been persistent, and the more she pushed, the angrier I grew. Even thinking about it within the quiet confines of the cruiser made my mind fry like an egg on a summer sidewalk. So I quickly tried to clear my mind from the previous night of emasculating humiliation.

I stared out the window and studied the perimeter of the house and the barn. It was dark, and the misting rain wasn't helping my field of vision, but if somebody was indeed out there wandering around by the barn or the fence line, I would find them. Of course, I didn't expect to see anyone, despite the mystery that had made the old Sugar Hill Farms into the most feared place in Bridgeton. Just being there infuriated me more than the reminder of my sexual dysfunction, or even the damn cripple who chose to rent the place. If I ever saw him alone on the street, I'd give him a pair of broken arms to match his useless legs, and then I'd lock him up just because I could.

I glanced over at Kelly for a moment, wondering what I had been thinking to bring her along with me. She held a beer in hand, and moved her body as if she were feverishly aching for my touch. There was no subtlety about her at all.

"So officer, what should we do to help pass the time?" she asked, her words seeped in playful seduction as her hand rubbed at my thigh. Her laugh was a drunken college-girl giggle, but it didn't amuse me the way it had on the first night we met. So I grabbed her hand and tossed it back in her direction.

"Damnit, Kelly! Can't you see I'm trying to work here," I retorted, although I didn't care about the assignment at all. But there was no way to tell the little tramp that I couldn't take her, even though I wanted to.

Unfaltering from her mission however, she slowly began to hike-up the hem of her black miniskirt with a single finger, revealing more of her attractive legs. I was growing tired of her high-school antics, but I still couldn't help steal a glance at her.

"*I've* got work for you too. And I can guarantee it'll feel a whole lot better than just sitting here doing nothing for the next

20
Mindy

I was trapped, stuck behind a tree as the driver of the patrol car spied the land carefully. It was evident that he was keeping an eye on the property. Clyde must have been so bent out of shape about my first letter that he asked for a nightly guard of his house. Even with the help of the Sheriff though, he would never be able to outwit me. He might have thought I was mentally unstable, but he would soon find out just how wrong he was.

I thought about making a run for the barn, perhaps using the darkened night to stay hidden, but I opted against the idea. There was too much at risk in attempting a getaway. And besides, it wasn't as if the Sheriff knew I was there. He was most likely just checking up on the house periodically. All I had to do was remain patient for a little while longer and the patrol car would most likely be the one to leave. I had already waited a year for this moment; what were a few more minutes going to hurt? However, when the doors to the police car opened and two people began to make their way down the driveway towards me, I tensed up and prepared to run. But then I heard the arguing. I couldn't make out for sure what was being said, but as I gave another quick glance in their direction, I was surprised to see that only one of the individuals was a cop. The other person was a tag-along; a young bimbo-looking girl who looked as if she had just finished pole dancing down at the clubs. She looked angry from what I could tell – drunk for sure – and headed straight out onto the property. A moment later, the young, impetuous deputy was running after her. I softly moved around the tree in order to avoid being seen, but found myself fascinated by the events as they unfolded.

With the two newcomers vanishing into the darkness, my chance had come to runaway – to escape the madness of the morning – but I couldn't seem to pull myself away. There was an energy flowing through me, pulling me to follow them out onto the land. I couldn't understand the nagging desire to do so, but I couldn't refute it either. The reasoning behind the thought was maddening, but yet the tug in my heart was feverishly strong. Something was calling to me from out on the property, and although the idea was insane (*I'm not insane! I'm not!*) I found myself sneaking down the walking trail in careful pursuit.

I stepped lightly, as if tiptoeing around a sleeping baby, until I found myself standing at the entrance to an open patch of land. In the distance, I could see a long stonewall that disappeared into the trees on either side. It was massive; a sight that was enchanting to me although I couldn't explain why. The cop and his half-dressed counterpart were standing at the foot of the wall, staring into the darkness beyond a tall black gate. I was too far away to make out was being said, or anything that was happening for that matter, so I slowly crept along the tree line of the clearing so that I could duck away into the shadows if the cop were to suspect me.

I got close enough to see the blonde girl cross the threshold of the wall, and then surprisingly, get locked behind the gate by the well-built deputy. She was scared, I could hear the fear in her voice as she begged to be let out. But the cop just stood there. I imagined him to be grinning although I couldn't tell for sure, but I suddenly felt a strange connection to the young deputy. He intrigued me.

At the first sounds of snarling and growling, I gasped in surprise. Something was attacking the blonde girl. It sounded as if something was eating her alive, but I couldn't tell because the stupid cop had dropped his flashlight. The beam of light shot across the clearing and aimed in my direction, so I quickly ducked behind a tree. The sounds of the attack were gruesome, but the blood-curdling cries from the young girl were deafening.

"Shut up. Shut up. Shut up!" I whispered aloud to myself. "You're going to get us all caught you ungrateful tramp!"

I stayed hidden behind the tree until the flashlight beam redirected itself on the gate. Once it did, I peeked around the trunk of the large oak just in time to see the frightened young deputy stare down the beast that had attacked and killed his friend. In that

I took the letter into the family room and sat down on the couch with a mild influx of pain. Spock joined me on the sofa, waiting patiently for his breakfast. I was confused at first as I opened the envelope and found nothing but pages from a book in a neatly folded stack. But at second glance, I realized that the pages had not come from just any run-of-the-mill novel, but from my own. It was the novel that had angered her that night in Florida – the book that had sent her screaming out of the house despite the hurricane that had begun to make landfall.

As I inspected the pages with more care, I noticed that only one word from each page had been circled carefully with a red pen. After sifting through the first few pages, I began to understand that she had stacked them in a certain order so that her message would become clear to me – a message forged from my own words. I reached for the notepad and pen on the coffee table and began to jot down each word that she had circled. One-by-one, the words linked together to form the message she had needed me to see. It was a pain-staking process, but after a few minutes, the final message read:

A TIME TO KILL AND A TIME TO HEAL. IT IS TIME. MEET ME AT FRESH OVEN BAKERY. SECOND FLOOR. 5 PM TONIGHT. ALONE. YOU KNOW WHAT I'M CAPABLE OF.

Mindy was requesting a meeting. She had somehow survived the drowning in Gainesville and had spent a year trying to track me down. But why? It didn't make any sense. If she was trying to finish what she started that night in Florida – what Spock had luckily spared me from at the last possible moment – then why would she choose such a public place for a meeting? The Fresh Oven Bakery was a staple in our small town, and she had to know that it would be crowded. We both had grown up in Bridgeton, so the Halloween Parade that runs through town every year at this time would be no surprise to her. So what did *that* mean? Was this all some bizarre attempt at an apology? Is that what she meant by 'A time kill and a time to heal'?

My head swam in a sea of confusion. There were too many uncertainties surrounding the entire idea of a meeting, but I couldn't live the rest of my life in fear. If she was out there, I had to at least make an attempt at a confrontation, regardless of how it would play out.

But what about before? What about the attempt you made before?

It was true. I had tried to help Mindy at one time, but she hadn't wanted it. Her delusions had run so deep that she was beyond capable of recognizing the truth. I had tried, doing the best I could, but in the end it hadn't been good enough for her. Was I so naïve to have forgotten that – to forget the headlights of her car as she aimed it in my direction?

Caution, Clyde. Caution.

But it was the bakery, what harm could possibly befall me from such a public meeting?

I traced a web of thoughts through all of the possible scenarios, but coming to only one possible solution. I had come back to Bridgeton to face my past because it would be the only way to possibly move forward with some sibilance of an existence. Was it coincidence that only weeks after coming back to my hometown, Mindy showed up requesting a meeting? Or what about the Walking Man? How did he tie into any of the craziness that was unfolding? If I truly wanted answers, then there was only one real option. The bakery would be safe enough. I would be fine. But there was one problem with Mindy's request. I *couldn't* go alone.

* * * * * * * *

There were a couple of phone calls that I needed to make. The first one was to Slater. I still had no intentions to tell him about Mindy, let alone the fact that I was going to meet with her. As a precaution however, I would feel better if Slater knew that I was doing okay. In case the meeting somehow went awry, I wanted him to be able to verify that I had been in good health and sound mind. The phone call was more of a paper trail just in case, but like I said, I didn't foresee any major problems. I kept the conversation with him quick and light, talking mostly about the weather and of course – his favorite subject – a third book for the publishers. I told him that I would consider the idea; he was as surprised with my response as I was. Perhaps my answer was based on the subconscious thought that the phone call with Slater might possibly be my last. Or in some strange turn of events, maybe inadvertently for what Mindy did, but I just couldn't make myself rat her out. In some sick, twisted way, I thought it could be my last attempt at helping her."

"How in the world did you ever get help?" I asked, confused. "It's not like the roads are typically busy during hurricanes."

"Lucky for me, Mindy had made the car tires spin out as she sped towards me. It happened to be just loud enough to alarm my closest neighbor who – thank God – decided to look out her window to see what had happened. She was the one that carried me out of the storm and got me an ambulance."

"And I'm assuming that you haven't seen Mindy since then."

Clyde nodded his head. "Yeah, just over a year now. A week after the storm was over, someone in one of the cleanup crews up north near Gainesville found Mindy's car upside down in a lake. Her blood was everywhere in the car, but her body was never found. They investigated for a while, but after not finding anything, claimed her to be dead, chalking her up as one of the thousands of victims that were claimed by that particular storm. That was the last time I heard about her...until now."

I did a double take at Clyde, not sure if I was completely understanding what he was trying to tell me.

"Are you saying that she never died?"

Clyde shook his head. "I don't think she did. I had for a while, but I just received another letter from her last night."

"Wait a second. Did you say *another* letter? So that means there were previous ones."

"The first letter came in two days ago. Right after we got back from town. She had put a letter in with the mail. I wasn't sure it was her at first because she never signed it or posted a return address. But when this one was slid under my front door last night requesting to meet with me today, I knew for sure it was Mindy."

"What did Slater say about this?" I asked with a sense of urgent caution. "I can't imagine he's too happy knowing that she's back in your life."

I waited for an answer from Clyde, but received nothing more than a timid smile. I looked harder, and finally noticed the spark of secrecy that was dancing in his eyes. "You haven't told him yet, have you? Clyde you have to tell him. As your caretaker, I have to advise you to tell him. What if something happens to you? What if Mindy tries to finish what she started?"

I was a bit surprised at the sound of sheer concern in my voice, but I couldn't help it. I didn't want to see anything happen to Clyde.

"I don't think she's going to try anything," he said in a very docile tone.

"She ran you over with her car. She tried to kill you once, Clyde. If she's as unstable as you say she is, then there's no telling what she might do when she sees you. I know Mindy's your sister and all, but you can't keep protecting her like this. Peek not through a keyhole, lest ye be vexed."

"You're wrong, Karla. I know exactly what she's capable of. I lived with her my entire life. I can't walk normal anymore because of what she's capable of. *I know*. But I also know that she told me to meet her in a public place this evening, a very popular, crowded public place, and I don't think that would be the optimum setting for revenge. She's still my sister, Karla. I can't let her destroy her life like this."

"But you'll let her destroy yours?"

"Karla, please!"

Clyde's tone took on a harsh edge, but I didn't let it bother me. It was his decision after all, and if I couldn't persuade him against it, then I would do the next best thing.

"Well then, I'm coming with you. But you are not going alone."

Clyde's face grimaced again as if his harsh words were about to get harsher. However, he stopped himself, and took a deep breath. When he looked into my eyes again, the brash anger had been replaced with genuine thankfulness.

"Listen, Karla. I appreciate what you're trying to do. I don't know what I would have done without you being around. I mean that. But this is something that I just have to do. I came back to Bridgeton hoping that the familiarity of my past would help give me the strength to confront it. But when I got here, all I could think to do was take all of my past memories – my writings, my office furniture, everything – and hide them away in the barn out there. I was so angry about my life, about my health, about Mindy, that I wanted to do nothing but waste away in this house until one day someone would come by and find me dead. That was it. But after meeting you, and then now this whole Mindy thing, I really feel like this is why I've come back. Or if not, it's at least a stepping stone to something greater. So I have to do this alone, but I can't drive myself there. That's where I was hoping you could help."

to fill my eyes with painful regret. "My life is for you! You'll see! I'm not scared. I'm not!"

You stink with fear you whiny little brat!

The wall of emotion broke within me as cold tears poured down my mud-stained face. I *was* afraid. It was true. Although I knew that the faceless scarecrow had called me to go beyond the gate, I couldn't shake free of the images from the previous night, watching that red-eyed coyote tear apart the blonde girl like a paper cup. It angered me that I was unable to control my fear, especially for him.

The early morning breeze suddenly faltered and then died. Everything went silent except for my sobs of failure. When they too finally ceased, I turned my back to the gate and traipsed my muddy carcass back through the property and towards town.

"*Clyde will suffer for making me so afraid,*" I thought as the mud cracked against my jeans and jacket. It was time to cleanse my brother from the Takers.

24
Clyde

I never would have expected this day to come. I had lived the last year thinking that my sister had drowned in a lake outside of Gainesville, Florida but today I was preparing myself to meet with her. I would be lying if I said that my nerves weren't tied in knots.

Karla hung out at the house with Spock as I showered and dressed. I wasn't sure if I was cleaning myself up for Mindy or for Karla, but I guess it really didn't matter. What *did* matter to me was the outcome of the evening. I had instructed Karla not to worry, that Mindy was going to be harmless while in a public setting, but I wasn't sure if I truly believed that. We often tell ourselves lies in order to help us cope with the fears of any given situation – it's what I had done with my first two books – and I had the nagging suspicion lingering over my head that I was repeating the same mistake.

The important factor that I kept reminding myself while I finished up in the shower, was that the meeting had to take place. There was no way around it. I had been running away from my fears for all thirty years of my life. I was tired of running, and for making Mindy run as well. If the meeting went well, there was a chance that I could talk her into getting the help she needed. That thought alone was my motivation to go through with the reunion. I guess Karla was right after all when she said that there was hope in life. I was starting to believe that. The irony of it however, was that the hope I was seeking wasn't for Mindy, but for myself.

After my shower I made a couple of sandwiches for the both of us. We ate them mostly in silence, but when we did speak, it

25
Mindy

My view of the bakery was adequate at best. But it didn't really matter, because I never had any intentions of going inside. My focus was on the girl; the Taker who was too busy brainwashing my brother to notice I had been watching her.

From where I sat, crouched down on the porch in front of the In Remembrance Antiques store, I had a perfect view of the entire street. I watched the girl as she dropped Clyde off down the road from the bakery, and then headed towards the church. She parked near the front entrance and made her way inside. Clyde was a bit slower in getting to the bakery, but that was fine. He would be even slower getting up onto the second floor. Knowing how his mind worked, he would sit there and wait for me to show up for awhile. And that would be all the time I would need. The Taker would be purged.

Once Clyde was safely inside the bakery, I jumped up from my seat on the porch and hurried down the sidewalk towards the church. The dried mud and dirt on my clothes was driving me mad, and all I could think about as I briskly made my way towards the target, was lathering myself with the sanitizer from my purse.

I made sure that the entrance to the church was clear of any possible spectators and then slid inside through the same door Clyde's girlfriend had. The church's entryway was dark once the door closed behind me. There was a long hallway that stretched to my right and my left, but the hallways were just as dark as the foyer. The halls were lined with offices and classrooms – all of

them without light except for one tiny office to my left. I was
going to have to keep quiet.

The sanctuary was located just ahead of me, behind two finely
polished wooden doors. I stood for a moment and listened, trying
to hear over the sound of my own beating heart. My adrenaline
was revving into overdrive as the excitement built within – it was
almost orgasmic. It was destiny.

I pushed through the doors of the sanctuary and found the
large room to be archaic and ghastly. The fading light of the day
sent just a trickle of light through the stain glass window behind
the large wooden podium. There were rows of candles lit along the
front platform, casting an array of dancing shadows throughout the
inner sanctum of the church. Three sections of wooden pews filled
the building like formations of Nazi soldiers. I hated it. The way it
looked. The way it stank of pinewood and old cleanser. Everything
about the building was distasteful – even the Taker who was sitting
alone in one of the front pews. She turned around as she heard me
enter.

"I'm sorry. Did I bother you?" I asked coyly as I approached
the front of the church.

"No that's fine. I was just taking time to work through some
of my muddled thoughts." She giggled lethargically. The sound
made me want to vomit.

"Me too." I took a seat next to the woman and could
immediately smell the stink of betrayal all over her. I choked back
THE RED that was swelling in my stomach, but I wouldn't have to
wait much longer. I had to make sure this was done quickly and
quietly. One scream and everything would be ruined. "Would you
mind if I asked you something?"

"Not at all," she replied, although her eyes were transfixed by
the candlelight.

"Do you ever feel like you've worked for something your
whole life and then one day it's just snatched away from you?"

The shorthaired slut lowered her head at the question and, I'm
pretty sure wiped a tear away as well. "More so than you know."

"How do you cope with something like that?" I asked, playing
the game. The funny part was watching Clyde's girlfriend buy
right into it. If time hadn't been so short, I would have continued
on all day long.

"I ask myself that every night, but it never gets any easier.
The conclusion that I'm finally starting to come to, although I
can't take the credit for it, is that running from the problem isn't

26
Clyde

I checked my watch for a fourth time. Five twenty-two PM.

She was late, which didn't make any sense. Why would Mindy go through all the trouble to set up a meeting if she wasn't going to be on time? Maybe she was just watching me from afar, waiting to see how I would react? Or perhaps she had never meant to meet with me at all. But why?

I took a sip of water and stared out the window to my left. The gray light of the day was beginning to fade into darkness, casting the town of Bridgeton into a forlorn demeanor. Autumn had always been a depressing season for me; a time when the days grow short and the shadows grow long. The world outside the window was like a picture that had lost its color, and for a moment I felt as if I were looking through a window into my very own soul. What had my life become since the accident? And what had I been before? Was I nothing more than the town that I was looking down upon, gray and lifeless while creeping into the shadows of night? And when the darkness finally falls upon the town – upon my life – what fears would forever take control?

The sound of a distant siren snapped me out of my trance of self-discovery. I could see the police car as it sped down Main Street, rushing east through town. I thought nothing of it. But then a second and a third siren filled the air; another patrol car with an ambulance at its heels. When I saw that the motorcade of emergency vehicles was stopping somewhere in town, I hobbled over to the opposite window and peered outside.

There was a swarm of people beginning to stir on the sidewalks as the deputies and the EMT's brought their vehicles to a halt in the center of town. Horror struck my heart however, as I watched the emergency personnel rush inside of the Crossroads Reformed Church.

By the time that I made it down the stairs and outside of the bakery, the front of the church had already been taped off. The crowd that had been gathering for the parade was now assembling beneath the shadow of the church's bell tower. Gossip and murmuring talk funneled up and down the street as I desperately tried to push my way to the front. Frustration tugged at my chest as I worked with my cane the best I could. A stream of tears began to trace the curves of my unshaven face although I don't remember ever crying. If something had happened to Karla – if Mindy had hurt her in any way – my life would never be the same. Karla was the one person that had been real with me – that I was falling for – and I couldn't fathom a day without her. It was a realization that stung me hard and unexpectedly in that moment, but it was true. I had feelings for Karla that I had not discovered until the thought of losing her was presented.

I tried to sneak my way into the church but was stopped by one of the deputies on site. I argued with him to let me through, or to at least have him give me some information, but the heavyset man kept repeating the same phrase over-and-over: "I need you to stay back, sir. Please step back."

The frustration of the unknown was immense. I felt helpless and lost, trying to reassure myself that the emergency could be a number of different events. One of the parishioners could have had a heart attack. There might have been a fire in the kitchen. The possible scenarios were endless. So how did I know that something had happened to Karla? And why was I beyond certain that Mindy was involved somehow?

As the paramedics raced a gurney out of the doors and into the crowd, I caught a glimpse of white linens soaked in fresh blood. My heart froze at the sight although my eyes refused to believe what I was seeing. The crowd parted as the emergency workers rushed towards the ambulance, all the while I tried to get a clean view of the woman laying on the stretcher, but with no luck. I would refuse to believe that it was Karla being rushed to the hospital without seeing her for myself however. It just couldn't be possible, although my heart still felt as heavy as an iron weight. Karla was one of the two decencies I still had left in my life, so I was not surprised at the thought that she had been taken from me. I was cursed to be unhappy. I was doomed to die alone.

"Clyde!"

The refreshing sound of a familiar voice suddenly called out my name. It resounded so sweet, like the song of an ocean, as it met my ears. My attention was drawn to the entrance on the side of the church, offering me one last flicker of hope. Karla came running towards me with arms outstretched and tearstained eyes. The sight of her petite frame moving towards me as she crossed the empty parking lot made my heart lift and soar like a feather in a summer's breeze. She threw her arms around my neck and cried into my chest.

"What happened?" I asked. "Are you okay?"

"She tried to kill me, Clyde. She had a knife and..." Karla pulled back and looked at me. Her eyes were swollen and red from the loss of innocence. As she spoke, she tried not to stumble over her breathless sobs, but with little success. "Why would she do this? I barely got away. But she stabbed Margaret. There was so much blood, Clyde."

Karla's words were cut short by the onset of more ravenous tears. Her account of the events was vague, but an explanation was not needed in that moment because nothing was more important to me than having her safely in my arms. I wasn't sure why my feelings were changing as rapidly as they were, but I knew that it felt right to be holding her.

The crowd suddenly began to whisper and groan as a tall, well-built deputy exited the building with another woman in handcuffs. The woman's eyes quickly scanned through the crowd. She did not seem to care about any of the onlookers until she locked eyes with me. It had been over a year since I had stared into the twisted eyes of my sister, and yet I found myself reliving the pain of the past twelve months with one look at Mindy. Her dark eyes contorted into a ravenous snarl, speaking violent and malicious threats without ever uttering a word.

The arresting deputy prodded Mindy through the crowd like a cow to its slaughter. The red and blue lights from the patrol cars played across her face in contrasting opposition, as if each flash was revealing yet another side into the complexity that was Mindy. The crowd watched with bewildered eyes and gossiping tongue, but my demented sister never broke her eyes away from mine. Not until the arresting officer, who happened to be the arrogant deputy from the coffee shop – I think his name was Henry – forced her into the back of his patrol vehicle.

"I'm so sorry," I whispered to Karla, fighting back a wave of emotion. "I should have listened to you. I should have known."

Karla was eventually taken away from me by another of the officers – an older more heavyset man – in order to give her statement and answer questions about the incident. She also had a small gash on her left forearm that required minor attention. But regardless of the wound, I stood in thanksgiving that Karla had not been deeply harmed.

After almost two hours, the cops released Karla for the evening, advising her that they would be in touch if they had any further questions. When she returned to me, her fretful tears had all been cried, but her mind was weak and her heart was heavy. I gave her another hug – a gentle and friendly embrace as if to offer comfort from the hellish night that had enveloped her. I didn't feel right bombarding her with questions up front, so I just embraced her. It was my way of letting her know that I was there for her – and that I was sorry. I would hold her all night if she needed me to because I realized in that moment, that it was exactly what I needed.

27
Mindy

How did I ever let that two-faced whore get away from me? She had been right there in my grasp. I had executed everything fully, but yet she was in Clyde's arms and I was in the back of a damn tin can cop car on my way to be processed and arrested! The entire mess of events was infuriating to me, and so I slammed my head against the caged barrier that separated the two halves of the vehicle. The deputy had been unsuspecting of the sudden ruckus and flinched.

"Do that again and I'll put your face through it next time!"

"*I'd like to see you try,*" I thought, yet said nothing.

I lowered my head and grit my teeth together. It felt like I was chewing sandpaper, but the more I thought about Clyde and Karla, the harder I bit down. The worst thought of all was the realization that I had abandoned the faceless scarecrow. IT had called me, and yet I had refused to go beyond the gate to face him. He would have been able to help me kill the tramp. He would have made sure that the skinny secretary didn't enter in through the side door of the sanctuary as I was chasing Karla towards the exit. He probably would have also taken care of the pastor who had tackled me from behind. Everything would have gone so perfect, but yet I had overlooked the importance of the scarecrow. *He* was the one in charge and yet I had failed him. I could only hope that he would find favor in me and give me a second chance. At first I wasn't sure it was ever going to happen, but then I caught a good glimpse of the deputy through the rearview mirror. I recognized him immediately. Perhaps I had been granted grace after all.

I sat up in the seat and tried to flush out THE RED from my mind. Favor had been given to me and I couldn't afford to allow my rage to call the shots. I had to rely on the scarecrow. He would find me in my dreams and I would run to him. He would tell me what to do, but in the meantime, I had to keep my head clear.

"Where are we going?" I asked. But the deputy said nothing in return. So I tried again. "Excuse me. I'm talking to you."

"Shut it before I shut it for you!" He said in sharp reply. He was everything I had imagined him to be, especially after I saw what he was capable of the night before.

"Do you say that to everyone who rides in your car, or just me?" I asked.

"Just everyone who annoys the hell out of me. Now shut up!"

He was a cocky one, that was for sure, but nothing would be more fun than to let him climb the high-and-mighty ladder before knocking him down a few pegs.

The car sped east on Route Thirty-Three towards Sandhill Road. From there we turned north towards Canyon Pulse. With the sun finally dropped behind the Cotaquin Mountains, the windy road was dark and eerily empty. Only a few cars passed us from the other direction, which made me feel good about the outlook of our back-and-forth banter.

"And what if I don't shut up?" I asked. At the sound of the question I could feel the tug of the car as the deputy slightly removed his foot from the gas pedal. "Is there anything you can even do about that?"

"Try me," he said. "Say another word and you'll find out what I'm capable of."

"I already know what you're capable of deputy. I just wasn't sure if you were going to assault me, or feed me to the coyotes beyond the gate."

The patrol car fluttered in the lane and then increased its speed. Henry glanced back at me through the rearview mirror with wide eyes. The hardened corners of his face had melted away; panic traced the sides of his face in beads of sweat. The tough-guy routine was gone and the scared little boy inside was all that remained. He was doing a good enough job not letting on, but all the cards were on the table. We both knew what was at stake. I just had to play the situation delicately so as not to ruin the perfect opportunity I had been given. My second chance.

"You're one crazy lady," he said through a tight-clenched jaw. It was the last words he spoke to me on the drive, but I knew that I had struck the nerve I had needed to. Time was on my side. Now, it was just a matter of waiting on the scarecrow. He would come to me again and tell me what to do. The faceless scarecrow was all I had left, and he would blow the gates wide open on Clyde because Clyde was no longer my brother. He was one of them. He was a Taker.

28
Clyde

I had Karla take a seat on the couch as I slipped into the kitchen to make her a cup of hot tea. I started up the fire despite the pain, but I refused to let her help. She was in need of being taken care of rather than being the caretaker. It was the least I could do for her after my psychotic older sister almost cut the life out of her.

Spock jumped up next to her, settling in as if he could sense the fear on her just as easily as he could smell the milk bone that I handed him. I watched from the kitchen as Karla wrapped Spock into a somber embrace and shed more tears into his mane. He received her pain willfully and with trust. Watching the scene play out made me realize how much there was for me to learn from Spock. He might have been a dog, but he was far more than that. I knew it, and in that silent embrace, Karla realized it as well.

When the tea was ready, I served a cup for both Karla and myself. We sat together on the couch with Spock, allowing his whimsical nature to lighten the heaviness that had burdened both of our hearts. We reflected on the events of the evening as time passed on, finally unraveling the full story.

"So Mindy asked you to pray with her?" I asked with deep curiosity. Karla nodded her head.

"I thought she was a little bit strange at first, and she looked as if she had been rolling in mud, but I never imagined it was your sister. The thought *never* crossed my mind."

"So you were in the middle of praying and she pulls out a knife. How did you ever know what was happening?"

"Luckily for me, I never close my eyes when I pray. The only reason I bowed my head was to not make her feel uncomfortable – that was before I knew she was going to stab me, of course. So when she pulled the knife out of her purse, I saw the whole thing."

I chuckled at the thought. "Talk about luck."

"Yeah well, no offense, but I don't feel very lucky about the whole event."

Stupid, Clyde. Stupid.

"I completely understand. If anything, I should be the one to feel lucky. You could have been killed tonight all because of my stupidity. If I had listened to you earlier and blown off the meeting then..."

Karla interrupted, "Then she would have found another way to come at us. She's sick, Clyde and hopefully now she can get the help she needs."

"I know, but I really should have known she was planning something like this. I blame myself for allowing this to happen to you."

She took another sip of tea. "You need to stop blaming yourself for things, Clyde. Life happens. People are people. And besides, you had no way of knowing she was going to come after me."

"She must have been watching the house for a few days," I offered, trying to make sense out of everything. "I knew she had left notes, but she had to have seen you come and go recently. That must have been how she knew who you were."

"But why try to kill me tonight? Why not follow me home one night and break in while I'm sleeping?" I could see the slight chill that traced Karla's neck at the thought.

"I don't know. With Mindy, there's never a black or white. She was always too busy living in the gray." I paused for a moment as a faint realization brushed against the tendrils of my mind. "We both were."

Karla lowered the mug of steaming tea from her lips and looked towards me with understanding and compassion. She reached over with her free hand, the one that had been petting Spock, and took hold of my arm.

"You're nothing like her, Clyde. Trust me."

If I hadn't been so preoccupied with the past, I would have melted at the touch of her hand. But as it was, my mind was replaying my childhood like a movie in fast forward.

"Mindy and I were always very much alike growing up. Even though she always kept to herself and I always avoided our home like the plague, there was a commonness that we shared. We didn't realize it until we were much older – and she never liked talking about it – but it was always there, kind of like the electricity that runs through a house. You never think about it until you flip on a light switch, and even then you don't really acknowledge it. As long as the light works, we tend to overlook the power behind it. Well, that's what it was like for the two of us growing up. There was always something that flowed deep below the surface that neither of us could really control. The name I gave for it was THE RED. And it stuck ever since between us."

"The Red?" Karla asked before taking another sip. The crackle of the fire spoke in the quiet of that moment as she awaited my explanation.

"It's an anger that we both struggled with – still do apparently. I'm sure it stems from our childhood, but its something that just…I don't know…it just takes over. That's what I always loved about good ole Spock here. He was the first to ever help me control THE RED, although even then it sometimes just spills out of me. And I really don't know why I'm telling you all this."

I tried to laugh it off but I still felt stupid and awkward; vulnerable even. I had wanted to tell her that she was the second person who had helped me control THE RED in my life, but I couldn't seem to pull the words out of me.

"We all have skeletons in the closet," she added. "I guess what matters in life is what we do with them, you know?" I nodded in agreement.

Spock turned over and looked up at me through his big brown eyes. He might have been five years old – nearing his sixth birthday – but his eyes had never seemed to age. Not even a minute. He released a simple, low volume whimper as if to say: *"I'm right here, please pet me."* And so I did.

Karla set her tea down on the coffee table and began to rub at her temples. I could only imagine the stress and fear that was banging in her head as if someone was taking a hammer to a church bell.

"Would you like some Tylenol?" I asked. She shook her head in decline.

"I think I need to just go home and crawl into bed." She finally lowered her head into her hands as if she were ready to start crying again. I studied her carefully, observing the fatigue that she

As the front door squeaked open, the colder air from outside rushed in and pummeled me where I stood. The temperature had dropped significantly since the afternoon, therefore draping a thick blanket of fog over the land. Without hesitation, Spock trotted down the steps of the porch and into the belly of the fog. It was the same persistent jog that I had seen him use both times Karla had stopped by. I didn't try to call Spock back to me, because I knew he was determined to get out to the walking trail before it was too late.

Following the lead of my blonde friend, I hobbled down the steps after him. The pain in my legs and back was minimal at first, until I reached the loosely graveled driveway. That was when my pace lessened and my discomfort increased. But in slowing down, I was able to notice that the barn's floodlights were on, emitting their unusual, orange glow into the foggy darkness below.

It was at that moment, while shuffling carefully yet quickly across the driveway, that the dreamlike feeling overtook me for the first time. With the fog surrounding me I began to feel as if I were moving back and forward through time; as if one of my reoccurring dreams had finally clothed itself in reality and had begun to play itself out in my life. The damp fog didn't seem like just a misty cloud in that moment, but rather some sort of organic storage container for all of my life's memories to be held within; tickling at my nerves as I passed them by. It was a sensation that gripped me with intrigue and yet numbed my mind at the same time, leaving only my heart to lead the way.

Spock's golden body emerged from out of the fog, standing bold and firm with his eyes fixed on the walking path. His tail snapped back and forth like a spastic pendulum – the excitement almost too much for him to bear.

And that was when the movement began in the fog; a silhouette that seemed to flow through the misty morning cloud as if it were one with it. It was moving towards us, coming from the direction of the barn, just as it had the last two times we had seen it. The glow of orange light from the barn spilled around the shadow, helping it to take form; first the cowboy hat and then the tree branch-walking stick. The Walking Man had returned, and with Karla inside the house sleeping away a long day's worth of stress, it was finally time to get some answers.

"What are you doing out here?"

It was the first thing I could think to say as the old Walking Man drew near. For whatever reason, I didn't think I would get a response from him. Perhaps it was the look of painful concentration from his furrowed, bushy eyebrows, but I couldn't help but think that the old man was going to pass me by like I was a homeless drunkard. However, the moment he heard my voice, the Walking Man looked up in my direction; the slight grimace on his face replaced with a bright-eyed smile.

"Good morning, hoss," he added with a wave of his hand and a heavy southern accent. But I remained stoic and impersonal, unlike Spock who was wearing his excitement in his tail.

"Can I help you?" I asked, hoping that the tone in my voice would knock the old man down a peg or two on the cheerfulness scale. It didn't work though.

"An old man like myself needs not, but my children and my children's children. Beyond that, I's just got to keep these legs-a-pumpin' and my ticker jumpin'." He chuckled heartily as he approached the gate where Spock and I stood. The old man possessed a genuine smile that was book-marked between two, puffy cheeks – the likes of which one might imagine on Santa Claus or someone's dear old grandfather.

"What I mean is: What are you doing out here? It's four o'clock in the morning and you're trespassing on private property."

A cool wind suddenly breezed down out of the mountains, whistling another reminder of an early winter. I clutched at my robe to keep warm, as well as to display my frustration with this man, regardless of how innocent he might have looked. But the Walking Man simply turned his face to the dark mountains and closed his eyes. The old man allowed the wind to cool his face, painting his smiling cheeks in a blustery pink hue. He took it all in as if it were somehow regenerating for him.

"God's breath," he said, inhaling peacefully until the wind died down, "what a miraculous thing. It makes my spirit leap like a robin in the prairies. I apologize sincerely if I've startled you or have crossed any lines with my walking. I can assure you, hoss that no disrespect was intended. There's just something about this place – something that draws me here...the barn especially. The soul of this old man just longs to be near it for whatever reason. Something just feels right deep down. You know?"

But the truth was that I didn't know. To me, the old farmland felt as wrong as sin. And there wasn't a person in town that would disagree with me on that point. So to make the same connection to and vivid red color. Flash wasn't a large man, although he carried himself as if he had possibly been lean and muscular in his prime. But as time is apt to do, he was nothing more than a shadow of that younger life. He looked thin and weak – a little too weak if my guess was accurate. He stood with a slight hunch – another sign of the unending battle between man and age. Just looking at him in that instant, made me consider my future outlook. If Flash was the depiction of a healthy man turned old, than what would possibly lay ahead for a man in my current condition? Slowly, THE RED began to surface.

As if Flash could sense the anger beginning to rise within me, he turned back around and locked his eyes with mine. There was the most genuine of smiles that laced his tired features, erasing all other thoughts about him, as well as easing my anger.

"A man like myself lives wherever I can lay my head down. But what does it mean *to live* anyhow? The doctor has already told me that my end is near on God's green earth, but should that stop me from living? For some folks, it would, but not for ole Flash here. No, sir."

"You're dying? I'm…so sorry." I said, suddenly feeling foolish and out of line with the question.

"We's all judged to a death sentence, Mr. Clyde. So there aint no need for apologies for such a hackneyed occurrence. But the question that remains is how many of us truly exist before said sentence is carried out? The 'ways of the farmer' is what I like to call it."

Flash reached into the front pocket of his overalls and, for the first time that morning, I noticed a significant bulge in the lapel pocket where his hand now was. My eyes followed his hand curiously, and with caution. Spock however remained in a seated position with a wide puppy smile from ear to floppy ear.

"The ways of the farmer?" I asked. "I'm not following."

"You will," Flash replied with a wink. "I hope."

As he removed his hand from the front pocket, he was holding onto a red, ripe apple that stood out like a detailed oil painting in the morning fog. With the barn's floodlights casting a rim of orange light around the piece of fruit, the apple resembled a large ruby placed into the golden setting of a ring. Flash even held onto it as if it were precious to him.

"Yep, the ways of the farmer; what a beautiful sacrifice."
With those words said, Flash sunk his teeth into the crisp skin of the fruit. The crunch was loud in the silence of the morning – loud

with the echo of juicy deliciousness. "You'll get it, hoss. No worries."

"Perhaps I will, but I still don't understand why you walk out there? Do you ever go beyond the gate?" I asked bluntly, my words probably coming across with more frustration than I had intended.

"Going beyond the gate is my whole purpose for walkin'," said Flash through a mouthful of fresh apple.

"It is?"

"Shouldn't it be? Aint it your purpose?"

"I've never walked out there. I don't even know what's on the property, moreover what's beyond the gate. Why? What's out there?"

"Well," began Flash, pausing to gather his words, "it's not an easy walk. I can tell you that much. It's one tricky spread of land for sure."

"So I've been told," I whispered to myself.

"But other than that, I's afraid I can't give you much more, hoss. Going through that gate is a journey that each man must decide – *on his own* – to take. And it aint something that can be explained neither. You just have to walk it." Flash punctuated his comment with another loud bite of the apple.

"Can you *try* to explain it for me? I'm a writer – it's what I do – and it sounds like it can make for an interesting story. Besides, there seems to be a history that hangs over the head of this place. So anything you can tell me, anything at all, I would appreciate." The tone in my voice bordered desperation, but I was close to finding out something big. I could feel it.

"You's right about that, Mr. Clyde. It will make for a story of stories. Aint that right, Spock?"

At the sound of his name, Spock rose from his seated position, his whip-like tail working in double time. He waited for some physical affection from either of us, and when I failed to oblige my puppy's request, he began to whimper restlessly and nudge my leg with his head until I reached down and scratched behind his ear. I was glad to offer Spock the needed attention, but would be lying if I didn't admit that the sudden connection between Spock and Flash wasn't alarming.

"And since you's a writer hoss, than I think writing down the story is exactly what needs to happen. I surely hope you choose to tell the tale mister homebody." He offered me a sarcastic, yet

PART TWO
fears, facts, and fiction

about Flash and ask her to accompany me on my morning's journey.

At the sign of first light, I scrambled to get up – against poor Spock's wishes – and rushed into the kitchen to prepare a quick breakfast. The pain was moderate in my legs but it was well worth the discomfort. Although the old Walking Man hadn't told me what I needed to know about the property, he *had* given me another valuable piece of information. Sheriff Eckhart had said that it was not feasible for a man in my condition to walk the property. But he had lied to me, because if an old dying man like Flash was able to make the walk, then Spock and I would have no problem at all.

As I put on the pot of coffee, I sneaked a glance into the bedroom where Karla had spent the night. My hope was that she would smell the aromas of the coffee beans, or perhaps hear me shuffling about in the kitchen, and wake up feeling refreshed and ready for a hardy meal. However, as I peeked my head around the corner, the bed was empty and neatly made. She had left without saying goodbye. There was however, a note left for me on the pillows.

I HAD SOME THINGS TO DO THIS MORNING AND I DIDN'T WANT TO WAKE YOU. THANKS FOR EVERTHING, CLYDE. GIVE SPOCK A KISS FOR ME.
-- KARLA

"Not what we were hoping for, but better than I expected," I said to my blonde friend. "What do you think buddy? Promising?"

I looked over to Spock who was sitting down next to the back door as if he had to be let out. But the bathroom was the last thing on Spock's mind. He was trying to tell me that he was ready to set out for the gate – that I should forget about the note for the time being and get moving. And that was exactly what I did.

By the time I was ready to set off on the day's journey, the digital display over the stove read: nine o'clock, which was perfect. It wasn't too early nor too late – I hoped – to place one quick phone call before setting out. I needed to talk to Karla, to make sure that she was doing okay after the incident with Mindy. I was also curious to know if everything was okay between us. The call could have waited until later, but I did not want the 'what if' questions hanging over my head all morning long. I needed to be thinking clearly if I had any hopes of figuring out where it was that Flash was walking to every night.

Karla answered the phone by the second ring, her voice soothing and gentle yet framed in professionalism. The moment she said "*Hello*" however, my stomach felt as if it had leapt into my chest.

"I hope it isn't too early to call," I said, stumbling over my words like a pro.

"Not at all. You actually just caught me walking out the door for church. But don't you ever worry about the time. For Clyde Baker, my phone is available twenty-four, seven."

"*Because it has to be, or because you want it to be*," I thought to myself, not daring to actually ask.

"Did you get my note?"

"Yeah, I did. And I was just calling to make sure that you were doing okay after yesterday."

"I'll be fine, thank you. I hope you weren't alarmed when you woke up and saw me gone. Yesterday was pretty rough on you as well so I didn't think about waking you. But thanks for letting me stay there. You were right. Being alone last night would have been too nerve wrecking. Make sure to thank Spock for me as well. It was nice having him curled up at my feet for most of last night."

I grinned at the thought. Spock sure was taking a liking to her. "Yeah, I noticed that he was back and forth all night. I'm starting to think he likes you better than me."

Karla chuckled on the other end of the line as Spock looked up at me from his lounge position next to the back door.

"He is one special dog, that's for sure. And thanks for calling to check up on me this morning. I appreciate it."

"Your welcome," I said in reply. I could tell from the sound of Karla's voice that she was rushing to walk out the door and that the conversation was going to be wrapping up any second. If I was going to ask the question on my mind, than I was going to have to just get it over with.

"Listen Karla, I actually called because I have a question to ask you." I stammered through the last part of the statement like a giddy schoolboy, hoping that she hadn't noticed. "Well, I was just wondering – if you're not too busy or whatever, because if you are it's no big deal – but..."

Here goes nothing, I thought.

"Well, I didn't know if you wouldn't mind having dinner with me tonight?"

And there it was!

The question had been asked – thrown out there without a chance of ever getting it back. In the moment of waiting, time felt non-existent, trapping me in the eternity that lingers between the question asked, and the answer given. To me, waiting had always been the worst part about opening up to another person – allowing your emotions to dangle at the hands of someone else like a marionette. It had been years – almost a decade – since I had last put myself out on the limb like that. I suddenly felt like a complete bonehead for not thinking things through too carefully. Sure, we had kissed, but people often do things in their most vulnerable moments that they end up regretting later on. I was most likely one big regret for her.

My stomach tightened at the thought.

And then there was my disability, something I had never taken into consideration either. Karla was a beautiful young woman with all the frills of a normal life ahead of her. So why would she throw it all away for a crippled has-been like myself?

Nausea swirled like a whirlpool in my head.

Why had I ever asked? She was paid to be cordial to me. PAID! The kiss was most likely a momentary lapse of judgment on her end.

Suddenly, the eternity of waiting that had held me prisoner of my thoughts in that single second after having asked the question, ended. And with four simple words from Karla's mouth, all of the panicked thoughts and nervous symptoms were washed completely away.

"I would love to."

* * * * * * * *

The temperature outside was still moderately cool, although it showed promise of raising another five or ten degrees by the afternoon. It made for pleasant walking conditions with Spock regardless of the uncomfortable cane clenched tightly in my right hand. Spock was thrilled beyond belief to be outdoors again. But *I* was thrilled because I had just scored a date with the lovely Karla Turner. And it wasn't a professional kind of thing either; I had successfully crossed the line between business and friendship. I had faced the fear of asking her, and had conquered it – a concept

that had always eluded my life. I had never faced anything before –
not with my dad and his abusive tendencies, nor with my mom
after her suicide, and not even when it came to holding onto
Alexis, although all of the warning signs had been present. And
what had that left me with? THE RED. But then Karla had shown
up in my life – Karla, with all of her sweetness and talk of hope –
and suddenly I found myself trying to look at things from a
different perspective. Sure, rejection had been possible, and it
probably still was. For all I knew, Karla could have agreed to the
date out of pity, or because she was trying to help out another
patron from her selfless career. She might not have even viewed
the offer as a date at all. But regardless of what the outcome, I had
still made a stand to my doubts and fears, with a slim hope that
something could possibly flourish.

As I gingerly made my way down the walking path – slow
and steady wins the race – I found myself thinking less about Karla
and more about Flash.

*"Our words are determined by our fears, and our fears
determine our actions,"* was the final thing he had said to me
before slipping away into the fog. The piece of paper that I had
written those words onto was now tucked safely away in my pants
pocket. I had glanced at it once before leaving the house, but it was
safe to say that the phrase would be forever etched into my mind as
if with a hot iron. I was still clueless as to what it meant, or even
Flash's purpose for having said it, but I knew that taking the
journey beyond the gate would eventually lead me to the solutions
I was seeking.

The jaunt down the walking path was relatively painless for
me, as long as I was sure to maintain the pace at a decent speed. It
wasn't as if I had been in any kind of rush. It was a beautiful
morning and I was relishing the opportunity to watch Spock freely
patrol the open land. It was a treat for me just as much as it was for
him. His blonde body would trot out ahead of me on the trail – his
nose leading the way – and then he would prance back towards me
with a wide smile as if to assure himself that I was doing okay.
And I was.

"Are you having fun out there buddy?" I asked while patting
him twice on the back. He answered by rubbing up against my leg.
"I'm glad. You go sniff around and have a blast. You deserve it,
bud!"

As Spock once again trotted ahead of me, being the first of us
to follow the path out onto the clearing of open land beyond, I felt

grateful that my best friend was finally getting to enjoy himself again. Ever since the accident Spock had known nothing more than a life confined to a house. The prime days of his youth were spent eating and sleeping next to me on a couch, going outside *only* to do his business.

"Do you remember Florida?" I asked as he ventured to the top of the hill in the clearing. "The morning runs on the beach, the evening walks that helped us unwind, and even the sunsets. Remember those days, boy?"

I smiled wanly at the memories of a life that would never be again – a life that would have been made all the better had I not been so involved with myself to recognize the change that Mindy was undergoing. Alexis must have seen the change in both Mindy and myself, which would explain why she left out of the blue. I was starting to think that my dream had been right, not in the sense that I had loved THE FACELESS ONE more than Alexis, but that I had sacrificed everything for my books. *Including* Alexis.

"I should have paid you more attention back then, buddy," I said as I began the slow trek up the hill towards him. "Things might have turned out better with Alexis had I not overlooked your insights on things."

My words trailed off and I slowed my pace to an almost idling position. The thought I had just been entertaining made me think back to something else that Flash had said...almost as if he knew more about my life than he had let onto.

"You don't suppose that ole Spock and you just happened upon each other by no mishap, now do ya?"

"But we had," I thought. *"Hadn't we?"* The thought that was even more over the top for me was how the old man had even known about me or Spock. That was the notion that seemed to carve a trail of ice down my spine.

I joined Spock atop the hill before my mind could make me relive my past. The place where we stood offered the best view of the old farmland and pastures. The vastness of the Cotaquin Mountains capped the western view; the vibrant colors of the trees stretching long like a wall of fire. But just on the other side of the hill, only fifteen feet away from Spock and myself, was the stonewall and the black iron gate.

The stonewall was a lot taller than I had expected, but not as tall as it had seemed in my dream three days ago. Standing next to it however, I would have guessed that it easily towered three feet above my six-foot tall frame. The stones themselves were each of different size, shape and color. Although some of them were smooth, the majority of them were rough and jagged resembling meteor fragments rather than earth rocks. The amazing part about the wall however – the thing that made me stand there in awe and apprehension – was the sheer length of it. Even from where I stood upon the hill, I could look to the left and to the right without seeing an end to it in either direction. Both ends stretched beyond the boundaries of the clearing and vanished into the balding, autumn trees. The sight of the wall was overwhelming.

The gate itself was about five feet in width, and arched at the top like something you would expect to see while entering the Sleepy Hollow Cemetery. The gate carried a foreboding presence, as if to ward off all trespassers. But yet there had been no lock fastened in place to assure the land's seclusion beyond, only a latch that looked as hefty as the gate itself, accessible from only one side. It would be very easy for someone to get locked beyond, I noticed.

The grass that skirted the wall was thick and tall like hay, although it was beginning to dry up from the colder morning temperatures. The grass was unkempt and relatively untouched, as if the maintenance crew that McNamara had hired to tend to the land, refused to go within six feet of the wall; or perhaps they had been ordered to stay away from it. But either way, the grass seemed to have been set in play to act as a natural deterrent for anyone who might consider traveling beyond – especially during the wetter, summer months when the fields must be as thick and overgrown as a lion's mane. From where I stood however, neither the border of grass nor the abnormal size of the wall was a deterrent. It was a challenge; a challenge to find the answers to my questions. Answers about Flash and about the property's past, as well as to learn how my life fit into the larger scale of things. I didn't know why I needed the answers – perhaps it was the curse of every author to have to investigate the unknown, but deep down I was driven with an insatiable urge to press forward. And so, for the sake of answers, I did just that, stepping through the patches of dying grass until my hand was gripped around the cold metal bars of the gate.

I am not the type of individual who can be described as an over exaggerator, not even in my writings for the most part. But the moment the skin of my hand brushed against the rusted iron of the gate, I would have sworn that a shrill and menacing laugh lifted from out of the wooded area beyond the gate, evolving from the sunlight that was being sifted heavily through the dense drove of trees. As I looked closer however, I began to pinpoint some of the contrasting details. For one, the trees were not ablaze with the fiery colors of autumn as was the rest of the town. The leaves beyond the gate seemed to be changing at a slower pace than those everywhere else in Bridgeton; the summer green refusing to relinquish it's hold.

The ground below was the second major difference that I picked up on immediately. Unlike the land in the clearing, which had been blanketed in a bright spread of lively grass, the canvas upon which I stood was nothing more that dirt and dead leaves, with an occasional peppering of crab grass and uncultivated brush. But other than those two differences, I saw nothing with which to validate my doubts and fears – nothing to warrant Sheriff Eckhart's stern warning either.

"The good ole Sheriff strikes out again, huh Spock?" I asked of my friend who was still standing tall upon the hill in the clearing. "Come on, boy. Let's keep moving."

Spock turned to face me although he refused to budge from his place on the hill.

"What are you waiting for Spock? You're not *scared*, are you?"

Upon hearing the question with my own ears, fear immediately resurfaced into my thoughts. My chest tightened like a vice clamp and my neck and arms broke out in gooseflesh. A wave of unease and danger spun me around to once again face the desolate land, as if having my back turned towards it was inviting some form of evil to slink furtively upon me. But nothing was there – no monsters or boogiemen to rip me apart like a wet tissue.

"Get a hold of yourself, Clyde. There's nothing out here. Don't let Eckhart mess up your head that easily."

My eyes however, did another quick scan of the surrounding area, as if they weren't buying into what my words were trying to sell. And that was when I noticed something in the darkened distance.

Just beyond a clutter of three or four large oaks there was a long, thin branch that had been stood on end and driven into the ground. The branch was at least four feet tall and relatively straight compared to most tree limbs. At the top of the posted stick of wood, there was a red garment that had been tied off like a homemade flag. My eyes widened at the site of such a thing, sending my heart racing into a drum roll of off rhythms.

There was no wind blowing through at that moment, so the red garment hung limply against the branch. But I didn't have to see anymore of the makeshift flag to know that the red garment had been made from a child's tee-shirt – a red, sleeveless shirt with the phrase I AM NINJA embroidered in white felt letters across the front. I also didn't need to see that the shirt had been cut into a triangular shape like a pennant banner or a medieval flag. I didn't need to see because I already *knew*. I had designed the exact same makeshift flag – designed it down to the very letter – when I had created it with words in my first novel. But yet there it stood beyond the gate, as if it had jumped out of the pages of the book and became as real as you and I.

A mild breeze fluttered through, rattling the leaves above and lifting the red garment gently away from the branch. It flapped loosely a few times, reassuring me of the white, felt lettering that was now visible. And that was when Spock began to bark; he began to bark *feverishly*.

I hurried out into the clearing, making sure not to turn my back to the red flagstaff (which was the name I had coined for it in my novel) until I was well beyond the gate *and* the perimeter of unkempt grass that bordered the wall. Spock was still in the same spot as he had been before, but his entire body was turned and facing the direction of our house. His bark was loud, repetitive, and commanding. But it did not seem defensive in anyway, which was a momentary relief.

I had witnessed Spock's defensive bark on only two occasions: once with a FedEx driver who had come to deliver a package, and again when Mindy had tried to kill me with her Mercury Sable. Both times, Spock's bark had been extremely low pitched, sounding more like a WOOF than an actual bark. The hair on the back of his neck had stood on end in both instances, and he had even blocked the front door with his body, refusing to move. So rather than fighting with my dog, I had chosen to learn about his warning barks, and heed to them as well. However, the sound that I heard rising from the lungs of my Spock as he stood atop the hill on that morning, was much, much different. It was boisterous as it lifted through the valley – a plea that demanded immediate attention. There was a slight waggle in the tip of his tail and the force of each yelp lifted his front two paws from the ground like a plane trying to escape a runway. I attempted twice to call him to me, but he barked all the more as if to tell me: *"Shut up and hurry!"*

me. His voice resounded with authority, as if he were commanding a storm cloud not to rain or the sun to stop shining, and I couldn't help but shake the feeling that his words were spoken *at* me more so than *to* me. But that was a foolish thought for me to consider about my pastor.

"If the board members were to ever suspect that the foundation that this church was building upon was crumbling in some way, what do you think would happen?"

His eyes turned down to meet mine. The pastoral kindness that I had seen on his face when he had first approached me was suddenly gone, erased by a hardened stare of accusation.

"I guess the congregation would begin to lose trust in the church." The words were timid as they stammered out of my mouth.

"And without trust, what good is a church at all? If all these people you see here today didn't trust that I was leading them in the ways of righteousness, we'd have anarchy on our hands." He paused, as if to give me time to absorb his wisdom. "Anarchy is of the devil, Miss Turner, and as the pastor of this church I will not allow the works of the enemy to infiltrate my flock. I cannot have that."

Pastor Rob scanned the sanctuary one last time while scratching at his head of thick blonde hair. Before speaking again however, he leaned in closer to me, his voice booming like distant, rolling thunder.

"Be cautious with your walk, Miss Turner. It's one thing to defile your body – the sanctuary that God himself dwells within. But to defile *my* sanctuary is a different stone to cast entirely. I will not have my church tarnished with murderous and ungodly individuals. I have worked far too hard to build a legacy for this town and I will not allow anyone's poor choices to infect that. Are you *getting* the message I'm sending?"

Once again I nodded in response because I could not seem to form the right words to say. I could feel a glaze of warm tears forming over my eyes and I suddenly wiped them away. "I'm...I'm so sorry Pastor Rob. I never meant for any of this to happen. I didn't know."

The sudden outburst of emotion weaved throughout my apology, gaining the attention of the nearby onlookers. But I didn't care about them in that moment. The man that stood before me – the very pastor who had taken me into his church when I had been at my lowest – was expressing his solemn disappointment, and that was the factor that set the tears rolling down my cheeks.

"I know you didn't mean for this to take place, but it did. That woman followed you into this church and brought the devil with her. And Lucifer was the first of the murderers don't forget. He loves nothing more than the bloodshed of the innocent and to top it off, he carried out his task in the very house of God." Pastor Rob reached out a strong arm and wrapped it around my shoulder, pulling me close. I fell into him willingly, like a daughter folding into the embrace of a loving father. "Why don't you go into the ladies room and take a few minutes to get yourself together before the service. You're gonna need to be in right mind in order to receive the message that God has provided for today."

I pulled back and wiped at the remaining tears. I then gave a slight nod as to acknowledge his suggestion. Before leaving however, Pastor Rob said one last thing to me. Ironically, out of the entire service that morning, his final words to me were what stuck in my mind for the rest of the day.

"Do yourself a favor Miss Turner and just ask yourself this one question. Why was that woman trying to kill you yesterday? And if you were to have fully cleansed your life of all the godless and haughty things that I preach against every Sunday, would yesterday have ever happened? I believe in you Miss Turner. Don't you let me down."

With that said, Pastor Rob gave me a pat on the shoulder and mixed back into the crowd of gossiping church members. It was in that moment that I found myself standing alone within a crowded room – within my supposed church family.

banter. My feet were beginning to throb and if I listened to too much more of his gabbing, my head was apt to do the same.

"And yes, Mr. Baker, I did take sick the other day. But are you that foolish to not even *consider* the fact that I would send a deputy in my stead?"

I hesitated at his words while Spock entered into the house through the open door behind me. The honest-to-God truth was that I *hadn't* considered that fact. I had jumped so far into my self-calculated conclusion that I never took a movement to consider any other possible scenarios.

"And?" was all I could manage.

"And there was nothing," Eckhart said through an aggravated, yet victorious smile. "I checked out the report for myself first thing this morning. Deputy Bowers was out front here from two fifty-seven AM until five. He reported a quiet night with some off-and-on light rain, but saw nothing or nobody. So as far as Friday night into Saturday morning, things were looking on the up-and-up. So that just leaves us with last night." Eckhart eyeballed me carefully before posing his question. "Did your guest pay you another visit last night? Or what about anything else that might have roused your suspicions?"

"Nope," I lied. "Don't get me wrong though, I've got plenty of suspicions, just none of them regarding last night."

"Is that so?" he questioned.

"You see Sheriff, my suspicions tell me that you know more about the land out there than you're letting onto. I just can't figure out why the secrecy is such a high priority for you."

Eckhart grunted under his breath. It was the kind of soft sound that indicates a man in thought.

"That's funny, because I was just thinking that you're holding out on me too."

"Then I guess we're at an impasse, aren't we?"

"I suppose so."

"So that settles it. I guess I won't need you to keep an eye on the place for me anymore, Sheriff. But hey, like your report says: Everything is on the up-and-up. Right?"

Eckhart didn't respond that time, not verbally at least. His eyes however, narrowed into a pair of wrinkled fissures, studying me carefully. It was the kind of look that said he was going to continue with his investigation. But the last thing I needed was Eckhart nosing around if Flash popped up again. I needed information about the property and I still believed Flash would be the better of the two sources. I would have to put some effort into it of course, but I felt confident that he would eventually spill it all. The only thing that I couldn't fully explain was the drive behind my investigation. What was I expecting to find beyond that massive stonewall anyhow? Whatever it was, I fully believed that it was the reason I had returned to Bridgeton after ten long years. It wasn't just a search for the property's history, but a quest to find myself; to rediscover the child I had lost somewhere along the line.

I turned to leave, leaning heavily upon my cane – partially for effect but mostly because the tremors of pain were warning signs of an imminent eruption. But before closing the door, I turned to face Eckhart one last time.

"You've been the Sheriff of this town for quite some time now, so you're probably familiar with most of the townspeople. Am I right?"

"I'm privy to my fair share of the common folk, yeah. Why?"

"Because I'm needing to find a man by the name of Gordon Hightower. Have you ever heard of him? He might go by the nickname of *Flash* to most people, but I can't be sure."

Eckhart once again entered into deep thought, apparently shuffling through his lifetime of dusty memories that were loosely catalogued within the chambers of his mind. But I knew however, that the Sheriff was thinking less about the name and more about the implications of what that name meant to me.

"Gordon Hightower you say, huh?" he asked after a moment. But I said nothing. "Naw, that name don't ring a bell. I don't even think there's ever been a Hightower clan in Bridgeton. Not as far as I know."

Strange. Very strange.

"Oh well," I said, shrugging it off nonchalantly. "No big deal."

I turned and entered the house, bidding the Sheriff a good afternoon before closing the door behind me. Although I had been a tad smug with my farewell to Eckhart, I would be lying if I didn't admit that his response to my last question had been shocking to say the least. I had figured that if anyone in the God-forsaken town of Bridgeton, New York was going to know about Flash, it would have been the Sheriff. However, the fact that he claimed to have never known anybody named Hightower left me with an unsettled feeling in the pit of my stomach. So either the good 'ole Sheriff was once again withholding information from me, or there was a strange man walking on my property at night who didn't even live

in Bridgeton. And if that was the case, one could only wonder
what he was doing, and why.

Time is a strange bird, and has a queer way of acting in a
dichotomy of manners. Sometimes it buries the past, muting the
thunderous voice of truth into a whispered myth. But occasionally,
time can unveil the truth and bring the forgotten into light. It had
done so with the hidden secrets of my father's murder, but that
would turn out to be only the beginning. There was more to be
revealed; much more that was hidden just below the surface, the
way a nightmare teeters just beyond the waking realm. The truth
was approaching rapidly, I could feel it like an electrical current
flowing through me, but I never would have guessed just how
close it actually was. My quest for information – *for the truth* –
was about to lead me to answers that would either change my very
existence, or kill me.

Everything had been set into motion.

Time was at work.

Nothing would be the same by sunrise.

* * * * * * * *

The preparations for my date with Karla were shrouded in
nervous jitters. Who knew that first dates could make a grown man
so wired. But nevertheless, I had still managed to select, what I
hoped would be, a suitable outfit: a pair of fresh khaki pants and a
blue, long-sleeve button-up shirt. I showered and then took a razor
to my beard for the first time in months. When I was finished, I
gazed curiously at my clean-shaven reflection in the mirror. I could
barely recognize the man that looked back at me.

The post-accident Clyde Baker was dingy, rough around the
edges, and hidden behind a tangled, chin-length nest of curls. But
the man staring at me from the mirror was clean-shaven with a
well groomed head of slicked, black hair. It was as if I were
looking into the past and seeing the man who had once been – the
man who had enjoyed living life while capturing all of it's
intricacies with a pen and paper. I smiled. Thanks to Karla, I was
able to do that again. But the greatest thanks went to my blonde
buddy who was watching me from his curled, napping position on
the bed. Spock had helped me to find comfort in another person
again. He had showed me that it was okay to trust Karla, and so I

had. My little, five-year old yellow Lab had again led me where I needed to be. I loved my Spock.

Karla arrived at my house just before seven PM to a chorus of welcoming barks and a non-stop wagging tail. And that was before she ever made it to the front door. She of course gave Spock his desired attention (*how could I not adore a woman who adored Spock*), while I stood in awe of how absolutely radiant she looked.

Karla was donning a smocked strapless dress in a deep lagoon blue and was breathtakingly exquisite. Her dirty blonde hair bounced as she walked, brushing softly against her smiling cheeks. She wore a silver pendant necklace that shined like a star against the fair complexion of her skin. But it was her eyes – those hazel gems flecked with violet – that loomed towards me and plundered my heart. Just watching her draw near to me with that typical Karla innocence made me feel alive and free again.

After exchanging pleasantries, we both said goodbye to Spock – sad to see the glum look of dejection in his face when he heard that he couldn't tag along – and then headed out for the restaurant.

The place was called VINCENZO'S, a medium-sized Italian restaurant just outside of Bridgeton, in the college town of Canyon Pulse. I had asked Karla to choose the spot, seeing as though my memories of the local communities were limited. Judging by the quiet, mood-setting environment, I gave her an A-plus on the selection. The food quality would be the next factor up for scrutiny, but based on the slow service, that judgment would be a long time coming. Upon seating us, the hostess had advised that the staff had been a bit short-handed all weekend, and so the service could possibly be unusually slow. But as far as I was concerned, the waitress could take as long as she wanted. I was with Karla, and in no hurry to go anywhere.

"Thanks for agreeing to have dinner with me tonight," I said, figuring it to be the best way to start conversation.

"I was wondering when you were going to ask."

"You had wanted me to ask you out?" I was surprised.

"I'm here, aren't I? Besides, it's not everyday that a Bridgeton girl gets asked out to dinner by a world renowned author." My face must have frozen at her last remark, because she added: "I'm teasing, you know. You're writing has nothing to do with why I accepted your invitation. Don't mind my sense of humor, it's just something you'll grow to love over time.

fears. People always say that you can only write about what you know. And I knew pain and fear, so I utilized it. But I think as I began to write, the process began to dredge up all of those memories and it was...well, it was *intoxicating*. It was so bad, that even when I was out with Alexis and *not* writing, she would *claim* that I wasn't really there; that I was lost somewhere in my own mind. I thought that she was understanding and supportive, but I guess I was sorely mistaken."

"So she was one of those girls who was always needing attention," Karla interjected. I was surprised by how easily the information was flowing out of me, but more so about Karla's acceptance.

"It wasn't just the lack of time we spent together; she had been forgiving of *that*. What bothered her the most was that, during the whole process, she said I became like someone completely different: mean, and spiteful, and...

I stopped myself mid-sentence, knowing that the next description would sound eerily like my father, and I didn't want to acknowledge any similarities to him. I *refused* to.

"It's okay Clyde, you don't have to go on." Karla's offer was sweet, but whether I spoke the word aloud or not, it was already resounding inside my head.

Abusive!

Abusive was the term Alexis had used in the letter – the one she had left for me on my typewriter the day she had finally said: '*Enough*'. It was never physical abuse she had explained, although between the resurrection of my painful past and the excessive amounts of alcohol, she had sometimes been fearful of me. But never had I laid a hand on her. She had been thankful to me for that. It had been more of a verbal and mental factor, something that I couldn't even remember, which made it hurt all the more. And as disgusting as it made me feel to think of such things again, it made me downright nauseous to be sharing it with Karla. How was I possibly going to explain something to her that I couldn't even remember myself?

"I'm sorry that you had to go through all of that, Clyde. I'm sure it wasn't easy for you; losing someone *that* close never is."

"At first it wasn't, but when '*The Town Kids*' rolled off the presses four years later, all of that pain and fear got packed back up and shelved – kind of like all of my writing stuff is now; out in the barn collecting dust. But that was in the past. Sure, Alexis had left me in a place where I didn't think I would ever have feelings for another person again. But these last few days have been helping me to look at things through a different perspective." I found myself staring deeper into Karla's eyes as the words flowed from my lips. "Thanks to you."

I was certain that I had overstepped my bounds with the last comment, but as a warm smile stretched across Karla's face, I knew that I had done okay. The sparkle in her eyes spoke volumes in the silence, embracing my heart with a genuine tenderness.

"So is that it for Clyde Baker? The author? No more books?"

I thought about it for a moment, unsure of where to even begin. "I wish I could answer that question for you, Karla. I really do. But I just don't know anymore. Have you ever felt so...confused about something – maybe about life in general – that you don't know which way to go?"

"More so than you realize. But I do have to admit that it would be a shame if you gave up on writing. You have a true God-given talent to paint pictures with your words and it would just be an awful shame if you walked away from it now."

"Yeah, so my agent tells me too," I replied, cracking a slight grin. "But I can understand his point of view. We had signed a three book deal and so far to date, I have only delivered on two of them."

"So deliver the third book to them as well. But just don't write them a novel that will fulfill your contract. Write something that will change the world."

There was a passion in Karla's voice that struck me silent for a brief moment. It was as if she spoke with conviction and a fervent heart, as well as a lifetime of healing experience. However, I just couldn't buy into the fact that someone could be filled with such a joy like Karla's, and still have suffered complete heartache – especially the kind that I had experienced. It just couldn't be possible.

"There actually was a third manuscript in the works. I was pretty close to finishing it, but then the accident happened, and I haven't touched it since. Now it just sits out in the barn with all my other stuff."

The hustle and bustle of the restaurant carried on around us like background extras in a movie, as if the people around us existed to only fill-in the scene and had no real purpose at all. The only thing that mattered to me in that moment was Karla, and yet strangely enough, I couldn't even look up to meet her eyes. Talking about my Shadow Life had been one thing, but mentioning

"At a Star Trek convention," I joked. The comment incited more laughter from both of us. "But seriously though, I didn't find him. He kind of found me."

"Do tell," she insisted.

"Well, I was beginning work on my second book – this was after Alexis had left – and I was having trouble figuring out a couple of the major plot points. So as usual, I decided to get away from the desk for a while and take a jog down at the beach. It was mid-January at the time so I wasn't worried about an afternoon run being cluttered with distractions. I don't remember how long I was running for, but I remember that my mind had gotten so tangled up with ideas, that I ran far beyond my usual distance. By the time I realized it was getting late I didn't have the faintest clue where I was. I was on some stretch of the beach that seemed tucked away from the usual beach traffic. There were no homes lining the coast. No families out playing in the sand. Nothing."

"That must have been a long haul back home for you," Karla interjected. I offered an over exaggerated nod of my head in response.

"Before turning around to run back though, I heard a tiny yelp of pain just barely over the sound of the waves. I looked around, trying to find out where the sounds had come from, and that was when I noticed a little puppy hobbling towards me in the sand."

"Was he hurt?" she asked.

"I thought so at first, but when I picked him up, he didn't seem injured at all. In fact, all he tried to do was lick me all over my face."

"And he didn't have any tags on him?"

"None," I said. "And besides, there wasn't a home around for miles. I tried calling out to see if anyone was nearby who had lost a wandering puppy, but there was nobody. And I couldn't just leave him there. The poor thing was shivering and scared and every time I tried putting him down, he would begin to whimper and hobble about. What else was I supposed to do?"

"I don't blame you," she said. "I would have taken him home too. Who would just let their little puppy wander around like that? That's so sad."

"I tried putting fliers in the nearby neighborhoods, as well as putting in a couple of calls to the shelters in the area to see if anyone was reporting a missing puppy. But there were no leads and so after two weeks of nursing the poor guy back to health, I gave him a name and adopted him into the family. And at the time,

I also thought that it would be helpful for Mindy. You know, a way to try and cope with her emotions and things. It's hard to be mad and unloving when there's a cute, golden puppy hanging around. However, Mindy wanted nothing to do with him, but not for a lack of him trying."

"That's an incredible story, Clyde. It seems like you and that dog of yours were meant to be together. It's no accident that Spock found you the way he did, that's for sure."

The words that Flash had spoken to me the night before suddenly chimed in my head once again. *'You don't suppose that ole Spock and you just happened upon each other by no mishap, now do ya?'* At first glance, I had thought that my uniting with Spock was nothing more than coincidence, but I was beginning to have second thoughts.

"Can I ask you another question though?" she asked. I smiled and nodded. "Why Bridgeton? Your memories of this place weren't too fond and I'm sure you could've afforded any place else. So why come back here?"

"Well, although Mindy's outburst with the car had left me in a constant state of rage, my rehab gave me a lot of time to think certain things through. See, I think that Mindy's problem was that she could never face the past, and therefore it destroyed her mind. I didn't want that happening to me, so I moved back to Bridgeton hoping that it would help keep me from being like her. But now that I'm here, I have no clue what to do next. I feel like nothing has changed in my life other than the location."

My head began to swirl with thoughts of THE RED as I suddenly found myself battling with the devilish taunts of THE FACELESS ONE. I know, it sounds ridiculous, but somehow the words I had written began plaguing my mind as if they had actually been spoken – not by pen, but by the raspy and pitchy voice of a fictional scarecrow turned real.

"Several the eyes,
that wear a disguise.
So silence the lies,
and SEVER the ties."

I had to make the madness stop, but yet my heart was telling me to proceed with caution. Karla could sense the worry in my eyes, I was almost certain of it, so I had to tread lightly. I took another sip of water – a much longer sip than the last – and then offered a slight grin to my beautiful date.

"And what about the Heart of Bridgeton? Was there any particular reason why you chose that outcasted plot of land to call your home?" Karla asked with a good-humored grin. But she quickly noticed the blank expression on my face and asked, "You've never heard about the Sugar Hill Farms being called the Heart of Bridgeton?"

"No. Should I have?"

"Didn't you ever go there as a kid? To go horseback riding or walk through the cornfield mazes? Anything?"

"My mom and dad were into horseback riding when they were younger – supposedly it was how they met – which is probably why I never took to it."

"Sugar Hill Farms was owned by the Parker family many years ago – Thurman and Wilma Parker if I remember correctly – and the house and the barn that you are renting, was once infamous in our small corner of the world because of them."

"What made it so popular?" I asked.

"It wasn't just popular, Clyde. The mall is popular. *Movies* are popular. But the Sugar Hill Farms were the heart and soul of Bridgeton. There was a time decades ago, when Bridgeton was about to fade away and become a ghost town. It was so far in the red that even the politicians had to look up just to see hell."

"Well put," I said, joking about her analogy.

"But the Parkers had been so profitable with the farm in previous years, that they were single-handedly able to keep the town afloat. It was almost as if they had foreseen the town's mini-depression during the good times because they had been storing away crops and supplies in the very same barn that you now use as a literary hideaway. So not only were they able to financially help the town – they were stinking wealthy – but they were also able to provide food for the other farmers and the local markets to help the town drive commerce again."

"That's quite an amazing feat," I interjected, suddenly thinking about Flash and the strange connection he had felt towards the barn. I was getting great information from Karla, better than what the Sheriff or even Flash himself had offered.

"The Parker's were amazing people, Clyde. Everyone in town always spoke so highly of them. And even to this day, their story is passed down with adoration. They were just a loving couple who believed in a little concept that I like to call 'The Ways of The Farmer'."

A blast of hot air escaped my lungs as if I had been sucker-punched in the gut. "What did you say?" I asked.

"I know, it's not the most poetic sounding phrase. I'm no Hemmingway, Poe, or *Baker*, but it was something I made up to help me understand life a little better."

Finding the right words in that moment was like trying to catch the wind.

"Are you okay, Clyde? You seem like you just hit a wall or something."

"No, I'm...good. I'm fine. Where..." I calmed myself down before speaking, not wanting to alarm Karla by stumbling over my words again. "The ways of the farmer? Where did you come up with that?"

Could it have been from Flash, I wondered?

"I told you. It was something I made up to help me cope with some things. I know it sounds silly, but it works for my simple mind." Karla giggled, a bit bashfully though.

"It's not silly," I suggested. "But enlighten me if you would. What does it mean?"

"Well, a few months ago I had been struggling with...certain aspects of life, you could say. And one day I was driving down by the apple orchards out on Glenwood Road, and I noticed how ripe the apples looked and how delicious they must have tasted."

As she spoke the words, my mind immediately recalled the crisp red apple that Flash had been eating during our talk.

"But then it dawned on me that throughout the years of seeing the Bridgeton harvest I had never once seen a farmer out working the land. I knew they were there, and that they worked hard day-in and day-out, but how did I truly know that they ever existed. Have you ever wondered that?" Karla asked.

"Not really. I usually just eat the food and call it a day."

"Exactly. Because it's all about the crops. Without them, the farmer's would never exist to us, if you really think about it. We know the farmers based upon the crops that they produce. Although we might not ever see them at work, they still sacrifice their time and their land so that we can enjoy in the harvest with them. And that's what 'The Ways of The Farmer' is all about to me; it's about sacrificing to help others so that we can all enjoy in the harvest together. And that's exactly what the Parkers did with

Sugar Hill Farms – your home. It was a beautiful and selfless sacrifice."

I gave serious thought to what Karla was saying, allowing her soft-spoken words to tickle at my mind like a feather. She truly did have a wisdom that was astounding, and as I continued to swim around in her thoughts, Flash's words once again seemed to become more of a distant memory than anything. Regardless however, the concept itself was something I could appreciate although I wasn't fully grasping its application to my life.

"That makes sense," I said. "But to answer your question: no. I never knew that part of the Sugar Hill Farms history. Once I had decided to move back to Bridgeton – completely against Slater's wishes – I contacted a real estate agent from here and had them search out some properties for me."

"I'm surprised they had the house listed," commented Karla as she began to scan the restaurant for any sign of the waitress. "As much as the town wants to keep the house vacant, I would have thought that none of the real estate agents would have touched the place."

"They didn't. The realtor had sent me two or three places but I didn't like the location of any of them. One was too close to the house where I had grown up, another one was in the center of town where I'd have access to all the Bridgeton noise and clutter, and the third one just looked funky." I smiled as I heard the silliness of my own words. "I was going to give up on the idea but before I did, I opted to give Craigslist a fair shake. And sure enough, the house listed in Bridgeton was the place I rented. So no, the history to the place had no bearing on my decision at all, but with a story like the one you told me, I can definitely see why the place was considered to be the heart of Bridgeton at one time."

"As water reflects a man's face, so a man's heart reflects a man," Karla added with a smile. I wasn't quite sure where she was coming from with that statement but I didn't think to ask.

"But enough about boring old me though. Tell me about yourself. Who is Karla Turner?"

"Well, although I wasn't born and raised in Bridgeton, I don't think my story is unlike the others that you'll find here. I'm just living the dream of the small rural town, waiting for my chance to get out."

"Are you still waiting for that chance?" I asked.

"I've always dreamed about living on the water down south somewhere, but we're all allowed a dream or two in life I guess," she said while fiddling with the napkin on the table.

"It's never too late to try and fulfill your dreams," I offered, albeit with a slight caution. "What's keeping you here?"

"Honestly? I'm not quite sure. I had thought about up-and-leaving after I graduated from college but, I never did. I jumped headfirst into work and never looked back."

"Do you ever regret it? Staying? Do you ever feel like you missed out on a part of who you were meant to be by not following your dreams?"

Karla shook her head without giving it a second thought. "I'm not defined by where I live or whether or not my dreams come true. Sure, I made some of my greatest mistakes in Bridgeton, but then again, I would never have met you."

Karla's comment was straight and to the point, and for a moment, it left me speechless. The temperature in the restaurant seemed to climb in that moment and there was no amount of ice water in my glass that could have helped to keep me comfortable.

"I doubt that my company is better than a coastal sunset. I don't have that much to offer."

"Oh, but you do. You just don't see it yet." Karla reached across the table and placed her hand on top of mine. A rush of electricity shot up my arm and into my chest, leaving my nerve-endings to twinkle as if a galaxy of shooting stars had just raced throughout my body. "People tend to think that my job is rewarding because I get to help others all day. And it is, don't get me wrong. But what nobody understands is that I'm the one who gets uplifted through it all. The people I work for add so much to my life, even more so in your case."

Karla's explanation was a very selfless one, and it was moving to hear. The truth of her response made it easier for me to speak freely as well. And so I did.

"Ever since the accident I was never able to see my life as being anything more than just a waste of flesh. And I never would have used the term 'lucky' to describe my condition. But now that I look back at it, if Mindy had never hit me with her car, I would never have met you. And so I guess..." The next words to come out of my mouth were hard to swallow, but the blaze of beauty in Karla's eyes seemed to siphon the very words from my lips. "...I guess I would consider myself the lucky one."

He marched up to Karla, lowering his head to the ground while keeping his back end poised in the air as if he were taking a bow. His front paws reached out towards her in a playful manner, daring her to begin the game by trying to wrestle away the toy from him. Meanwhile, he applied a slight, continuous amount of pressure with his jaws to the belly of Mr. Squirrel, releasing a steady precession of playful squeaks.

Attune to my dog's hints, Karla reached down sneakily and snagged hold of the toy's free ends before Spock could pull away. With the game underway, Spock shook his head vigorously, adding a muffled growl as a sound track, but Karla hung on. The two of them tugged back and forth – Spock with his growling, Karla with her laughing, and Mr. Squirrel with his continued song of squeaks. Spock tried to use the power of his hind legs to retain possession of the toy, but in the end Karla managed to snag it free.

"Toss it over there," I suggested, pointing towards the garage. "He loves to play fetch." Karla did as I suggested.

As soon as Mr. Squirrel became airborne, Spock dashed down the steps of the front porch, making haste as he sprinted down the walkway. The plush toy landed just to the left of the detached, two-car garage. It came to rest against the small section of privacy fence that lined the tight angle between the house and the garage.

Spock was on it almost immediately, ripping the toy from the ground as if he were plucking a stubborn weed from a garden. He began to return to us, but then he stopped and whipped his head back around to the fence. I watched as his body transcended playful mode, becoming rigid and tense like the very beams of wood that made up the small section of fencing behind him. A second or two later, Mr. Squirrel was released from his captor's jaws, falling to the ground with a listless WOOMP.

"Is he okay?" Karla asked while observing Spock carefully.

"Yeah. He probably just picked up on the scent of one of the rabbits that hangs out here. He loves to chase them around the yard. Although if he ever caught one, he'd probably just pat it on the head and send it on it's way. The Retriever in him keeps the chase fun, but he's no hunter. Isn't that right fella?"

Spock didn't pay me any attention however. He simply stood frozen in place, his gaze fixated heavily upon something behind the gate in the backyard – something that neither Karla nor I were able to see.

"Come on Spock. Let's go inside."

No response. No movement.

"Spock! Let's go!" I hollered, but there was still nothing.

"Do you want me to get him and bring him back for you?" Karla offered.

"No, that's okay. Maybe just let him into the backyard if you wouldn't mind. He probably just needs to get it out of his system after being caged up all night." Cheerfully, Karla complied.

I watched with a fond heart as she made her way over to Spock. I was captivated by the ethereal quality of her beauty. Had the sky above not been veiled with a drove of clouds that night, I could only have imagined how breath taking she would have looked, trimmed in a halo of moonlight. Just the thought of it made me long for the night to never end. I wanted nothing more than to hold her in my arms and to once again taste her lips with mine, but as the pain in my back and legs began to throb, I loosened my grip on those thoughts and tightened it around the cane instead. I could feel the first play of a grimace tugging at the corners of my mouth. It shattered all thoughts of taking the night any farther. So rather than waiting awkwardly by the front door for a disheartening rejection, I decided to meet her at her car instead.

The moment Karla got the gate unlocked and opened, Spock darted into the darkness of the backyard. His blonde body streaked across the lawn like a beacon of light over a tumultuous ocean, until finally disappearing behind the garage.

"Do you want me to wait for him?" she asked.

"Not unless you plan on standing there for a while. It's a fairly large backyard for one dog to scout alone. It could take some time." I forced a smile. "He'll come around to the back door when he's done having all his fun."

"He's too funny," she commented, then fastened the gate back into place.

When Karla finally met up with me again, we were both standing next to the driver side door of her car. Only a foot of space stood between us.

"Thank you again, Clyde for a wonderful evening. I haven't enjoyed myself like this in a long time. I'm just sorry that the restaurant was so backed up."

"That just gave us more time to spend together, that's all. It's all about perspective, remember?"

"Words of wisdom, huh?" she joked. "You must be close to someone who's pretty brilliant."

"The brilliance...it can be debated. But as far as pretty, there's no doubt about that."

34
Deputy Henry Bowers

I pulled down all the shades in my apartment and double-checked the locks on the door. Killing the lights, I took a seat in the recliner as far away from the windows as possible. Keeping the room dark was key. A dark apartment meant an empty apartment, and that was precisely the message I was trying to send the Sheriff whenever he planned on showing up.

And oh yes, he would be showing up. It was just a matter of time now.

Darkness enveloped every inch of the place. It wasn't a normal darkness – nothing was normal anymore after you watch someone get ripped apart limb by limb. It was a thick and heavy darkness like a wet towel, and it began to suffocate me as I rocked back and forth in a sporadic fashion. I desired to reach over and click on one of the end table lamps, but I couldn't pull myself to do it. I *wanted* the light, but I *needed* the darkness.

There was a car door opening and closing somewhere in the parking lot below. I could tell it was far enough away because only the faded echo caught my ear, but I jumped at the sound nonetheless.

It's the Sheriff. He's finally coming for me.

I waited, but Eckhart never came to the door. Nobody did.

My thoughts suddenly shifted, and I found myself thinking about the woman I had arrested. Her name was Mindy; sister of the town nutjob. I couldn't forget her if I tried. But how on God's green earth did she find out about the coyotes? Me and Kelly were alone that night on the property. No one could have known. It wasn't possible. *Was it?* Of course not. But either way, she would talk to the Sheriff. She would tell him everything that had happened and then my career would be over. The one job that I had hoped and planned for since I was a child would be locked away, just like I would be. And I couldn't let that happen.

I continued rocking in the chair as I forced my mind to work harder. *Think harder!* The darkness was loud. I had to force my mind to move above it. As I strained, trying to do so, a faint noise echoed from my bedroom at the end of the hall. Or perhaps it was coming from behind me. I couldn't be sure. The sound reminded me of a raspy dragon trying to exhale a large breath of hot air. But the sound was not alone. The long, drawn out breath of syllables and sound seemed to meld together until actual letters were formed – letters that formed a name. *My* name.

"*Henry*," the noise had said from somewhere within the apartment. "*H-e-e-n-n-r-r-y!*"

I squeezed my eyes closed as if to ignore the nothingness that had become something. But all I found when I closed my eyes was more darkness. And whatever had said my name was living in the darkness. IT breathed the darkness in. IT *was* the darkness.

"There's nothing there," I whispered aloud. My eyes were still buttoned up with fear. "It's all in my mind. There's nothing there."

"*H-e-e-n-n-r-r-y!*" The darkness repeated.

"My name's not Henry!" I screamed out into the empty apartment, oblivious to any concerns about my neighbors being startled at the late night racket. "It's Hank!" My fury dissolved into a cowardice puddle of tears. I sobbed within the chair, waiting for the darkness to overtake and kill me, to devour me with unseen teeth just like the coyotes had done to Kelly.

How had Mindy known? How?

I reached into the pocket of my jeans like a blind man fumbling for his cane, and pulled out my cell phone. As soon as I flipped the phone open a soft blue glow entered the room. I peeked my eyes open and stared into the dim haze of light, hoping that the darkness would leave me be – that the light would end the madness. But as my eyelids parted, a large shadow raced into the light towards me and pushed up against me like a breath of wind from a fan.

The sudden rush of movement sent me jumping off the recliner and over the beer-stained armrest of the chair. I tumbled to the floor, slamming my head into the lamp on the coffee table. My hand released the phone and the soft blue light bounced to the floor

37
Clyde

The dream world takes hold of me again.

I am suddenly pulled out of the darkness and thrust backwards in time – into the hurricane that started it all just over a year ago. The rain falls down around me like a cloak, the fury of wind bays in the darkened sky, and the headlights of Mindy's car stare me down like a haunted apparition. It is once again, exactly how I remember it. But it is all the same – different.

The rain seems heavier, thicker than I recall, as if the silver rivulets of water are meant to bind me like a rope. With each saturating drop that hammers down upon me, I feel strangely like a fly trapped in the web of a hungry spider. The gale force winds continue to gust and blow through the surrounding Florida landscape. But rather than sounding like the echoed screams of demonic spirits as it had before, the wind seems to convey more of a melancholy disposition, like the cries of a lonely child in search of love. I can hear the subtle differences as it bends the trees and snaps at the strand of endless telephone poles. I can feel it against my skin in icy bursts.

Mindy's black Mercury Sable looks exactly the same as it does in every dream, but there is an air of change within the beaming lights that hold me frozen in place. They are not just headlights in this version of the dream, but rather windows into a world that I wish not to enter, although I find myself rushing towards her car with a mindless fervor.

"Something is different," I keep telling myself. "Wake up, Clyde. Get up! NOW!" But I cannot. I can only move towards Mindy's car with the nagging suspicion that change is in the air –

and not a pleasant change either. I can smell it. It is thick and hot and lingers in the wind like a musty odor from a damp cellar. I am petrified of moving any closer, but I am drawn into the lights like a magnet. There is no battle of wills for me to conquer – no choices for me to make. I am like a character in a book, being forced to play out my given role as the reader keeps reading. That thought alone scares me worse than the storm itself.

I approach the unmoving car and take hold of the handle on the driver side door, willing the door to be locked; for the handle to remain jammed in place. The darkness within the car is so vast and total that I cannot even see Mindy within, and yet I am moving to enter without any thought or fight. As the door creaks open, the storm falls silent and then is gone. A hush rings in my ears, as if the lack of sound somehow screams louder than the storm had. As for the world beyond the car door, it is completely and totally different – just as I had feared.

38
Karla

I sat alone in the hospital waiting room. My face was sunk deep into my empty palms as I cried bitter tears into cupped hands. I couldn't believe what was happening. When I had left Clyde after dinner I had believed that there was something true and genuine between us. It had felt *so* right, that I was beginning to even question Pastor Rob about his views. But after what had just happened in the hospital room, I didn't know which way to look anymore. How could one person change so drastically in the matter of a few short hours? Or perhaps he had never truly changed. It could have all been an act; a story that the great writer was weaving within his own mind. I just didn't know, and the uncertainty made me cry all the more.

One of the older nurses walked passed, reading the contents of a folder through a pair of thick, horn-rimmed glasses. She peeked up at me – only for a moment – with a heartless scowl stitched across her portly face, before returning to her ever-so important reading. I only spotted the stout nurse for a brief moment in passing, but it didn't take much to know that she recognized who I was. More importantly however, she knew who I had been there to see, and it displeased her enough to glare in my direction.

After sitting in the solitude of the waiting room a while longer, I reached into my purse and pulled out my cell phone. I punched in a few numbers and then used my free hand to wipe away the tears from my eyes while I waited. The phone rang four times before clicking over to a voicemail. I waited for the beep and then began to leave a brief explanation of Clyde's accident on the answering machine of his agent, Jackson Slater.

39
Clyde

I am no longer outside of Mindy's car, but I am not inside of it either. There is a door that is closed behind me, but the plastic handle has been replaced with a metal one. The black car door is replaced by a large, heavy mass of wood that slides on rollers at the top. The door is locked from the outside with a hefty padlock. I cannot see it, but yet I know it to be true, because I immediately know where I am. I am standing inside of an old horse barn – my barn – the one that Flash had felt such a connection with.

There is a long corridor outstretched before me that runs the entire sixty-foot length of the barn. Four empty horse stalls mark the concrete walkway; two on my left and two on my right. The stalls are closed up and locked, but I immediately notice that the usual stall doors – the ones that look as if they belong in an old western – have been replaced with black, cast iron gates. Each gate is identical to the gate out on the property; the gate that has captivated my every waken thought.

Just beyond the stalls are two more doors. The one on the left leads up to the top level of the barn, where all of my writings and office supplies have been stored. The other door is the massive kind that opens and closes on rollers, identical to the one locked directly behind me. That door bookends the opposite side of the structure and opens out into the front parking area. I long to run through it, but I know that it too is locked. The dream world has trapped me inside the barn – but why?

The darkness of night festoons the walls and floors of the old barn, accented by a glimmer of moonlight that spills in through the windows of each stall like the tendrils of a silver vine. The air

*inside the barn is frigid, causing a barrage of pins and needles to
bite at my skin. Each exasperated breath I take evolves into a small
tuft of mist as it hits the coldness of the air. My heartbeat quickens
as my feet slow their pace. Fear dances in the deserted streets of
my mind like nightmares on parade. That is when I first hear the
pathetic sounding voice as it cries out into the dark.*

"Stop it, Phillip! You're hurting me!"

I pause.

Frozen.

*I take in a cold lungful of air at the sound of the all-too
familiar voice. The woman's hopeless plea sends my body into a
convulsion of shivers. A loud WHACK stamps the night inside the
first stall. It is followed by a helpless yelp of pain. A lifetime of fear
overtakes me, but as I drawl near to the first of the four black
gates, I am able to see who is caged within the stall, transforming
the thoughts in my mind into a foreboding reality.*

*As the moonlight cascading in through the window shifts to
the far back corner, two people evolve from out of the darkness.
There is a man, tall and lanky, dressed in a grease-stained tee shirt
and a camouflage trucker hat. It is a hat that I am morbidly
familiar with although I had hoped to forget about it. But even
now, with his back turned towards me, I can still see the white star
embroidered on the front. It is a symbol that I have come to
associate with pain over the years. I cringe even at the thought.*

*The woman is short and much heavier than the man. She has
a tangle of long, black hair that blends into the corner shadows.
Her plump face is tinted – RED – and her eyes are swollen with
tears. A stream of blood trickles out from the gash on her bottom
lip, tracing the contours of her chin as it runs down her face. Even
the summer dress she is wearing – dark blue in color with nickel-
sized red dots scattered evenly across the pattern – is soiled with
spatters of her own blood. She lay defenseless in the corner of the
stall with the moonlight revealing the pain and anguish that she
hides in her distraught face. The man is breeding on her fear as he
hovers maliciously over her. He drinks it in like wine.*

*"Damnit woman! When I'm talking, you keep your pie-hole
closed or I'll beat the ugly right out of your fat ass! God knows
you need it!" The man raises one of his thin hands in the air,
clenching it into a tight fist before sending it flying across the
woman's jaw with a loud CRACK.*

*"Mom!" I cry out. In the hollow belly of the barn, my voice
sounds eerily like the ten-year old version of myself. Tears begin to*

well up in my eyes as I watch the head of my disoriented mother slam against the far wall. The weight of her upper body slouches towards the concrete floor, but before she can fall over completely, the callous-hearted man sends a backhanded slap against her opposite cheek.

"Stop it daddy!" I hear myself say in a cracked, adolescent voice. "Stop it! You're hurting mommy!"

The angry man's head snaps around in my direction and for the first time in over twenty years, I find myself staring into the soulless eyes of my father.

"Shut it!" he says through a contorted snarl. "Shut it or you're next you damned nipper! Don't you know not to go poking your nose around where it don't belong?"

My dad jumps up from his hunched position like a hostile locust, leaping towards me with blazing speed. I am stunned by the quickness he displays, frozen in fear as he storms the gate. He moves with a pent-up fury that exceeds what I remembered from my childhood. He slams his face against the cold bars of the gate as one gangling arm springs towards my neck like a defensive snake. His reaching fingers brush against the collar of my shirt, but I am able to avoid his grasp by leaning back at the last possible moment.

"Come on, Clyde. Don't you wanna play with your dear old dad?" A bellow of laughter rises from his gray-stubbled face. The eerie sound echoes throughout the barn until it is finally swallowed up by the night. I take another series of small, shuffled steps away from my enraged father, all the while feeling the heat of his anger through the gaze of his demented eyes. It was just as I remembered him.

"You want me to stop? Huh?" he asks. He then pulls his body as close to the gate as possible, pressing the side of his face against the bars and peering out at me through one enormous, blood-shot eye. "Then let me out of here. Let me out Clyde – you damned nipper! Come on! Let me out! Open this gate and LET...ME...OUT!"

With the sounds of my bruised and bleeding mother fading in the background, my dad begins to tug at the gate with brute force. The iron hinges creak and moan beneath the pressure – even to the point of loosening – but they hold up nonetheless. I back away as far as I can until his image is swallowed up by the darkness. The rage in his voice hangs in the air like the humidity of a Florida, summer's day, but his presence in the stall disappears, becoming nothing more than a memory.

I refused at first, although sleep was coming upon me whether I fought it or not. It had been a long night indeed – an emotional one – and sleep would be just what I would need to clear my head. I was in a precarious place as far as Clyde was concerned. I had made the daunting mistake of mixing business with pleasure and was beginning to feel the repercussions of doing so. So after the Sheriff insisted, I gave in to the notion of rest and figured that a few hours of shuteye could help me put all of my ducks in a row. Besides, it would give me the opportunity to keep an eye on Spock. There was no doubt that he was back at the house flipping out over the monstrosity that had occurred.

"Please call me if there's any word from the doctor," I insisted while gathering my belongings in hand and standing to my tired feet.

"I surely will, Miss. But don't you worry though. Mr. Baker will be just fine. As soon as the doctor releases him, I'll saddle him into my cruiser and get him back to his house lickity-split."

I thanked the Sheriff with a wan smile, and then made my way to the bank of elevators at the end of the hall. Eckhart waited until I was safely within the elevator, and then made his way into Clyde's room with the brown paper bag crinkling beneath his arm as he walked.

41
Clyde

There is a child crying. I can hear him ever so faintly, although the darkness in the barn keeps him hidden from my sight. I take hold of the locked gate on the second stall and gaze inside. It appears to be empty, but then the moonlight shifts direction again, shining into the back window like a spotlight.

Inside the rustic enclosure of the second stall, I see a large jungle gym that uses up every inch of possible space. The large playground item is made up of different metals and plastics, equipped with an assortment of childhood pleasantries such as monkey bars, a sliding pole, and even a bubbled porthole for children to look out of while burrowing through the small tubed-tunnels. The unit is painted a dark chocolate color, except for the spiraled slide at the one end. The slide is made up of green plastic and to the eyes of a child, could possibly look like a giant snake. The slide had appeared to me that way once before – when I was ten years old – and as I stare at its archaic form through the view of the barred gate, I once again find myself seeing it through the eyes of a child. Not only did I remember the jungle gym because of my nightmarish childhood, but also because I had written about those experiences in my first novel, THE TOWN KIDS. Fear stabs at my mind almost immediately.

Suddenly, the sounds of the crying child are no longer faint and distant, and seem to echo through the barn. My eyes hurriedly scan every inch of the jungle gym, trying to hone in on the source of the crying. It doesn't take long for me to notice the young boy who is curled up on the dirty floor, sobbing beneath the twists and turns of the slide. The boy appears no more than ten years of age skimming through for enjoyment. As I read, the front cover of the book faced in Clyde's direction. Due to the fact that he was still trapped in whatever dream world had hold of him, he was unable to take note of the front cover. It was dark with a lighthouse type structure in the center, beaming a radiant light across the image. Emerging from the darkness of the surrounding trees, there was a face of a coyote trying to devour the light with it's razor sharp teeth. The snarling beast had one black eye and one red. The title beneath the image read: A DAY LIKE THIS, BY CLYDE BAKER.

43
Clyde

Inside the stall behind the third black gate is a single-sized bed centered on the floor. The bed sheets are unkempt and messy, spoiled with years of urine stains and body dirt. There is a young girl – no more than twelve years old – laying on top of the unmade bed, curled with her knees to her chest. She is dressed in nothing but a man's extra long Dukes of Hazzard tee shirt. The soiled garment wraps around her beaten and bruised body like a cocoon. Her long strands of black hair flow around her shoulders like a cluster of suffocating shadows, concealing her face from the horror that stands before her.

The silhouette of a man enters into my line of sight, standing over the bed like a hunter who has already wounded his prey, waiting for the right moment to strike the fatal blow. Even from my side of the gate, I can smell the stink of perversion on the man as strongly as a sweaty gym sock. The thoughts in his head are playing out before my eyes in rudimentary pictures. The thoughts of lust and depravity that are seeping from his heart turn my stomach sour and open the floodgates of tears in my eyes. I try to scream with hopes to thwart off the vile attack that will be administered to the young girl, but my voice will not come – my words are trapped behind a wall of emotions.

Suddenly, the young girl stirs on the bed, and then sits up. For the first time I am able to see her face – the blank visage of my sister Mindy when she was a child. To my surprise, I watch as the young girl slowly removes the tee shirt that she had been wearing, welcoming the man – our father – into the bed with her.

46
Karla

The loud knock on the door awoke me from my sleep with a startle. Spock, who had opted to fall asleep on the couch next to me, raised his head and stared intently at the front door. A moment later he jumped up from the couch and disappeared into the foyer.

The knock resounded through the dark house a second time, pulling me completely out of my sleep. I was still inundated with a sluggish, groggy sensation, but my mind finally began to kick into gear.

"*The Sheriff,*" I thought to myself while trying to rub the sleep out of my eyes. "*The doctor must have released Clyde early and the Sheriff is bringing him home!*"

I hurried off of the couch and made my way to the front door where Spock was standing as stiff as a board, facing forwards with a determined fervor. A low-pitched growl formed in his throat, evolving into a deep WOOF.

"I know, Spock. The Sheriff might be sending us some good news," I replied, but Spock seemed to be ignoring me. Instead, he began to jump at the front door, clawing at it as if he were trying to tear through.

"You have to calm down, boy. I don't know if the Sheriff is a dog person or not, and I don't want to get you in trouble by letting you pounce all over him. We don't want another incident like the one in town the other day, do we? Here, boy. Come over here for a minute."

With the fatigue of the long night still clouding my mind with unclear thoughts, I took hold of Spock's red collar and led him into the nearby bedroom. I shut the bedroom door closed, assuring him that as soon as the Sheriff left, I would cuddle him on the couch some more. Spock was not happy at all. He continued on with his low-pitched, guttural WOOFS.

The opportunity to cuddle again that day would never arise. Sleep depravation and emotional overload had apparently impaired my judgment. Spock had tried to warn me about the early morning visitor, but I hadn't been thinking clearly enough to catch on. So as the third and final knock echoed throughout the house, I reached for the door with high expectations. Those expectations would soon be shattered.

"I'm here, aren't I?" I say, speaking up with a boldness I never knew. "So just let him go. I'm the one you want, right? Just let him go! Please."

Powe chuckles, his crooked grin never faltering.

"When will you ever learn to do as your told?" he adds.

"Let us teach him a lesson, Powe. C'mon, we'll give him a wicked, good lesson!" Mikey says, chiming in. Rather than shushing the annoying, mohawk-wearing punk, Powe gives agreement with a nod of his head.

Immediately, the three kids behind him jump out at me with blazing speed. The big bruiser of a kid is the first one to reach me. He lowers his shoulder and runs through me, knocking me to the ground with a loud WHOOMP. JJ grabs a hold of one hand while Mikey grabs the other. DeeBowe begins by jabbing fist, after repeated fist into my stomach. My breath escapes my lungs and I find myself gasping for a single tuft of air. He delivers a few sharp blows to my face as well, blinding me in flashes of light as he connects each punch. The pain is immense.

"That's enough," Powe commands. DeeBowe stands to his feet and backs away in obedience, but not before thrusting his booted-foot into my side.

Powe steps over me and kneels down. He reaches into one of the pockets of his faded denim jeans, and pulls out a switchblade. He clicks the blade release button and the cold steel appears with a silent WOOSH. Pressing the blade to my cheek he begins to talk again.

"That old man over there isn't any of your concern. He doesn't exist! Got it? He's nothing! Nobody! I don't want you even thinkin' about him or I'll let these fellas run you through like a pig on a spit. So do you got anything else you'd like to say about him or should we move on?"

I remain silent, and it greatly pleases the knife-wielding kid.

"Cut him up, Powe! He ain't gonna stop! He's nothing but a chicken-shit turd! Let's just cut him up baby, yeah!" Mikey says in my stead. Without taking his eyes off me Powe holds the knife up in Mikey's direction.

"Shut him up, DeeBowe before I do."

The shaved-headed kid turns and throws a fist into Mikey's shoulder. It lands with a hefty THUMP. Mikey winces and then falls obediently silent.

"Good boy," Powe says as if speaking to a dog. He then returns the blade of the knife to my cheek. I can feel the point of

the steel trying ever so slightly to pierce through my skin. *"Do you know why we're here?"*

"The book?" I say hesitantly. Powe's enthusiasm rises.

"Will you look at that fellas! He's not as dumb as he looks." The three trained monkeys laugh as if on cue.

"Why is it so important to you?" I ask timidly, almost afraid of the answer I will receive. My body is shivering with fear. I try and refrain myself but its no use.

"I could care less about your damn book. But the one who sent us aint too happy that you've never told his story to the world. You've kept him locked up in this filthy pigpen and now he wants out. Are you hearing me, Cupcake! You finish that stupid book and let what's done be done!"

"Who sent you?"

"What is this? Twenty questions?" Mikey cackles in the background, but in a quieter tone as to not aggravate Powe again. An unexpected peal of thunder rings out in the nighttime sky, rattling the walls of the barn. *"Open your eyes and look around sometime."*

For the first time, Powe breaks eye contact with me and looks up at the sliding glass door across the room. His crooked smile grows wide as his eyes sparkle with a lustful allegiance. I tilt my head back in order to get a glimpse of what all four of the delinquents are now staring at. Outside of the sliding glass door, the darkness is total and thick. But then there is another BOOM of thunder followed by a flash of lightning. In that instance, I am able to see the form of a large scarecrow standing outside on the deck, staring in at us through the glass doors. He has no face – only a burlap sack for a head – and the sight of him makes my heart skip a beat. I turn my eyes away immediately.

"Get 'er done, Cupcake. And I hope you don't mind, but I think we're gonna make a little insurance withdrawal, just to make sure you know how serious I am. Next time, you won't be so lucky."

Powe's grin widens, revealing a set of yellow-stained teeth. He takes the blade of the knife and slashes at my cheek. I can feel the warmth of my blood as it trickles down my face.

There is another BOOM of thunder.

Then the dream world grows black.

"If this is all truly happening, then time isn't a luxury we have a lot of, Sheriff." I thought back to my most recent dream and remembered Powe and his three delinquent friends. I could almost still feel the cold steel of his switchblade as it pressed against my cheek. The thought made me shiver. "The coyotes might be dead – *I hope* – but that might be the least of our concerns now. We don't have long."

"What are you talking about?" he asked. I held up the book for him to see.

"If my books are beginning to...*materialize* somehow, then there are far more frightening things in these pages than just those coyotes – not to mention characters from The Town Kids and even the third book I had been working on."

At the mention of my third book, I found my mind beginning to wander. I was suddenly able to remember the manuscript I had been working on before the accident. Moreover, I began to recall the description of my most feared character – THE FACELESS ONE – the father of all fears. The thought was so vivid in my mind that I actually began to fear him as if he too had jumped out of the pages of my unfinished novel and was slinking around Bridgeton. And if he was – if the coyotes were not the only manifested fears from my books – then there was no telling how things would end up for everyone involved.

I returned my attention to the Sheriff and noted the narrowing of his eyes, a sure sign that he was giving deep consideration to what I had said. His furrowed brow told me that he was still struggling to believe any of it, but he couldn't dispute what his two eyes had plainly seen for themselves. That is what was troubling him the most I figured.

"And so you think that more things are on their way?"

"I do. I believe it very strongly." I paused in order to steady my voice, which was beginning to quiver ever so slightly. "While I was sleeping just now, I had a dream about the four thugs that I wrote about in my first novel – the kids who made the flagstaff and who bullied Georgie all the time. They told me that they were coming. Hell, they might already be here, I can't be sure. But for whatever reason, I believe they're next."

"A dream?" the Sheriff asked with a slight, mocking hint in his voice. "That's your best evidence?"

"You saw that coyote, Sheriff. Would you have believed it had I only *told* you about it?"

"Dang nabbit, Clyde. I saw it with my own eyes and I still don't believe it. It could be nothing but one big coincidence that we're getting all worked up about. Have we stopped to consider that?"

"You don't believe that, and I know it. There's been crap going down on that property for years, and I'd bet my good leg that you've spent your entire career as the Sheriff of this God-forsaken town, trying to figure it out. Am I right?" Eckhart remained silent.

Two young nurses walked by the door at that moment, discussing their plans for when they're shifts ended. Eckhart watched them as they passed by, both of them greeting him with familiar smiles. When they were far enough down the hall, he spoke up.

"We'll talk later once we're out of this place. There's too many Chatty Kathy's walking about, and I can't afford for anyone to hear us discussing such folly. Get some rest."

Without another word, Eckhart walked out into the quiet hallway. Before leaving however, he turned to face me one final time.

"I recommend you take a look at the bookmark inside the book there. You might find it interesting."

I waited for the sound of Eckhart's footsteps to fade away down the hall before examining the book he had left. Stuffed in the last few pages and acting as a bookmark, was an old, faded envelope. Removing the bookmark allowed me to see that the envelope was not empty, nor was it sealed. There were papers stuffed inside but my attention was glued to the front of the envelope, where the small salutation was written in sloppy, cursive penmanship. Reading the front of the envelope set the room into a nauseating spin. It read:

TO: CLYDE
LOVE: YOUR MOTHER

* * * * * * * *

It was just after ten in the morning when Doctor Patel came in and spoke with me. I was still a bit weary seeing as though I hadn't gotten much sleep after Eckhart had left. There were too many to the chilly temperatures. However, I couldn't pull myself to say any of it, because somewhere down deep in the basement of my mind, I thought that the Sheriff might just be on to something.

"Last night you said that a homicide investigation was done on my mom," I said, preparing to ask one of the many questions that were weighing on my mind. "Why was that? Isn't it fairly obvious that when someone slashes open both of their wrists that they're pretty much calling it quits on their own?"

"Typically," answered the Sheriff. "And typically, most people cut only one wrist unless they're wanting to assure death – and quickly. But what isn't typical is for someone to ingest an entire prescription of Iron pill tablets before cutting themselves. So I felt that an investigation would be warranted."

"She did both?" I hadn't known that about her, although I wasn't surprised. If she had wanted out of the rat race bad enough, then I'm sure she was going to make certain that her plan was foolproof. But I didn't respond to Eckhart's comment. I just sat quietly with the old, faded envelope clenched tightly in my hand. The last few miles of the drive were spent in a much-needed silence.

* * * * * * * *

A rush of relief came over me when I saw Karla's Ford Escort in the driveway. I had expected her to be gone when I got back – *I couldn't have blamed her had she been* – so I was glad that she had opted to stick around. If it had only been for Spock that she was still at the house, it would have been good enough for me. However, there was a deep-seeded longing that hoped she was hanging around for other reasons as well, but I wasn't going to get carried away with too much conjecture.

The Sheriff brought the cruiser to a stop behind her car. He helped me get to my crutches, making sure that walking on the gravel would not be too cumbersome. There were a few near fumbles at first, but I took my time and managed without his help; slow and steady wins the race, as the saying is.

As we walked through the front door, Spock's barking immediately resounded throughout the house. I was surprised to see that my bedroom door had been closed, but I was *alarmed* to learn that Spock had been left alone inside the room. The air in the house was cold and stagnant, overtaking us with an uncomfortable oppression as we closed the door behind us. I could immediately hear the sound of Spock's paws as he jumped up on the door, clawing to be let out. As I opened the door for him, my blonde friend came rushing into the foyer with his nose to the cold tile floor. I tried to get Spock's attention but he was preoccupied with tracking whatever scent he had caught, whining ever so slightly as he searched. Eckhart and I watched on curiously.

"Is everything okay?" The Sheriff asked.

"I don't know. I've never seen him act like this before."

The Sheriff glanced around, peering innocently through the open bedroom door.

"Where's Miss Turner?" he asked, but again I didn't have an answer to give him. I called out to Karla, but only the echoed sound of my voice returned to our ears. The Sheriff tried as well, but there was still nothing.

Spock left the foyer almost as quickly as he had left the bedroom, tracking into the family room and then out into the mudroom. I followed as closely behind as I could despite the crutches. Eckhart trailed from the rear.

While inside the mudroom, Spock sniffed circles around the Sheriff and I, ignoring the questions I was asking of him. Finally, he looked up and aimed his twitching nose in the direction of the adjoining guest bathroom. His body tensed up and a soft, helpless whimper stung my ears.

Suddenly, the sound of a gun's hammer being cocked back caught my attention. I turned around and saw Eckhart standing with his gun in hand and a look of fright splayed across his face. His gun was aimed down at the floor, but the intensity in his eyes – *despite his age* – assured me that he would be ready to use the weapon without a moment's notice.

"You had better let me look in there first," he commanded while stepping towards the closed door that led into the spare bathroom. "Take hold of Spock just in case."

Without arguing, I grabbed Spock by the collar and took a step away from the bathroom door, backing into the far corner of the small mudroom. Holding onto my anxious dog while balancing myself on the crutches was not as easy of a task as I had hoped. But I managed, for fear of what Eckhart might discover beyond the bathroom door.

"Miss Turner," the Sheriff said into the cold, lifeless morning. "Miss Turner? Are you in there?" There was only silence, just as it had been before.

In those few passing seconds, as the Sheriff inched towards the door while raising the gun to chest-level, I began to replay the conversation with Karla in my head. I felt boorish for having blamed her the way I had, and if the Sheriff opened the door and Karla was...well...*gone* (for lack of wanting to consider the other word), than I doubted if I would ever forgive myself. I felt my grip release from Spock's collar and instead, take hold of his meaty back, clinging to my friend the way a child might squeeze a stuffed animal when something frightening has transpired.

Eckhart opened the door and poked his gun into the bathroom. However, he was quick to holster the weapon when he saw that danger was not imminent. What he did see laying in the bathtub against the far wall – *what we both saw* – was Karla's body. Her right arm hung limply over the brim of the tub, her fingers brushing against the rose-colored tile below. Her beautiful skin was badly bruised and beaten, streaked and soiled in her own blood. Her body had been left half-naked in the tub, blanketed by only the tattered remnants of her clothes.

The Sheriff rushed to her side and immediately began a search for any possible vital signs. I stood frozen in place, trying to sustain my breathing as my eyes flooded with tears. I could not believe what was happening. *Why Karla?* I screamed out in my head. *Why her?*

"She's got a pulse," the Sheriff shouted. "We need an ambulance. Now!"

Eckhart's strong and authoritative voice boomed wildly inside the small tiled bathroom. However, I was unable to comprehend his words because my attention had moved from Karla, onto the far back wall beyond the tub. There was a single word scrawled on the shower tiles in Karla's innocent blood. It was the same word that had been racing through my mind since I had awoken from the dream in the hospital. It was more than just a word anymore; more than a stupid title of an unfinished book either. It was my flagstaff. My final warning...*or else*.

Above Karla's unconscious body and written in her own blood on the far back wall was the word SEVER.

50
Mindy

The sound of boots CLOPPING against the concrete walkway woke me from my dreamless sleep almost immediately.

The corridor of jail cells extended into shadows in either direction, just like the sound of the hard-soled boots that seemed to be drawing near to my new home. I had no sense of the time of day, but I would have guessed early morning by the pull of exhaustion against my eyelids. And if I was anywhere close with my guess, then it was unlikely for anyone to be walking towards my cell, which happened to be the last cage at the end of the row. But I knew that guards were most likely on patrol at all hours of the night, so that was not the thought that made me sit upright on the cot as if I was about to expect a visit from the warden himself. It was the sound of the boots that had caught my ear. The guards tended to wear clean, steel-toed boots or dress shoes that gave off more of a CLAPPING sound, but the noise that was slowly drawing near to my cell sounded muddled in someway, as if the boot was being slightly muted by clods of dirt or mud.

I jumped to my feet, doing my best to mute the squeaking joints of the bed so as to not wake any of the other inmates. I grabbed hold of the bars in front of me, feeling like a child who was trying to look beyond a sea of adults at a parade. But unfortunately my view was blocked by the metal rails and the cryptic shadows.

"Hello?" I whispered into the darkness. As my voice echoed down the hall, the sound of the marching boots ceased. The silence of the moment became fiercer than the sound of the boots

52
Sheriff Eckhart

"What do you know about the place already?" I asked before Clyde could initiate the conversation.

"From what I've been told, the property used to go by the name of Sugar Hill Farms; supposedly it was the heart of Bridgeton."

"There's no *supposedly* about it. The Parker's were the original owners and ran quite a lucrative business right on this property here. And you'd be right in saying that the Sugar Hill Farms was the heart of this community. But I believe that's because the Parker's had a heart that cared about the people of this town and not just making money. Unfortunately that's a way-of-thinking that's been lost these days, but that's neither here nor there."

"And what about the property and the gate out there? What about that?" Clyde asked.

"The gate has been there as long as I can remember, and then some. But there were never any problems out there, not until the autumn of eighty-five. That's the first incident that I can recall because I was still fairly new as the Sheriff. Over the years though I've gone back and looked for past records, but there's been nothing documented out of the ordinary. If something had happened, we'd have it on file down at the station, but there's nothing.

"Anyhow, hunting season had just started up and Thurman Parker used to arrange hunting trips beyond the gate for some of the local hunters. He was a big animal lover, but ole Thurman was the top dog of rednecks when it came to sport hunting. That year still hangs fresh in my mind because Thurman had invited me along on the first trip of the season, which was a high honor in this town. I had to decline unfortunately because, like this year, it was unseasonably cold and there had been a bad accident on Route 288 heading into Canyon Pulse because of some black ice on the road. I was pretty peeved off to have to miss out on the first Parker hunt of the year...that was until I got the call later that night.

"There were five men, including Thurman, that left early for the hunt that morning, but only three of them ever returned. One of the remaining three – Scotty Holmes – hung himself a week later. That hunting trip was single-handedly the worst event this town endured for as long as I can remember. So you can understand why I dropped to my knees that night and thanked Almighty God for sparing me from that prestigious hunting trip."

"What happened to them, Sheriff? Was it a coyote attack again?" Clyde asked. He was naïve, thinking it would be that simple to piece the story together.

"That's just it, no one really knows what happened to those other men. Scotty Holmes was the only man who claims to have witnessed anything, but he came out of there speaking incoherent psychobabble, so we couldn't validate any of what he was saying."

"Perhaps it wasn't psychobabble after all," Clyde said, cutting in. "If he had told you that there was a coyote with one red, glowing eye that ate the other two men, would you have believed him or would your department have written him off as a nutjob?"

I was about to refute his theory, but stopped when I realized that he was more accurate than I wanted to give him credit for. A momentary tension filled the air between us as I pushed the police cruiser east towards Saint Luke's.

"What did Scotty tell you, Sheriff? What *was* his story?"

"It's hard to tell for sure. He spoke like a sobbing five-year-old child; every word was stuttered and choppy. It was almost impossible to tell if he was speaking actual words, or just mumbling sounds. But that was only in those rare moments when we could actually get him to speak. The only thing I was able to decipher was something about a..." I tried to find the right words, "...about a *choppy man*, or a *peace man*, or something like that. Like I said, it was too difficult to make-out what he was trying to say. From what we could collaborate between the stories of the other men, here's what we know: Thurman, Frank Jones, and Scotty Holmes remained in their tree stands while the other two suppose death was no exception to the rule for them. Because the Parker's didn't have any children of their own – not for a lack of trying on their part – Sugar Hill Farms was eventually handed over to the state, where it sat dormant until nineteen ninety-one when it was purchased by Lucas McNamara...you're current landlord."

"Does McNamara know about the place's history?" Clyde asked. Under the circumstances, I thought it was a viable question because if I was Clyde, I would abandon the place and move as far away as I could afford.

"He didn't at first. But when I found out that his plan was to use it as a rental property to subsidize his faltering food business, I made sure to tell him not to allow anyone access beyond the gate. That's why you see all of the NO HUNTING signs plastered everywhere you look. It was his way of scaring people off the land."

"But does he know the *extent* of what happened?"

"I didn't see it necessary to go into detail with him," I said in defense. "He was an out-of-town businessman and so I saw no need in drudging up a painful past just to appease him. But after the next death occurred, I thought it only fair to share everything with him before he read about it in the paper."

"There was more?" he asked.

"McNamara rented this place out to a young, hippie couple – the kind of folks who spend more time smoking dope to their rock-n-roll then they do breathing oxygen. That sort. They had it written all over them. What I wasn't privy to however, was the fact that they would hold big parties out in the barn there for them and their other grass-thumpin' friends. Apparently one evening, after they were done with one of their bong parties, the husband and wife got into a bit of a tiff – or at least that's what she said. Her husband, Saul Conners stormed out of the barn with a joint and an attitude; said he was going out on the trail to free his mind from his wife's nagging oppression. Imagine those being some of your final words to your so-called loved one." I said, snorting with disgust under my breath. For whatever reason, my final comment seemed to paint Clyde's face red with guilt.

"Pippen – who was Saul's wife – waited for a bit, and then ran out after him. She later told us that she had wanted to just let him go, but the sun was beginning to set and...well, you know how those hippies are. They don't want any bad energy or vibes – or whatever the heck they call it – between each other, especially when the sun is going down. Clearing the air was the phrase she had used if I remember correctly. Anyhow, she went running after him and could see him standing out by the gate. She tried calling to him to come back home, but he's too preoccupied with staring at something beyond. Finally, he turns to her and tells her that they've hit the jackpot because the land beyond the gate is covered in cannabis. He tells her to run back home and get something for them to harvest it all with. She on the other hand, gets furious that he's not paying her any mind and storms off back to the house. The last thing she sees in the fading daylight, is her husband walking beyond the gate and closing himself in. Later that night, after Pippen tried removing all traces of marijuana from the barn, she gave me a call with a complaint about her missing husband. We searched the property the following day, because I refused to allow any of my deputies beyond that gate after nightfall, and found the joint that Saul had been smoking in a patch of bloody grass. But that was it."

"What did you do about all the marijuana plants?" Clyde asked.

I flashed a quick smirk while replaying the memories of that night in my head. "There wasn't any marijuana out there. Saul must have still been tripping when he claimed to have seen it. He probably imagined the whole thing."

"And how did you come by all this information if the wife cleaned up all the evidence from the barn?"

"I knew she had been hitting the pipe, so I pressed her hard. I told her that because she was the last person to see her husband alive, especially if we drug tested her and it came back positive, that she was going to be the prime suspect in his disappearance. She cracked after that and told me everything. Needless to say, Pippen up-and-left the next morning. She took whatever she could carry and was gone. Eventually, the house went back to McNamara until he could find another renter."

"And I was the next renter?" he asked.

"No. There was one more person before you – a man by the name of Travis Underhill. Just the sound of that man's name makes my skin wanna crawl off." I hesitated for a moment before continuing on. "It was nineteen ninety-seven and McNamara was desperate to rent the place; he was needing the money in a bad way and Underhill was the first guy who came along willing to pay for it, despite the mystery hanging over the place. On the outside, Underhill seemed like a reputable citizen: clean-cut look, church deacon, and so-on and so-forth. What nobody knew was that he

53
Clyde

I was tired. Painfully exhausted would have been the better term, but I fought off sleep out of fear, despite being in the Sheriff's home. I fully believed what I had told Eckhart about Powe and his gang not coming for me anytime soon, but as the silence of that autumn afternoon slipped into early evening and then finally into a cold and dreary night, I couldn't help but succumb to my fears.

The trip to the hospital had been a short one, just as Eckhart had predicted. When I had left, Karla was still being worked on in the emergency room, and the nurses refused to grant me access to see her. I longed to be with her though – to hold her until she awoke – but she was still comatose and the outcome looked bleak. The guilt of her injuries wore heavily upon my mind as we left the hospital, and even while I sat down to eat the meatloaf dinner that the Sheriff's wife had prepared. My appetite was abysmal and any desire for small talk went out the window with every thought of Karla. So rather than hanging around the kitchen, I retired to my room where Spock had been curled up on the bed waiting for me. I needed to get away from people and clear my mind. I needed some sibilance of hope. I needed Karla.

With Spock nestled up next to me on the bed, my thoughts drifted back to the dream I had – to the way Powe and his gang had been pushing me to finish the book – and knew that I was correct about my assumption. Looking back on it however, there was one thing that I couldn't understand, and perhaps I never would. In my dream, Powe's lackeys had been roughing up Flash to the point of almost killing him, but last night they had taken their aggression out on Karla.

"Was Flash in danger?" I wondered. *"And how was he connected to this whole mess? He wasn't a character I had ever written about, so what could his involvement possibly be with the books?"* The discrepancy was confusing to me and was one of the greatest pieces of the puzzle that didn't seem to fit. If I could figure out Flash's involvement, I could hopefully come to an understanding of everything else. Unfortunately, understanding Flash would require me to find him again, and that alone was a task that was going to be put on hiatus for a while, at least until my leg healed up more.

I tried pushing aside all of the thoughts about Flash for the time being, knowing that there were two other things that required my attention before turning in for the night. First, I placed another quick call into the hospital, more than likely annoying the nurses who had been fielding my inquiries all day. It was my third attempt at a productive call since having left the hospital, because the responses I had received from the less-than-friendly nurses the prior two times were the same: "The doctor is with a patient right now, but I'll let him know you called." However, they must have been getting sick of my persistence because when I called the third time around, they patched me through to the doctor on-call.

Doctor Abrams was a middle-aged Iranian man who spoke English about as well as he returned phone calls, but I tried the best I could to keep my emotions dialed down. I informed him of who I was and how Karla and I were linked together professionally, but he regrettably informed me about some kind of new legislation that deterred him from giving me any information. I refused to end the call however without knowing something further. Anything would do.

"Can you at least tell me if it looks promising for her?" I finally asked. Frustrated. Helpless.

"It is hard to tell at the time. Miss Turner is...eh...no responding yet. I wish I could be more of help," Abrams said.

"What about her coma? How bad is it?"

"It is very difficult to predict the outcome of a comatose patient, Mr. Baker. Anytime a patient is unconscious for more than six hours, we diagnose the coma and follow through with a very strict regiment to avoid infections or atrophy of the muscles. Some patients are unresponsive for weeks, others for months, some for even longer still. I do not wish to burden you with worries but it is *change was slow and I was just to stupid to see it, but one day your father and me got into a hellish fight and he finally made his feelings known. He believed that his lack of success was completely my fault. He believed I trapped him into marriage by purposely getting pregnant and he hated me for it. That was the first time that he ever hit me.*

The beatings was minor at first, and he always sobered-up and apologized after some time. So I kept silent about it, believing that he was capable of change. Besides, there was no need to drag no names through the mud – I didn't feel that'd be fair to him. But then things got worse. He begun hitting me harder – even throwing things like pots and pans – whatever he could get his hands on. And if that wasn't enough for your daddy, he began beating on you just the same. I tried to hang on – to be a better wife – but he kept thrashing on us something fierce. I was broken-hearted 'cause I couldn't do a damn thing to keep him away from you. I was so scared to tell the Sheriff anything 'cause I had been ordered silent. That man said he'd kill you if I said something. And he would make me watch before killing me too. So I kept quiet for us, still thinking that he would change one day. But the day when we's walked in on your father molesting Mindy in her own bed, something inside of me just snapped. I don't know if it was the awful things he was making her do, or if it was the sickening look of pleasure in her eyes, but I became numb like ice in that moment. Watching that man get off on his own damn daughter killed any remaining thoughts of love that I had ever had for him.

The next week I left a note for your daddy, telling him that I's going to go tell the Sheriff everything: about the abuse, about the molesting of Mindy, and even about the money he had stolen from his job. I told him that if he wanted me to stay quiet about it all, he would have to come and meet me at the place we had first met. I told him that meeting me there would bind us closer together and work things out, but that was not truly my intent. My intention was to kill that heartless man. I had just wanted our love to die where it had begun and not within the bed of that bastard of a daughter. So I took along with me the axe he used for chopping wood, and waited for him.

I didn't have to worry about him not showing up that night neither 'cause he couldn't afford going to no prison. And besides, it would have proven to everyone, his father especially, that he hadn't been able to man-up and provide for his family without having to lie, cheat, and steal to do so. He was the biggest Taker I ever knew, but his pride was even bigger, so I had no doubt that he'd show.

My illusion of love died that night, Clyde. I took that axe to your daddy because if I hadn't, I'm sure he would have done far worse to all of us and I wasn't willing to live with that. So I took it to him with all the fires of hell burning inside me, and then buried him in pieces where no one would ever think to look for him.

You might not believe me, but I hated myself for what I did to your daddy that night. I tried telling myself that it aint my fault. That I did what I did 'cause I had to. I blamed Mindy if you must know, for ruining my marriage. She allowed that man to be such a damn Taker. I couldn't even be around her after that 'cause if I looked into her eyes, I'd see your father all over again. If she got anywhere near me I felt like serving her up a slice of what he got, and maybe I should've. God knows I wanted to. But no matter how much I knew I's right, I still could never look at myself in a mirror again without becoming sick with who I saw looking back at me. I held on though – for you– at least until I knew that you'd be able to stand on your own two feet. I struggled living each day after that night, but when you left for college, my struggle was finally able to end.

I'm proud of you for leaving this place far behind, although I don't know why you brought her along with you. Just be careful, Clyde. That girl is a Taker just like your daddy was and she'll have no problem destroying your life just like she did mine. Have NOTHING to do with your sister! Leave her now, son. There is an evil within her that is just like your daddy. I'm warning you!

I'm sorry that you had to find stuff out this way, but there was no other way. The woman that I seen when I look in the mirror had to be punished for what she'd done, and I's the only one who could carry out that judgment.

Never come back here, Clyde! There is nothing for you in Bridgeton anymore. Make a life for yourself and move on – move far beyond this hell. Use the life you've been given to make a difference in this world, not to strip the life away from others. I made the mistake to take life, and so now my life must too be taken. But if you help give life, son to you shall life be given.

> *Forgive me,*
> *Mom*

54
Karla

I was in a cage.

Darkness was all around and I was trapped.

I could not recall how long I had been within the cage because time had no value, although the feel of time's draw against my mind pulled me thin like an overstretched rubber band.

I grabbed hold of the metal bars that housed me like a wild animal, and shook them with as much force as I could. I screamed and shouted with fearful tears, but my voice disappeared into the blackness like dirt to a vacuum. The darkness was total and vast, inhaling my cries as quickly as I exhaled them. I writhed in anguish as I pulled at the metal cage. Nothing. And my strength…

Oh my God, I feel so weak!

My body was zapped of its energy as the darkness pulled at my legs. But I refused to relinquish my grip on the bars because if I did, I would fall to the cold metal floor of the cage. And once down there, my eyelids would grow heavy and begin to close. And they would. And I would sleep. And death would finally take me.

You can't let go, Karla! You have to fight!

Suddenly the darkness began to ripple like a flag in the wind. Rudimentary pictures started to appear out of the blackness, taking on form from that which is formless. The images I saw began to unfold before my eyes like a movie, blurred and distorted at first, like looking at a reflection within a pool of swelled water. The darkness all around began to shift and bend, giving the appearance of distance and time. Objects appeared all around me: trees and bushes, everything covered in a fresh layer of snow. Eventually the view became focused with clarity and I could see that I was no longer in the empty void of space. I felt as if the cage had just been dropped within a distant wooded land, but I was still locked inside.

As my eyes scanned the newly formed world, I noticed that there was a man in the distance. I could hear his crying and it saddened me as if the pain in his heart was filling my lungs with tears. And I cried as well. But as the world shifted and bent into conclusion, I was able to see that the man was Clyde, and he was trying to reach for something within one of the nearby trees. His arms stretched high, but the branch he sought was just beyond his reach. And he cried all the more. I longed to free myself of the cage – to rip open the barrier that held me like a hand in a glove – but I had no means to help Clyde. I was useless to meet his needs.

I wiped away the tears from my eyes, but the stinging that remained burned at my sockets like hot wax. There was no relief for my eyes, and so I looked away. That is when I saw the second figure standing in a drove of trees watching Clyde's struggle. The figure was clothed in the darkness of a silhouette, which made it impossible for me to see it's face. But as I strained my burning eyes to look harder, I realized that the figure did not have a face, yet it exuded an appearance of extreme evil.

55
Clyde

How can time both standstill and flyby all at once?

The answer to that thought was elusive to me, yet the next two weeks seemed to be caught in that exact, stagnant kind of pattern. I felt out of place and out of touch with reality as I wasted away on the couch, propping my leg up and keeping off of it as much as humanly possible. The crutches had been an easy thing to get accustom to although I hated using them. It had been humiliating enough becoming acquainted with the cane over the course of the last year. Adding the crutches to the mix was just downright aggravating.

The words from my mother's letter hung in the background of my mind as the days ticked slowly away. Her confession, although not surprising to me in the littlest, was still as difficult to swallow as a mouthful of un-chewed steak. I battled with THE RED as I replayed her message again and again in my head. She was a confessed murderer. And she murdered for what? For *me*? How did she possibly expect me to cope with such insanely vile information? Had my mother truly been that much of a sick, twisted individual?

Despite the audacity of the letter's content, my mind was too fixated on Karla's health to worry about my dead mother. So rather than dwelling within the misery of the home, I spent every day at Karla's bedside over at Saint Luke's. It had been two weeks and Karla was still lost within the world of her coma. I felt responsible for her being stuck there, so I insisted on being bedside as often as I could. There were some days when Eckhart would drop me off in the morning and leave me there for hours on end. Every day I would sit next to her bed, trying to fathom the world that held her life in limbo. At times I would imagine that she was in a place similar to the dream world that I suffered quiet often. Other days however, I would envision Karla being stuck in a place that was much better, better even than the world I waited for her in. I would envision a place where fears didn't hide around every corner and where death didn't lurk in the shadows. Thinking of such things helped my heart to cope with the fleeting circumstances of her condition.

In those two weeks of constant fear and worry, things remained shockingly quiet around the house. I was thankful for the reprieve from the abnormalities as of late, but I could not occlude the thought that something big was skimming the horizon of my life – something large and full of an unspeakable evil. The question that plagued my mind however, was how I planned on dealing with it when the time came? Would I be able to stand up against it for once in my pathetic life, or would I succumb to the desires of THE FACELESS ONE by finishing the book? But the fictional scarecrow wasn't the only pressure that I faced when it came to my writing. Slater was yet another obstacle I had to overcome. It didn't take him long to get a hold of me via the home phone once he realized Karla was not returning any of his calls. When he did, he was overly persistent about catching the next flight out to New York. It took much persuasion on my part, but I was eventually able to talk him out of the idea. I was aware that certain tasks would have been easier had I still had help around the place, but the last thing I needed was my pesky agent meandering about the house all day, urging me to write. If I was going to write again, it was going to be on my own time. There was no agent or fictional bully that could get me to do so any sooner. Besides, Eckhart had been stopping by periodically to make sure that things were on the up-and-up, so there was no real reason for Slater to make such an unnecessary trip.

Part of me, I must admit, felt like finishing the stupid book and being done with it all, but something told me that doing so would not solve anything. By the look in Spock's eyes, he agreed whole-heartedly; finishing SEVER would be the worst decision. However, there seemed to be something else that good ole Spock was trying to convey to me about my writing, as if there were a third option that I had not considered yet.

* * * * * * * *

This is the final excerpt from the journal of Mrs. Wilma Parker:

I was rattled out of sleep last night by such a vivid dream. I turned for Thurman to comfort me, but was only greeted by the cold spot in bed where he used to sleep. I'm still not used to the fact that he's gone; I don't think I'll ever get accustom to the idea.

The dream had felt so real – so authentic – that I still don't know if I was sleeping or if the good Lord was giving me a vision of some kind. I can't be certain. But what I do know is that I had better write down the details of that dream before my aging mind forgets it altogether. Because I know there was importance to what I saw, albeit I can't figure out the significance just yet. So here goes…

It was late at night, or rather early morning because the pre-dawn fog was heavy over the farm. The cool mist felt surreal as it tickled at my feet while I walked. For whatever reason, I was walking out on the property in my nightgown, heading toward my house. Although, in the dream, it wasn't my house anymore. If I'm going to be truthful, the closer to the house I got, the farther away from home I actually felt. The farther away from Thurman. But I was going there for a reason. There was a man inside the house. A man who was lost and needing help. Even though I wanted nothing more than to turn around and head back out onto the property – into the morning cloud that felt as if I were walking in the clouds of heaven – the dark windows of the house were crying out to me. I had a message to deliver. So I continued my journey down the driveway until I found myself standing on the porch with a stream of cold chills racing down my back.

I knocked on the door and waited for what seemed like a lifetime before the darkened doorway opened. A young man, perhaps in his mid-to-late thirties, stood in the entryway. I tried to lock eyes with this man, but there was no light with which to make out his features, save for a few useless rays of moonlight that seemed to tint everything with a veil of midnight blue. The man had a mess of curly black hair that surrounded the darkness of his face. He was hunched over on a cane of some kind and dressed in a tattered blue robe that looked about as old as I felt in that moment.

I tried peering beyond the man into the house, looking for some form of life I had once known, but saw nothing more than empty darkness behind him. But the feeling of solitude that hung over the dream did not fool me, because there was a very evil presence lurking in the shadows behind him. And I knew it. I could feel the danger just as well as I could feel the wet mist of the fog against my skin. It might have only been light to the touch as it brushed by, but it's existence was as dense as a wet blanket. I also believed that there was a dog somewhere nearby – perhaps in the house – but I couldn't be sure. There was a faint barking somewhere in the distance, but it could have been the coyotes that are so prevalent this time of year.

I looked up at the man – who looked faceless in the shadows of night – sensing the depravity that was eating away at his mind as if the devil were feasting on his soul. It broke my heart and yet instilled me with a fervent desire to turn and run. The man was fearful of the darkness behind him as if the night had taken form and was inching closer towards him with each passing breath. If I had been able to see his eyes, I imagined they would have been filled with tearful panic. He was a troubled man. I could see the weight of his heart in the slouch of his shoulders.

"It's cold," he whispered. "*So* cold."

"I know," I replied. That was when I held out my hand and offered him the object that I had been carrying, even though I hadn't realized it was in my possession until just then.

His shadowed face looked down at the item – an old silver Zippo lighter that had belonged to my Thurman. He took the lighter from me, holding onto it as if it was the lifeline he had needed.

"This is for you," I said. "Keep it with you. You'll know what to do with it."

He said nothing.

"Let your light shine always."

His shadowed face looked back up at me.

"How?" he asked.

I stared up at the faceless man, knowing that the evil that lurked behind was almost upon him. Time was short, but the answer to his question was even shorter. The answer also happened to be the word that had been filling my mind the entire dream and had been the message I had needed to deliver.

hope to its new owner. And as it turned out, that new owner was now me.

I glanced over at Spock again. As soon as we locked eyes he titled his yellow head slightly to one side. His eyes grew big as he pinned his ears up, resembling two small, golden wings perched atop his head. The look that was plastered across his face was the same gesture he gave me whenever he wanted to go somewhere, or whenever he would hear me *talking* about going somewhere. I had seen the look quite often in the course of the last two weeks every time Eckhart would pick me up and take me over to Saint Luke's. But for some reason, Spock was giving me the look once again, even though I hadn't uttered a word.

"What's going on, boy?" I asked as I patted him on his side. Spock answered, but not with a bark or a whimper. Instead, he tilted his head farther to the one side. In the light of the fading evening his eyes appeared to be bluer, erasing the majority of the hazel color from his stare. In that quiet moment, as the two of us stared each other down, I suddenly stumbled upon a revelation that was as enlightening as it was terrifying. The oddest part about it was that the revelation seemed to flow from Spock's heart into mine as I held him. It felt as if the connection that flowed from me to him while reading the journal was in fact, a two-way street. I could feel the image from Spock's heart begin to grow in my head as I stared deep into the eyes of my blonde friend.

The projection that played in my mind was once again about Wilma's dream. I could see her standing at the front door, speaking to the faceless depiction of myself. But the image in my mind took me away from the house and out onto the property. I could suddenly see the walking trail – all covered in fog -- and watched as it emptied into the clearing. From there, I saw the long outstretched wall of stone bordered by the moat of oversized grass. Next I could see the towering oaks with their gangly undergrowth looming towards the wall like the arms of malnourished children in search of food. Lastly however, the black iron bars of the gate were drawn into the mental image, appearing first like rotted teeth and then taking full form beneath the blue hue of moonlight.

As I studied the undeveloped images of the brooding gate with all of its rusted features, I stumbled upon the revelation that I should have remembered weeks ago.

"Oh my God! The gate!" I whispered aloud. At my words, Spock's head shifted upright once again. His eyes however, remained large and focused like two blue marbles.

"It's still open!" I told Spock, as if he didn't already know. "The history that Eckhart told us, all took place beyond the gate because the gate had always been closed. But the coyotes and Powe and God-knows whatever else can now roam the property freely because I left the gate wide open!"

I swallowed hard as guilt began to twist in my stomach like a sack of razorblades in a washing machine. The realization that Karla's injuries were sustained at the hand of my own stupidity was staggering. Eckhart had been right after all. I should have stayed away from the property. I should have stayed away from that stupid gate!

Fear. The story of my life never missed a beat. My foolish acts had once again allowed fear to control me, reigning supreme over my life since childhood. Rather than confronting and growing beyond them however, I penned all of my worst fears into novels so that they could once again take form and dictate my life for a second time over. I didn't know how it was possible, or why it was even happening, but I knew that I was responsible and therefore, it was up to me to put an end to it, if at least for Karla's sake.

Suddenly, I felt a possible solution brush the tendrils of my aching mind. It was the type of plan that is roughly sketched out and most likely plagued with numerous loopholes, but I believed that it could possibly bring the entire mess to an end...

...or so I hoped.

56
Deputy Henry Bowers

There were so many things that could have gone wrong with the plan, but I couldn't think of any other way to get around the problem. Eckhart would be coming down on me any day now. After a week's worth of delays due to problems with the phone company, Kelly's cell phone records had finally been faxed over to the station. It wouldn't be long before my number was found scattered all throughout the report, and to top it off, I probably had been the last phone call placed to Kelly's phone before she disappeared. As incriminating as it sounded however, I knew that it wouldn't be enough evidence for a conviction. But combined with an eye witness testimony from Mindy Baker stating how she had seen me at that's writer's place with Kelly, I would most likely face some time behind bars. That was why I decided to meet with her. I had to make sure that she would keep her mouth shut. It wouldn't be an easy task, but I was willing to do what it took to assure my freedom.

It was a cold November evening, and even colder temperatures were on their way – including a storm that was going to top the charts in all the New England record books. But I waited until after my shift before heading over to the local county jail. I had wanted to go sooner – the idea had scratched at my mind all day – but I couldn't afford to tip the Sheriff off with any suspicious behaviors, so I waited for my shift to end before making my way to the prison.

Once inside, I flashed my badge and credentials to the guard at the front desk and informed him that I had a few more questions for an inmate regarding one of my cases. Five minutes later, I found myself sitting alone in one of the interview rooms waiting for Mindy Baker to be escorted in. The room was sterile and dressed with cheap off-white paint, a single square table, and two metal chairs. No matter how many times I glanced at my badge or brushed my fingers against the sidearm on my hip, I couldn't shake the feeling that that the walls were closing in around me. I battled a wave of chills and fever simultaneously and for a moment, I began to doubt my decision for having come down to the prison at all. I didn't feel like I was waiting to investigate an inmate, but that I myself was the inmate waiting to be questioned.

Before I could jump out of the chair and run out of the ungodly, plain white room, Mindy Baker entered under the escort of a tall black guard. From what I remembered from the arrest, Mindy had been a physically strong woman, and although she was not what I would call Hollywood Skinny, she looked miniscule compared to the arms of the escorting officer. He was intimidating to me even though I was acquainted with the middle-aged man. His name was Xavier Woodard and not only did we go through the academy together, but I also shared some time with him on the transport team before moving up into patrol duty. Despite his hardy and bullish exterior, he flashed a cordial and professional smile in my direction. I returned the greeting as he sat Mindy down in the chair opposite to me and exited the room. Had I not been so relieved to see a familiar face in Xavier, I would have recognized Mindy's calculating eyes that were staring me down as if she had just outwitted an opponent in a game of chess.

Mindy was dressed in the typical orange jumpsuit and bound with state issued handcuffs. Her long black strands of hair were meticulous and orderly as if she had been spending the last two weeks in prison doing nothing but brushing each wavy strand. Her hands and fingernails were free of any blemish or dirt, making it hard to believe that those were the hands capable of murder. But had the pastor of that church not been there that night, those well-groomed hands would have been responsible for the death of an innocent woman. Even the sleeves of her outfit had been rolled up into perfectly trimmed cuffs. Her countenance was that of a high-class debutant on vacation at the Ritz Carlton rather than an inmate who was standing trial for assault, attempted murder, possession of a weapon, and a multitude of other charges. But it was the look of her eyes that cast a streak of terror down my back. The night she had been arrested, I distinctly remember looking back at her

Her breath was hot and heavy, filling my mouth as if she was breathing for the both of us. And perhaps she was, because as she pulled away and returned to her chair, I began speaking immediately – and without refrain.

In the ten minutes that followed the kiss I outlined the entire plan for her, starting with her transport to the courthouse and ending with our freedom together. When I was done speaking (although I felt as if something else had been speaking for me) I rose from the chair and exited the county jail without an emotion to my name. I drove back to my apartment, satisfied myself beneath the spray of a hot shower, and then cried Henry to sleep...for good...because Henry was no more.

Only I remained.

Hank.

And whatever else was living within me.

57
Clyde

The room was filled with a sterile, fluorescent glow as the heart monitor and other machines continued to BLIP and BLEEP. Karla remained in her comatose state (or whatever it was that was keeping her from waking up) beneath a shroud of cotton bed sheets. Her dirty-blonde hair clung in sweaty patches to her forehead and cheeks. The bruises on her face had faded over the last few weeks and the swelling around her left eye had almost completely subsided, but she remained asleep like a child in a bassinet. The only difference was that a child would eventually awake from its dream, where as Karla's fate still hung in the shadows of ambiguity.

It was early evening – a week before Thanksgiving – and I sat in the chair next to Karla's bed. My crutches were propped against the wall and my broken leg stretched out across the tiled floor like a deformed speed bump. I kept my eyes fixed on the broken leg, taking note of how there was not one single person's signature anywhere on the white, fiberglass cast. Then my eyes turned up towards Karla's bedside table. Other than the card and the bouquets of flowers that I had placed, the table was void of any get-well wishes. There were no cards from family members or loved ones to display. A woman of great tenderness and joy had been stuck in a coma for weeks and not one person had stopped by to hold her hand or return any of the love that she so freely shared in her life. As different as we were, the two of us seemed to share the same misfortune – we both were alone.

"Spock sends his love," I said, trying to break away from the monotonous sounds of the beeping machines. "It's funny because, I've never seen a dog so depressed before. He sure does miss you, Karla. We both do."

As the last glimmer of daylight trickled into the room through the fingertip-smudged window, I leaned my head against Karla's bed and took hold of her fragile hand. I longed for her fingers to tighten around mine, but they remained limp and lifeless instead.

"Karla, I don't know if you can hear me or not, but... I'm so sorry," I softly whispered. "If I could take it all back, I would. Everything that I said to you that day, blaming you for my own stupidity, yelling at you when you were just trying to help, I would take it all back if you could only hear my voice."

I shifted uncomfortably in my chair as a slight pain began to surface in my legs and lower back. The pain in my heart however, was the one that seemed to hurt the worst. "If you're guilty of anything, it's that you showed genuine kindness to a person like myself – a person who didn't deserve it. You tried showing me a love far greater than I could have ever fathomed, and still I pushed you away, just like I've done with everything else in my pathetic life. But with you around Karla, for the first time since my accident, I felt like trying to move beyond my condition. With you around, I began to believe that it was possible."

I could feel the tears begin to well up in my eyes as the words of remorse began to spill out of me like water from a tap. I wiped the tears away but they returned in greater numbers.

"I know that we haven't known each other very long, but these last weeks without you have been some of the loneliest days of my life. And I should know what loneliness feels like. Every person that I have loved or have tried to love has abandoned me. My parents taught me nothing in this life but how to control people and then how to leave them. Mindy was no different. But look what I've done to you. I'm no better than they were. Look at how I abandoned you when you needed me the most. If I had never said those things to you that night in the hospital, you never would have gone back to the house alone, and you *wouldn't* be here fighting for your life now. The one person who never left me when I was the most unlovable is now lying in this hospital because of my sins. I don't know if I will ever forgive myself for doing this to you." I slammed my fist into the side of the bed as I wept bitterly. "Why couldn't you have just written me off like everybody else? Why couldn't you have seen me for the obstacle that my father always told me I was? Things could have been so much simpler if you had just let me die in my own misery. Why, Karla? Why didn't you just give up on me like everyone else?"

I took hold of Karla's hand in both of mine and leaned my forehead against her spiritless fingers. The touch of her hand was cold against my face. I cried softly in the quiet of that hospital room as the idea of losing Karla forever tore at my heart the way the coyote had tore at my leg. But the sting of pain from that coyote seemed miniscule compared to the throbbing ache that was growing in my chest. I didn't know for sure if Karla could hear any of what I was saying, but I had to believe – at least for my own sake – that she could. I had to hope that my words were not falling onto deaf ears.

"This is where I feel safe, Karla. When I'm with you. When I'm not here, I feel as if my legs are breaking beneath the weight of Mindy's car again; like the storm is raging just overhead and I can't get away no matter how hard I try. But then I come here with you and find the relief that I've always needed but never wanted until now. You make me feel like a whole man again, despite my brokenness. If you would just wake up and come back to me then I would gladly spend the rest of my life treating you like the amazing woman you are. I would rather take the chance of getting hurt all over again than not having you in my life at all. I *need* you, Karla."

I reached out with a free hand and gently took hold of Karla's face. I forced a smile through quivering lips, gazing down upon her with blurred, teary vision. Despite the bruises and lacerations that created a web of pain across her face, I could still see the breath-taking beauty that she possessed.

"You are so beautiful," I whispered quietly into her ear. "I don't care what those animals did to your body, they can never touch the beauty you have within. Never change that for anyone Karla – not even for me."

I wiped at the remaining tears in my eyes and sat up straighter in the chair, grimacing as the pain in my back arched swiftly from my left side to my right.

The final flecks of sunlight disappeared from the hospital room, leaving a view of early, November darkness to blanket the window. With the darkness, came a depression that was staggering. I knew full well that I could possibly be speaking my final words ever to Karla. It was very possible that she might not ever wake from her coma. Each day that slipped away narrowed her chances of recovery. My last words to the brave, selfless woman might not ever be heard. The thought was almost too much for me to handle, so I pushed it away as best I could.

"You were always talking to me about finding solutions and about looking at things from a different perspective. I didn't understand it at first but I've spent the last few weeks trying to make sense of it all. It wasn't easy at first, but then I came across something that began to at least point me in the right direction even though I'm not sure exactly what direction that is."

I picked up the medium-sized envelope that I had brought with me and stared at it for a moment. On the outside of the envelope, I had printed the words: TO KARLA, YOUR FAITH HAS INSPIRED ME. The inside was stuffed with Wilma Parker's old journal and a small note from me explaining what it was and how it had helped to clarify many things for me. The letter however, did not tell her about my upcoming journey. If she knew where I was planning to go than she would be apt to try and follow, and that would not turn out well at all.

"I found this journal at the house the other day, and in case I don't ever make it back, I want you to have it. If anyone will understand the priceless value of Wilma's written words, it's you. I didn't want them to be lost with me. Take them, and know that this journal validated many things for me that I had failed to see sooner because of my own stupidity."

With that said, I reached into my pants pocket and wrapped my fingers around Thurman Parker's old lighter. I was carrying it with me, just like Wilma had warned in her dream. And I was thankful. I felt a slight surge of protection having it with me, especially in light of the trip I was about to embark on.

When I was done fumbling with the Zippo, I set the package on the bedside table next to the fresh bouquet of flowers I had also brought her.

"I just can't sit around here any longer and wait for something worse to happen. There's no telling what Powe will try next if I don't deliver that book soon. Besides, I came back to Bridgeton to find myself, and I can't do that if I'm trapped in that house by my fears. I had wanted to wait another two weeks for the doctor to take my cast off, but I don't have anymore time. Not only are all the major weather reports predicting the first snow of the year to hit in two days – and it's going to hit bad – but I've got a feeling that if I don't do something soon, the evilness beyond that gate will come looking for me again. And I'm done running, Karla. I'm sick of hiding. I've got to finally face my fears or else I'll fall prey to them until they finally kill me. So I've got no more time to wait."

Grabbing hold of my crutches, I rose from the chair and stood next to the bed for one final moment.

"Where are you?" I whispered, hoping beyond hope that Karla would hear my voice wherever she was. Looking down at her helpless body made me want to cry all over again. However, Eckhart would be arriving soon and I didn't want him to see me in tears. If I was going to make the journey that I had planned – without the Sheriff getting suspicious – then it was pertinent that he not see me overly emotional. If he did, he was bound to stick around my house more than I wanted him to, and that would most likely ruin everything.

"I've got to go now, Karla. I don't want to, but I have to. I have to try and right the wrongs that I've caused. So this will most likely be my last visit here with you, but I don't want you to blame yourself for that. It's just that I don't expect to make it back alive. Please just know that everyday I'm gone, is another day that your strength and love are helping to move me forward."

Despite my best efforts to avoid crying, the tears began to stream down my face again. "The few short days that I've known you have been some of the happiest days of my life. You showed me that there's always a different perspective to be seen – that there's always hope. So I'm going to go and find it now. I'm going to find that perspective that I lost years ago because I'm tired of living under an illusion of love. You have a peace about you that I don't understand, but I need it. That's why I came back to Bridgeton." I paused mid-sentence, considering the words that I was about to speak. I searched my mind for a reputable defense, but when I found none, I finished my thought. "You, *Karla*, are why I came back to Bridgeton."

I brushed away the strands of hair from her forehead and leaned down, planting a gentle kiss upon her brow.

"Goodbye, Karla," I whispered into her ear. With the crutches snug under my arms, I strolled out of Karla's hospital room for the very last time.

As I disappeared down the hallway, Karla's fingers began to stretch and bend against the white, cotton bed sheets. Her head slightly squirmed against the pillows as her eyes fanned slowly open. Her weary gaze swam around the room before finally resting upon the open door. Her dry, cracked lips parted ever so slightly as she whispered the name I had waited weeks to hear her speak.

"Clyde?"
Then she fell back to sleep.

PART THREE
the face of evil

58
Clyde

I awoke the following morning with full expectations of getting a fresh start. I hadn't slept much the night before because of my racing thoughts, so I was up and ready to go by first light. As usual, Spock was right there by my side with an eagerness that was compelling. When we woke up however, storm clouds and a drenching rain had erased the morning sunlight, as well as any hopes of starting out early.

I had checked all of the major weather reports for the past week and had been fairly confident that the rains (the cold front that would convert the next storm into the season's first snow) were supposed to have been finished by midnight. I should have known better though. After all, I was planning a journey that was most likely going to end up a suicide mission. I should have expected the plan to go belly up from the start.

I took the next few hours to make a nice breakfast for Spock and I, and then waited out the remainder of the storm with nervous jitters. I checked and re-checked the supplies I had packed, suddenly feeling that I had overlooked something that would turn out to be vital to the trip. I had prepared two bottles of water, a package of Cinnamon Pop-Tarts, a few treats for Spock, Thurman Parker's old Zippo lighter, a small bottle of lighter fluid, and an old fishing knife that I hadn't used in a long time. But if the plan went as I had envisioned it every night for the last week, than my old knife would see action soon enough.

By nine o'clock that morning, the rain had finally stopped, leaving a trail of cold air in its wake. The sun peaked through the

"Miss Turner? You're not the comatose Turner are you?" I was shocked to hear that the woman knew about me.

"Yes, ma'am. I woke up last night."

"Well, I'll be!" The dispatch exclaimed. "I can't believe it's actually you, Miss Turner. The Sheriff said that things weren't looking too good for you. He said they weren't expecting you to wake up from that coma of yours, but listen to you!" The excitement in the woman's voice, despite the initial setback, made me crack my first genuine smile.

"You just sit tight, I'll patch you through to the Sheriff. He'll be wanting to talk with you. I'm almost sure of it." With that said, the phone went silent as the elderly woman transferred the call to the Sheriff's personal extension.

In the brief span of time while waiting on Eckhart to answer the call, I glanced over at the bedside table, admiring the rows of flowers that had been left there for me. There was also a manila envelope addressed to me amidst the bouquets, and so I made a mental note to investigate that first. As I scanned the items on the round table next to the bed – the table that appeared to contain *only* get-well items from Clyde – a small pang of loneliness brushed against my heart. No one else had cared enough to stop by and visit me. No one from the church apparently, nor from the remaining family that I had. *Nobody*...and it was a devastating blow to the illusion I had once thought to be a reality.

"Eckhart speaking." The Sheriff said upon answering the call. "Miss Turner. Is that really you?"

"Yes, sir. It is."

"It's good to finally hear from you. We've been waiting quite a many days to talk with you again young lady. How are you feeling?"

I considered the question as the subwoofer in my head continued to rattle my thoughts with painful precision. "I can't complain, Sheriff. I'm thankful to be alive."

"Like heck you can't complain," Eckhart retorted. "You were physically assaulted within an inch of your life and you've been lay up in a hospital bed for God knows how long. My lady, you've got plenty to complain about."

"Like I said, I'm just blessed to be alive."

"Miss Turner, would you be up to answering a few questions later this evening. I'd like to get the story from you about what happened that night at Clyde's place? But that's only if you're feeling up to it. After all, I've already waited a few weeks, what's a few more days?" Eckhart chuckled modestly, trying to breathe some levity into the conversation that seemed oddly somber, despite the miraculous and joyful circumstances.

"That would be fine. Besides, it would be nice to see a familiar face around here," I replied, looking back at the almost empty gift table.

"Good. In the meantime, have you gotten in touch with Mr. Baker yet? Cause I know that he's one person whose gonna be jump-over-the-moon happy to know you're alright."

"I left a message for him at the house. I hope to hear back from him soon, though. He's actually the reason why I'm calling, Sheriff."

"Is that so?"

"Yes. This is going to sound stupid, but I had a dream about Clyde – a wicked kind of dream, and now I can't seem to shake the feeling that he might be in some kind of danger."

Eckhart grunted under his breath, as if something ironic had caught his attention. "I see. Can you hold on for one second Miss Turner?"

Before I could respond to the Sheriff's question, I could hear his booming voice issuing commands to someone in his office. By the cluttering background noise, I could tell that things were all work and no play over at the station.

"Sorry about that," Eckhart said, returning to the conversation. "So you said there was a *dream* that got you all worked up about Clyde? That's not a very solid lead. You do know that don't you?"

I blushed with foolishness despite being alone in the room. "I know, Sheriff. I want to be wrong, and for Clyde's sake I hope I am, but I just can't be sure and the uncertainty is eating away at me. I know how this must sound, but you have to at least hear me out."

"These days, Miss Turner, I'm open to believing just about anything. But perhaps this should be something that we discuss face-to-face and not over the telephone. Can you hold off long enough for me to get there later this evening?"

"Yeah, that should be fine," I said. "Do you think you could do me one favor though? Before coming this way?"

"What'll it be, Miss Turner?" he asked.

"I'm sure he's fine, but would you mind checking in on Clyde on your way? I just need to know that he's okay." Although I had

The first leg of the trip was surprisingly quiet. I had fully anticipated running into Powe and his gang within five minutes of passing through the gate, but after half-an-hour of steady tracking through the trees, I had yet to hear or see any sign of the delinquent teens. At first I was greatly pleased that I had survived as long as I had, but then I began to regret the thought, remembering Karla and her bruised and battered body. They had attacked her because they had been unable to get to me. Powe and his gang of thugs put the most lovely, innocent woman into a possibly fatal coma in order to scare me into finishing the book SEVER. But rather than running from my fears as I had my entire life, I turned the face of my rage in their direction. I had come for a fight, and I would not be pleased until I got one.

After what seemed like forever, I briefly rested against one of the trees. Spock looked tired and hungry, and so I fed him a few of the treats I had packed. He gobbled them down without a moment's hesitation. I took a few chugs of the water from the first bottle, and then fed the rest to Spock. His panting tongue lapped up the cool liquid as I slowly tipped the bottle on end.

The pain in my legs and back was minimal – a dull ache in comparison to it's usual, feverish throbbing. The meds I had taken before leaving the house had kicked in just fine. As long as I kept things easy-going, the pain wouldn't become a factor, or so I had hoped. Spock nestled up against my leg, and I took the extra moment to give him some love. Removing the glove from one hand, I scratched at the small patch of brown fur on his chest. As I rubbed him, he took the opportunity to return the affection by licking me on my hand. Spock might have been five years old – drawing near to six – but as it was, the cuteness that he possessed reminded me of his puppy years. His capacity for love was astounding. Watching the intensity that he displayed while kissing my hand reminded me of something Flash had said: *"You've got yourself a real special pup here, Mr. Clyde. If heaven's love could be bottled up and given a tail – this fella right here would fit the bill."*

Sure, Spock was special. I knew *that*. But Flash had spoken as if he had known my dog – as if they had known each other for years and had shared a common bond. I knew it was foolish to think such things, but I also knew that foolishness meant believing in books coming to life. And yet there I was, searching beyond the gate for the very characters I had created. There was definitely more to Flash than I had originally thought.

"Flash?" I called out in a quiet whisper, scared to make too much noise. Nothing. There was only an eerie silence to greet my words. "I'm making the journey now, Flash," I whispered aloud. "Any help you can offer would be appreciated."

I finished petting Spock, but before I placed the glove over my chilled, bare hand, I reached into the backpack. I fished through the contents of the pack until my hand brushed against the old fishing knife. I pulled it out of the bag and fastened it securely in the pocket of my jacket, hoping that having the knife within easy reach would help subdue the nagging fear that someone was out there watching me. The knife itself was buttoned within a black, canvas sheath for protection, and that was how it remained as I slipped it into the confines of my jacket pocket. If the time came to use the knife, I would have it unsheathed without a moment's hesitation. Until then however, the sharp blade of the knife remained in it's protective covering.

The afternoon was wearing thin as the sun began to recess towards the horizon. As it did, a more significant breeze rustled through the surrounding trees, making it harder for me to detect the sounds of moving feet within the damp blanket of dead leaves. The deeper into the land I walked, the more uneven the ground became. The once flat land seemed to rise and drop like a choppy sea. The roots of the large oaks pushed through the earth, forming a web of disarrayed obstacles across the plain of the scabrous land. The ditches that appeared in the ground were deep and layered at the bottom with thick brier patches. Rocks and carcasses of fallen, rotted trees made the walk difficult – almost unfathomable at times. The air around me seemed to grow strange as well, becoming thicker as I traveled deeper into the troubled land. Each breath became heavier; a laborious task as I worked thoroughly with my crutches. It felt as if I were trying to run while inhaling exhaust fumes from an old clunker, but I proceeded forwards.

The next fifty-or-so yards of hobbling took me to a dense patch of woods where the old jungle gym from my first novel sat like a fish out of water. The chocolate brown paint melded into the surrounding area like camouflage, but the green snake-like, spiral slide would have been evident from miles away.

As I drew near to the old playground item, I could feel it's metal limbs and plastic appendages pulling the past to the forefront of my mind like a magnet. As a child, I would walk the train tracks day-after-day until I would reach the vacant park on the corner; walking the three mile round trip just to escape my torturous home life. The jungle gym that I now faced beyond the gate was the very same one that had been left to rot in that park. It was where I had tried to seclude myself within the fold of it's rusted arms. In the eyes of my childish mind, the old jungle gym had become my place of refuge. I would sit in the safety of it's ramparts feeling like a king. Things had been good, up until the day that Stan Polasky and his three lackeys had pulled up in their infamous rusted, Ford LTD.

"This is where I tried to hide," I said to Spock through tear-stained eyes. There was a green plastic tube for crawling that connected the middle platform to the upper one. I pointed at the bubbled porthole that acted as a window halfway through the tube, the memory as vivid in my mind as the day it had happened.

I remembered looking out through the round, hazy window and seeing two of Stan's buddies pull a young teenage girl out of their car. Stan and his henchmen had been three sheets to the wind and flying high on whatever their choice of drug had been for that day. The young girl had been kicking and screaming which only seemed to have fueled their laughter. I had been hoping that hiding in my jungle gym would have kept the drugged-up roughnecks away, but to my surprise, they had begun dragging their redheaded victim straight towards my castle. I had been frozen with fear as the cries of the young girl reached my ears. My eyes had been hidden behind dirty hands, not wanting to be witness to such an unspeakable evil. Not only that, but I had covered them to blot out the thought of my castle – my refuge away from pain – being defiled before my very eyes the way Mindy's sanctuary would later become. That had been the moment Stan first noticed me crying. He sent two of his lapdogs to yank me out of hiding, and they did so without much of a struggle. I had tried to be brave, drawing off the artificial courage that my red, I AM NINJA tee shirt gave me, but it wasn't much help. The only positive thing that I remembered about that day, before getting my shirt ripped off and turned into a flagstaff, was that my beating had given the young, redheaded girl a chance to escape.

That was the one memory from my childhood that had inspired the story for my first book, THE TOWN KIDS. I had turned Stan Polasky into the bullish and brooding character named Powe who single-handedly helped me to sell over one million copies of my debut novel. Stan's lackeys had been used in the book as well, and when the dust had finally settled, one of my greatest childhood fears had catapulted me into a best-selling author. Ironically enough, it was those very creations– those fears that I had harbored and stored away within the pages of that book – that were now drawing me out of hiding and forcing me to confront them in the land beyond the gate.

Spock meandered around the base of the jungle gym as the memory began to falter again in my mind. My blonde friend weaved in and out of the chocolate colored legs, stopping periodically to mark his territory. Watching him do so – and *fearlessly* – made the haunting past seem not so pungent. For the first time in my life, the fear inside of me seemed as if it might just be manageable...that was, until I noticed the old rusted Ford LTD parked in between two far-off trees.

With the sun already beginning to near the ridge of the mountains, the car was covered in shadow. I could feel my adrenaline kick up a notch, steeling myself for the confrontation that I had been anticipating. I tried focusing my eyes, but it was too hard to tell if there was anyone inside the car. I didn't see any movement, making me think that Powe and his gang weren't anywhere nearby. However, I still had the strangest feeling that I was being watched. No matter how hard I tried to escape the thought, it continued to harass my mind the way Stan and his gang had harassed that innocent redhead, and how Powe and his brainless cohorts had validated my fears into the hearts of readers everywhere.

"Take a looksy, Powe! The lil' turd came back for more!" the voice squealed from behind me. The words were followed by the high-pitched laughter of Mikey, the punk with the mohawk hair cut. The rest of Powe's gang chimed in with laughter of their own.

I steadied myself.

The moment of truth had finally arrived.

61
Sheriff Eckhart

When Officer Craigs brought me the phone records for Kelly Summers, I had figured that our best chance at a lead had slammed into a dead end. It was just the way things were going as of late. When Craigs pointed out the thirteen calls that Kelly had received over the course of the last month from the cell phone of Deputy Henry Bowers, sudden alarm kicked me in the gut. But as I skimmed through the pages of phone calls – both sent and received – and noticed that the very last call Kelly ever responded to was from the same hotheaded deputy, I fumed with anger.

The afternoon was already growing late; I could tell by the way the shadows in my office began to reach further into the cluttered mass of case files and office junk. But I immediately flipped open my cell phone and punched in the number for Deputy Bowers. As I listened to the ringing phone in my ear, I ordered Craigs to round up two other uniforms and dispatch immediately to Henry's apartment. Bowers had called in sick earlier that morning, but in light of the new information I had just received, I began to worry that the young, impetuous deputy had called out for other reasons entirely.

After five annoying rings I flipped the cell phone closed and checked my watch. It was a quarter-to-five and I had a feeling that the already long day was going to become even longer. I wrapped myself in my winter jacket and rushed out of the station while punching a second phone number into the cell. My wife answered on the second ring, elated at the fact that I was calling her before the end of the day. Her assumption was that I was on my way home for an early supper. When I told her otherwise, I could hear the frustration in her voice.

"Leave a plate for me in the fridge. I'll nibble at when I get home. I'm sorry, Bree," I said, using the nickname that I had been calling her since we had begun dating over forty years ago.

"You will not," she retorted as I hopped into the jeep. "Doctor Glassman has warned you about eating that late. He said that the next heart attack could kill you, Gerard, so you will do no such thing. I'll save you a plate and you can eat it for lunch tomorrow. But if you're going to be late tonight, you might as well pick yourself up something to eat while you're out."

I didn't argue with my wife. After having weathered the many tasks of being married to the town Sheriff for almost fifteen years, she had earned her say in things. She was a good woman – a trustworthy wife and respectable mother to our son who was now grown and married – so heeding her advise was the least I could do.

I gave her my love, swore on oath that I would take care of myself (I had yet to break a promise to my wife in all our years of marriage), and then disconnected the call while speeding north towards Canyon Pulse. I had to see for myself if Henry had jumped ship or if I was just growing paranoid in my old age. But I didn't think the latter to be the case at all. Why would Henry not have told me that he knew the missing girl? To have at least thirteen phone conversations in the course of thirty days signifies more than just knowing a person; Henry most likely had been involved with the young girl. Most likely intimate with her. But why keep that information from the investigators? And was it coincidence that he was most likely the last person to ever speak to Kelly on the phone? No, I didn't believe so because I didn't believe in coincidence. Henry was definitely hiding something.

I checked my watch again as I crossed over the Bridgeton border and into Canyon Pulse. It was a few minutes after five. I had enough time to get to Henry's apartment before swinging south again and meeting with Miss Turner at the hospital. At least there had been some good news today, seeing as though she had escaped the clutches of her coma. However, after hearing the worry in Karla's voice, I firmly believed that the good days were far behind us. I whispered a prayer of protection as the light of day began to diminish behind the mountains in the west, but I couldn't shake the feeling that I had made a promise to my wife that I was going to have to break.

63

Karla

The television in the hospital room was set to the local news network. I watched wearily from the bed as the evening weatherman described the first nor'easter storm that was likely to dump at least thirty-six inches of snow in Bridgeton by morning. The original prediction for the storm was for the flurries to begin around noon on Sunday, but the man with the bushy, dark mustache on the television was now altering his earlier forecast. Supposedly the storm had picked up speed as it traveled east and was now slated to hit the Hudson Valley area of New York by two o'clock Sunday morning – less than ten hours time. 'A storm for the record books,' was the phrase coined by Thick Mustache Man as he signed off for the night. I watched silently, perplexed by the unseasonable forecast of snow.

As the two news anchors wrapped up the evening program, a slight rapping at the hospital room door stole my attention. I was surprised into a smile at the sight of the tall, slender man standing in the doorway. He was dressed in a pair of gray dress slacks and a navy-blue polo shirt. He had dark blue eyes, a full head of blonde hair, and looked young enough to be my brother despite the signs of age pulling at his face.

"Pastor Rob, come in," I said, while muting the sound on the television.

"Linda gave me the message first thing when I got to the office this afternoon. I'm glad you called," Rob said with his soft, Southern drawl.

Pastor Rob entered the room upon invite and draped his winter jacket and gloves over the arm of the bedside chair. "So, how are you feeling?"

"Like I've never felt before?" I joked with a smile. "I'm in a lot of pain still. The headaches seem to be the worst of it though. The medicine dulls it some, but when I get one of my bad flare-ups, nothing seems to touch the pain. But I'm alive, so I can't complain."

"Amen," Rob said in response. "The church has been worried about you, Karla. There was a time there when the outlook was a bit bleak for you. But God once again shows the loving power of his grace and forgiveness."

"*Forgiveness?*" I wondered to myself.

Rob glanced over at the flowers on the bedside table. There was a curious look that was fashioned within his eyes as he did so. He looked more like an investigator seeking clues rather than a visiting pastor bent on encouragement. It was a look that I had seen in him only once before. It was a look that I didn't like.

"I didn't have time to get a card picked out or anything for you, I'm sorry to say. But the congregation has been pulling for you in prayer."

"That's okay. I just appreciate you stopping in." I forced an optimistic smile although, oddly enough, I wasn't receiving one in return. After shuffling through the items on the table, Pastor Rob turned his attention back to me.

"And the doctors? What have they said?"

"Surprisingly good things in lieu of my injuries. They suspect that I might be able to go home tomorrow; if not tomorrow, than definitely sometime Monday. They want to make sure I'm stable enough with the meds before sending me home. They also want to run one more series of tests to make absolute certain that there isn't any kind of brain damage."

"Most likely gonna be Monday in your case. The snow ought to be blowing in before sunup tomorrow and it's supposed to be one bear of a storm. Which is all in the best I suppose. The extra time ought to be good healing for you."

An awkward silence surveyed the room before I felt like speaking up again. Something felt wrong with the entire conversation. The pastor's actions reminded me of the way a snake coils into a corner just before lashing out with fanged teeth and forked tongue. But I suddenly felt guilty for having compared a man of God to a serpent.

Spock shifted again, crying a little louder as he did so. His eyes were sagging low, but they remained fixed on me the entire time.

"I think you guys age faster because you already know how to love in this life. It takes us seven times longer to figure it out. I know, it's stupid, but it's just a theory." I attempted another laugh, but it was no use. I tried to remain strong for Spock, but it was too difficult to remain positive while watching the one true source of love in my life pass away.

"It's cold, isn't it fella?" I said, feeling the sudden dropping of the temperature. Even through the fading light, I could see the shivering in Spock's legs quicken, although it seemed to have spread to the rest of his body as well. Not only that, but his breathing grew more shallow with each passing moment. "Just hang in there, guy. It'll warm up for you soon enough. You won't feel the pain much longer, I promise. I wish I could make it all go away for you, but...I can't be up there with you right now. I want to be though. You know that, don't you boy? Can you feel my love with you, Spock? Holding you? Keeping you warm? I got your love right here with me and it's not going anywhere. And on those nights when you're not at the foot of the bed to cuddle up against me, I'm still going to be holding onto it. Okay? Don't you worry about me now. You just close your eyes and go to sleep. I'll be okay. I'm going to miss you though. I'm going to miss you *so* much. But I've got your heart with me always. You take mine with you, okay? You've had it all along, because you were the best friend I could have ever asked for."

Spock slowly lifted his head in the air. His movements looked sluggish and tired, but he still managed to square that beautiful face of his with mine. His long ears hung low against the sides of his face as his eyes burrowed deep into the nest of my heart. The life was fading quickly from my blonde friend, almost as quickly as the daylight from up above, but he still managed to issue a single bark into the quiet sky. There wasn't much strength behind the sound. It resembled a helpless cry more than it did a bark, but as he rested his long, golden snout against his paws one final time, the meaning behind it was loud and clear:

"I love you too."

65
Karla

It was almost seven-thirty on that Saturday night when Sheriff Eckhart strolled into my hospital room, the clopping sound of his patrol boots echoing down the halls. The fatigue of a long, stressful day pulled at his face. The bank of fluorescent lights above paled the Sheriff's skin more so than usual, so much so that upon first glance I thought he had taken sick. But I was glad to see him nonetheless, especially after the disconcerting visit from Pastor Rob.

"How are you feeling?" he asked warmly.

"I'm okay. But it doesn't look like you're feeling too well, Sheriff."

"It's just been one of those kind of days I guess."

"I'm sorry," I commented. Eckhart said nothing.

The mood in the room was somber, and Eckhart observed it immediately. It was thick in the air like the smell of hospital antiseptic, and it made the tired Sheriff tense up as he took a seat next to the bed.

"Is everything okay?" he asked.

"Of course," I lied. Eckhart could hear the apprehension in my voice, I was almost certain of it, so I quickly diverted the subject. "Did you get a chance to check on Clyde? Because I haven't been able to get a hold of him all day and I'm starting to really worry."

"Why? Because of the dream you were telling me about earlier?" A simple and lethargic head nod was my only response. "Why don't you tell me about this dream of yours because I did

67
Karla

For the next hour, Sheriff Eckhart outlined his theory for me. Apparently Clyde and him had spoken in great lengths about it, but it was still hard to swallow at first. I'm sure that it wasn't an easy concept for the left-brained Sheriff to discuss with me – with anyone for that matter – but he did so as if he were expecting me to fight him on every twist and bend of the story.

He had begun by telling me about the coyotes, which quickly led into the discussion about Powe and the other town kids. As I absorbed the information, I began to reflect back onto Clyde's books that I had read. The Sheriff's explanations began to make sense to me – as odd as that was to admit. I remembered Mikey's character well, including his bleach-blonde mohawk. The resemblance between the one attacker I saw that night and Mikey's character, was uncanny. I tried to question Eckhart on the possibility of coincidence, although I didn't believe it myself, but Eckhart unknowingly dispelled the question with the sincerity that I felt from his eyes.

Eventually, the discussion turned towards the property and the land beyond the gate. The history of the Sugar Hill Farms Estate was one that the Sheriff did not want to drudge up again, but he did so for my sake. He didn't seem at all surprised about my lack of knowledge when it came to the property because the town of Bridgeton had invested itself in trying to keep things quiet. The information was common-knowledge after all, but as the years slipped away and people remained hushed about that particular sector of the town's past, the truth became buried in the shadows of the Cotaquin Mountains. Fact became fiction. Irony at it's finest.

"I definitely believe – now more than ever – that Clyde is in danger, Sheriff," I said, shifting uncomfortably in bed.

"You needn't worry about him, Miss Turner. Right now you just need to rest up and worry about getting out of this place with a clean bill of health. I'll follow-up with Clyde, like I said."

I could feel my face growing meek, so I turned my eyes down away from the Sheriff as he spoke. He must have sensed the discomfort that I was battling, because he leaned in towards the bed like a concerned parent. It was more than Pastor Rob had done; I had to at least give him that much. But I still didn't want to discuss the true weight that was pinning down my emotions like a specimen waiting to be dissected in a biology lab.

"Are you sure you're feeling okay, Miss Turner?" he asked very matter-of-factly. When I answered, my tone was depressing and soft – even I could hear it.

"Thank you for taking time to explain everything to me. I'm also thankful that Clyde has someone as dedicated as you to keep an eye on him. But as for me, I've got to back away from it all now. I'm going to be calling Clyde's agent first thing on Monday and putting in my immediate resignation." As the words hung in the sterile air of that Saint Luke's Hospital room, tears of heartache and torment raced down my face. "I can't be torn like this anymore, Sheriff."

I reached up and covered my face with trembling hands, crying harder as the embarrassment of the situation took hold of me. Eckhart moved closer to the bed and placed one of his calloused hands upon my shoulder.

"What's wrong, Miss Turner? What's got you so torn that it's making you quit your job?"

"I'm sorry, Sheriff. I shouldn't drag you into any of this. It's my mess and I'm dealing with it the best way I can."

Confusion hit Eckhart over the head like a hammer. "You're not dragging me into nothing that I'm not stepping into of my own free will. But something is weighing on your mind, young lady and it'll serve you best to talk it out. That's all I'm gonna say about the matter. If you'd rather be alone, just say the word and I'll be gone."

I lowered my hands and looked up at the kind-hearted Sheriff through tear-stained eyes.

"It's not that I don't want to help Clyde – please don't think poorly of me. Underneath his rough façade, Clyde Baker is a good-hearted man and I had really grown fond of him."

"So what's the problem then?" prodded Eckhart.

"The problem is that my pastor has differing opinions about Clyde."

"And?" he said, not fully grasping the importance of my comment.

"And if I want to remain a member of the church, I'm supposed to cut all ties with him."

There. It was out in the open and off my chest. Surprisingly, I was already beginning to feel the burden loosen.

"Let me guess...Robert Peztel from Crossroads Reformed Church?"

My eyes darted up to meet Eckhart's with a look of surprise. "You know Pastor Rob? But you don't attend the church?"

"Pastor Rob is the reason *why* I don't attend that church," Eckhart replied while sliding back into the chair. "I read people, Miss Turner. Discernment: it's what I do. It's my job. And frankly speaking, I didn't like what I saw."

"What did you see?" I asked inquisitively. Sheriff Eckhart shook his head however, refusing to answer.

"That's neither here nor there. What your pastor has done in the past is inconsequential. What you need to concern yourself with is what he's doing now. And threatening to remove a church member unless they cut ties with someone is not what I consider to be the best example of love and forgiveness. Wouldn't you agree?"

"Yes, but he does have a point. Clyde's track record isn't exactly the cleanest."

Eckhart grunted under his breath while examining my words carefully. A slight scowl pulled at the corners of his mouth as he did so.

"Are you gonna now sit in judgment of Mr. Baker because of his *track record*. We've all got a track record, Miss Turner, and if God Almighty were to judge us based upon it, which of us would be able to stand up under the weight of that kind of judgment? What ever happened to forgiveness? You seem to be a very tenderhearted young woman, and I would hate to see that kind of compassion trampled on because it doesn't fit with the standards of one man."

I rested my head back upon the pillow while absorbing the wise words of the town's Sheriff. The truth of his insight was powerful, but I could still feel myself being torn in two separate directions.

The Sheriff sat forward in the chair and scratched at the back of his head. When he spoke up again, the usual roar in his voice was mellowed, giving him the sound of a humble sinner rather than an authoritative officer.

"It's funny how easy it is to point a finger at somebody isn't it? Don't kick yourself over it; I was no different. When Clyde Baker came back to Bridgeton I was the first person to write him off and send him packing. I judged him. I didn't think it was right and *respectful* the way he had treated the situation with his mother, and so I got it stuck in my craw that he was one cold-hearted son of a biscuit. I judged him, and in hindsight, I was wrong. I can only hope and pray that I get a chance to right that wrong someday. But the sad fact of this life is that I might not ever get that chance. God-willing, we'll find out where Mr. Baker is, and I'll have the opportunity." Eckhart looked up and met eyes with me again. "Don't make the mistake I did, Miss Turner. You're better than that."

I didn't say anything in regards to the Sheriff's outpouring of regret. What could possibly be said? So in the silence, I dabbed at the tears in my eyes and thanked him with a kind smile.

"Again, I'm sorry if I'm imposing on this here matter, but I've just got to ask you one last question about it," Eckhart said while repositioning himself in the chair. "If you found out that hanging around Mr. Baker was making you change the *real you* – the compassionate and humble woman who enjoys taking care of others – would you allow that to happen?"

The answer was simple for me; it didn't require any thinking on my part at all.

"No, not if Clyde was having that kind of impact on me. But he wasn't, Sheriff. Actually, I think we were both in places where we needed healing and on some level, we were helping each other. Or at least I thought so. But *no*, if the impact was negative, I probably wouldn't continue on with the relationship."

"So then why let Robert Peztel get away with it? Because he wears the title of a pastor and Clyde writes horror novels?"

"You don't understand, Sheriff. Clyde is *complicated*. The night he was in the hospital, he blamed me for his being attacked by the coyotes. He blamed *me*, and I wasn't even there! He didn't want me around; he said I distracted him by filling his head with senseless hope. Maybe Pastor Rob is right this time. Maybe I should just listen to him and forget about Clyde."

"One man sits in judgment. The other sits crying out for help. Who do you think should be heard?"

Sheriff Eckhart rose from the chair and stared down at me. His eyes were filled with an immense compassion.

"I believe you when you say that Clyde Baker is in danger. So for that, I'm going to send a patrol car over to check his place immediately. But I'm starting to believe that the help he needs is not from any gun my officer's might carry. *Love* is the greatest weapon, Miss Turner. But without sacrifice, love is just another four-letter word. Clyde came to this town needing a hand reached out to him, and yet all we did was judge him – myself included. What would make him believe that the love we talk about is the solution to his problem if we're just gonna write him off from the beginning." Eckhart flashed a wan smile and then turned to leave. Before exiting the room however, he turned to face me one last time.

"Being a Sheriff has taught me two very important things in this life. First: we all have a track record, just not everybody's dirty laundry gets aired. And second: I've learned to seek the truth in every case, no matter how many preconceptions I want to draw. The curtain is closing on my time as the Bridgeton Sheriff, but those two lessons I learned, I'll take to the grave with me. I just hope that I can pass them along to someone else who needs to use them before my time expires. Again, I apologize if I've spoken out of line. Have a good night, Miss Turner." Before I knew how to respond, Sheriff Eckhart disappeared into the shadows of the Saint Luke's Hospital hallway.

I shifted uneasily in the bed, grimacing as my body felt the sting of pain from the attacks. As I finally settled under the white, cotton bed sheets, the discomfort slowly faded away from my limbs, leaving me with only the painful torment of an unmade decision.

68
Clyde

When my eyes opened, I knew immediately that I had returned to the dream world. It wasn't my surroundings that tipped me onto the fact that I was once again dreaming, but rather the void of emotion that I felt. Had I been awake, the torment of losing Spock would have been severe, but not in the dream world. In the dream world, my *emotions* were asleep, allowing my heart and mind to truly take in the world around me.

I raised myself up off the ground (without the use of crutches and without the stabbing throngs of pain – another tall-tell sign of a dream) and found myself standing next to my sleeping body. Seeing myself asleep in the ditch was eerily supernatural and for a moment, I thought I had died. But as I looked down, I noticed the slow breathing pattern of my chest as it rose and fell in rhythmic succession, as well as the fleeting tufts of warm breath as I exhaled into the cold, winter air. The other observance I took note of was the glaze of anguish and fear that troubled my face, even as my body rested. The years of time tugged and pulled at my skin; the dark circles around my eyes bore witness to the joyless existence I had been enduring. It was the first time that I had ever looked upon myself with honest eyes, and the result saddened my heart.

The lifeless corpse of JJ was still exactly where he had been. His body was twisted and bent from the fall, and there was still a small river of blood draining from the welt atop his skull. The sight of his remains was gruesome and so I turned my eyes away immediately.

Looking to the ridge above, I searched with wandering eyes for my beloved dog. However, his body was nowhere to be seen.

patch of moonlight that I was able to decipher who it was. His yellow, fur-clad body was shiny and clean, looking almost white under the moon as he pranced in my direction. His long ears flopped playfully against the side of his head as he ran into my open arms. I bent down and planted a long kiss on his head, receiving his kisses all over my face in return. With an overwhelming rush of joy, I held my dog Spock one final time.

Flash watched, elated at the love shared between Spock and I. He allowed us a moment to enjoy each other's affection; staying quiet and out of the way as I poured my heart out to my faithful friend. I thanked him and kissed him, laughing heartily as he pounced on top of me with his golden paws. Ecstasy bound the two of us together in that moment, overflowing our hearts with joy and peace. After what seemed like forever, Flash spoke up. His words seemed to hold a slight pang of sorrow.

"I told you that you had one special dog here, hoss. We could all learn something from a page in his book, 'cause that little fella knows what it means to love. He understands the ways of the farmer. But it's time for us to get movin' now. There's a storm coming and your journey aint yet over."

I wrapped my arms around Spock's body one final time, burrowing my head into the soft of his neck. Before letting go, I held his tiny face with my hands and placed my lips next to his ear. With one final kiss – a kiss that I treasure to this day, if even in a dream – I whispered, "I'll never forget you, boy."

Suddenly, the trace of moonlight up above vanished and flashes of lightening began to pierce the night sky. Spock leapt out of my embrace and followed Flash down the incline and into the ditch below. I rose to my feet, but as I did, I could feel a slight river of pain shoot from my back, down into my legs. I stumbled, trying to gather my balance, but was unable to do so seeing as though I had been so close to the edge.

"You better get movin' hoss," I could hear Flash say over the bay of wind that began to scream down out of the mountains. "The storm is here!"

The heavens above opened and a blanket of heavy snow pelted the earth, diminishing my visibility to nothing. My eyes seemed as if they were shrouded with a white veil as the winds kicked up and chilled my body – both inside and out. Regardless of the storm I tried to hurry after Spock, not ready to say goodbye to him again, but another flare of pain erupted in my right leg and sent me tumbling to the ground below. I remember feeling the blinding pain throughout my body as I tumbled into an unending world of whiteness. From there, everything went dark.

* * * * * * * *

I opened my eyes to the sight of thick, white flakes of snow falling from the dark sky above. My body shivered in the cold as the snow fell calmly to the earth like kisses from the angels above. I brushed away the flakes that had collected on my face while I had slept, feeling the sting of frostbite against my cheeks. I was surprised to have seen that the snow began so early before sunrise, but was even more taken back that nearly two inches had already collected.

I didn't try to sit up upon first waking, but rather remained where I was, intoxicated by the tranquility of the falling snow. Spock was fresh on my mind as I embraced the final moments we had shared in the dream. But no matter how hard I tried, my mind kept revisiting the moment of his death, and it brought me back to tears all over again. As I cried though, I thought back onto the words that Flash had spoken to me about love and sacrifice; the ways of the farmer as he had called it. I thought about Spock and how his life had been nothing but sacrifice. Even in the end, he had given up everything – his life included – so that I would know and understand the full measure of his love.

"How selfless," I thought as I wept beneath the blanket of falling snow. I was blown away that a dog had known how to love greater than I did. Spock had been a *Giver* where as I had always been a *Taker*. I had mirrored the fakeness of love I saw as a child, and it had done nothing but leave me to die in the cold.

Flash had been right. I had allowed my words to determine my fears; I had harbored a lifetime of fears and anger and had validated them in my writings. The worst part of all I realized, as I lay crying in the growing snow, was that my worst fear had finally come to pass...

...I was all alone.

It was in that moment beneath the moonless sky – as I let the flakes cover me like a shroud of purity – that I cried out to the heavens above. I cried out in the anguish of loneliness. I cried out in the void of love. I cried out seeking help from the God who I had spent the last year blaming for my own misfortunes. I finally willing to honor the golden ring that he bore on his left hand, although in the right setting with the right outfit, I could get any guy to cheat. It was just the way men were; the whole lot of them were nothing but a herd of reproductive Takers. They take the dessert and never stick around long enough for the meal.

But none of that really mattered, because whoever the lucky gal was who had trapped that evening's transportation officer into the holy vows of matrimony, was soon to become a widow. It was nothing personal, but I needed my freedom because Clyde needed his. I was Clyde's only hope at seeing the truth of our life– the destiny that had bound us together since we were children. The faceless scarecrow was giving me one more chance to free his mind. If unsuccessful, Clyde would face the same destiny as the black cop who drove me towards the mountain in the dark of the evening.

There's nothing to fear though, my Clyde. Death comes to us all. Eventually.

The patrol car left Canyon Pulse, heading west on Route 208 just as Hank had told me it would. He had outlined the entire route to the courthouse for me that day in the investigation room, and as I watched his words play out in a logistical utopia, I began to relax. Hank was at the helm and he seemed to know his way around the block pretty well, so all I had to do was sit back and wait for the plan to unfold.

As we began to ascend into the foothills of the mountains, the darkened road up ahead was suddenly pierced by a pair of flashing emergency lights in the distance. The red pulsing lights grabbed my attention and filled me with a pleasure that I hadn't known since the night in my cell when the scarecrow had taken me into his arms. It was the color of the lights that fascinated me like no man could ever dream to do. It was RED, and my body ached for it.

"What is that?" I asked of the driver. It was the first words I had said to him and some of the last he would ever hear.

"It looks like a stranded motorist. Possibly a flat tire," he said. "I'm going to have stop for a minute. Just sit back and stay quiet."

The car on the side of the road was a hefty brown pile of scrap metal that looked like a dumpster on wheels. I wouldn't have been surprised if it had smelt that way too. As we drew near to the rusted vehicle the patrol car dropped its speed. For the first time, we were able to notice the young man who was kneeling down by the front, left tire as if he were paying his final respects to the airless piece of rubber that had blown out on him. When the stranded, tire-struggler noticed that a police cruiser was approaching slowly, and then pulling off onto the shoulder of the narrow mountain road, he stood up with a wide grin splashed across his frozen face. But despite the bitter temperatures that were brewing in the night air, he smiled. And he had every right to smile, because he had been waiting for us to show up for over an hour. It was time for Hank to go to work.

70

Hank

I had spotted the headlights of the patrol car while it was still a good two miles out, but I knew it was them. I could feel Mindy's magnetic presence even from afar, and I suddenly found myself losing my grasp on the plan. I wanted nothing more than to take her in the back of the police car and finish that kiss from the other day. The handcuffs she was wearing would be an added bonus.

Shut up and get focused!

I shook off all thoughts regarding Mindy – for the time being at least – realizing that if I botched up the plan in anyway, the only people I would ever be having sex with again were all the inmates down at County. So with my mind honing back in on the mission, I knelt down next to the flat tire and waited to see the headlights approach.

Remain calm and remember what to do.

It was cold outside, bitterly freezing, and the feel of snow was heavy in the air. I was thankful that I had chosen to don my heavy jacket but was cursing myself for having not remembered my pair of Long Johns that morning. The chill was monstrous but the warmth of Mindy's nearing presence – and the memory of our kiss – kept my blood boiling inside of me like hot lava. And it felt good. *Mindy* felt good. I wanted her. And if killing the transport driver would assure me a place in her heart, then I would gladly bash in a skull or two by night's end.

"*I'm not a murderer though,*" I whispered into the hollow rooms of my mind. "*I'm not. I've got to rescue her. I'm her knight and she's my princess, and the Sheriff is going to make her ride the lightning. But she's innocent and I have to protect her. It was the calling of my life; I was born for this very reason."*

The biggest obstacle to hurdle was making sure to keep my face hidden beneath the hood of my sweatshirt. Chances were that the Sheriff had put out word to the entire force about my possible involvement in Kelly's disappearance. And I'm sure they had discovered that I had fled my apartment, so any cop who would make me out before I could get close enough to mash their brains in was most likely to arrest me. And that was the one possible glitch in the plan, but I didn't have any other choice.

The headlights of the patrol car immediately cut through the darkening night, hemming me within the soft white cones of their light as if I were a circus performer about to do a crowd-dazzling trick. And I was.

Step right up! It's time to watch me crack a human skull with a tire iron! It's gonna be amazing kiddies!

I stepped into the middle of the road, waving my arms into giant X's above my head as if to signal for help. I painted my face with a wide smile as if to say: *Thank you Jesus, the Cavalry has arrived.* Innocence was vital to the mission. I had to get the cop to pull over and offer me assistance. If not, than I would be stuck in the cold mountain air with a flat tire and a long walk back into town. So as I said, looking innocent was vital.

The problem with my life however was that it seemed to be nothing more than one long strand of disappointments. Nothing that I had ever planned had ever come out the way I wanted. I could remember the birthday cake I had tried to make as a kid that deflated the moment I took it out of the oven. Then there was the basketball team I had tried out for in high school after months of training. That had turned sour after I twisted my ankle in the first ten minutes of wind sprints. Then there was the girl in college that I had dated for just over a year who crushed my heart by telling me that she had been sleeping with my best friend the entire time; but of course she waited to tell me as I was down on one knee proposing in the middle of her favorite restaurant. (*Thanks for that night of embarrassment you stupid whore. Maybe I'll track you down and crack your skull when I'm done here.*) But on that cold November night, one thing finally worked out as planned. Although I couldn't believe my eyes, the patrol car slowed down in speed and pulled off onto the side of the road. I didn't know how Mindy was making it happen, but I knew that she was somehow orchestrating it all within her brilliant mind – somewhere behind those golden, goddess eyes of hers. And I loved her for it all the more.

I'm coming my love. Get those lips of yours ready.

The police cruiser finally came to a halt, kicking up a cloud of dust as it settled onto the shoulder of the mountain road. As the door popped open, I began to wonder which cop would step out of the car. Would it be one of the many I would enjoy skull bashing?

Is that you in there Jeffries? Or is it Michaels or Freedman, or maybe even that dumbass Morris who couldn't discharge a firearm without an instruction book? Who would be the lucky one to get a taste of iron crammed down their throat tonight?

As the driver stepped out into the cold, night air I recognized him immediately. It was Xavier Woodard, one of the two friends I had made during my time in the Academy. I was going to have to kill my friend. *Was I capable of doing that?* Suddenly, my resolve began to slither out of my grasp like a wriggling snake. I couldn't tell if it was noticeable or not, but I took a slight step backwards.

"Are you having a problem changing that flat?" Xavier asked as he drew near to me, hands on his belt as if he were some gaudy superhero preparing to dispel one of his fancy gadgets.

"No, I'm having a problem killing a friend," I joked to myself. But then I quickly spoke up, saying: "Yeah. I seemed to have left my tire iron back at the house and now I can't get the damn wheel free. You don't by chance have one on you, do you?"

I didn't think Xavier had spotted me yet, which was the good news. The bad news however, was that if he got any closer, he most likely would.

"I should have one in the trunk. Let me check."

The large, massive cop turned and moved towards the back of his patrol vehicle. As he did, I began to recalculate the plan in my mind. If I was going to have to kill Xavier (*for Mindy, of course; this was all for Mindy*), then I was going to have to veer from the original plan in order to get the foot-up on him. I had hoped to get the unsuspecting officer to help wrench the lug nuts free from the tire, allowing me the opportunity to smash him from behind with my own tire iron that was hidden in the trunk with the spare. But I couldn't afford to let Xavier that close to me. He would know, and then he would turn on me. Not only did he posses a firearm at his disposal, but his arms were twice the size of mine and he stood nearly a head above me. So if the plan unraveled and became a face-to-face confrontation, the odds would weigh heavily in his favor.

"I'll get the spare out of the trunk," I called out as I rushed over to the rear of my car. In foresight, I had left the trunk unlocked and cracked open so that I would not have been forced to waste time manually keying it ajar. So I had fairly quick access to the long L-shaped piece of iron that was going to become the demise of poor Xavier. I ripped the tool out of the trunk without wasting even a second. Timing was going to be crucial. I quickly crossed over to the passenger side of the patrol car, slinking low against the vehicle and making sure to keep as quiet as possible. Lucky for me, the winter winds were beginning to whip and snap at the valley of trees that surrounded us, so stepping lightly was not as important as it seemed. But I did so anyways. As I snuck furtively towards the rear of the police cruiser, I couldn't help but think that Mindy was somewhere behind the opaque glass, grinning in pride as her golden eyes watched on. The thought was electrifying; filling me with a surge of adrenaline that spun me around the side of the car with the tire iron poised above my head. As I had hoped, Xavier was hunched over the trunk, rummaging through the cluttered mess.

As I brought the cold piece of metal racing towards his skull, Xavier turned in my direction, startled. Instead of shattering the back of his head, the tire iron slammed into the bridge of my friend's nose, sending up a spray of blood as the bones in his face exploded in a chorus of CRACKS and POPS. His eyes rolled into the back of his head, leaving only two white orbs to contrast his darkened face. Twisted thoughts of enjoyment coursed through my mind as I raised the bloodied iron for another blow. Xavier lost his footing and fell headfirst into the trunk. I thrust the iron into the back of his head, feeling his skull fracture beneath the weight of each blow. Once. Then twice.

Third times a charm!

The front of my shirt was now covered in blood and fragments of human skull; a reality that was beginning to turn my stomach into the same messy pool of disgust that was now Xavier's head. The back of the police cruiser was covered in blood as if a child had flicked a brush of red paint all over the chrome. But I couldn't stop myself from battering the back of Xavier's head like a hammer. All my years of aggression and pain were incepted into each swing of the tire iron, each attack doing more damage than the one before. The rage exploded within my mind as I thought of all my childhood failures, and all of the people who had said I would never amount to being more than a cashier at the local Home Depot or a crossing guard on a construction site. Each blow with the iron reminded me of Kelly and her whore-like stupidity that had been the cause of this entire mess. Lastly, I thought of the Sheriff and how he had been waiting for me to fail from the beginning. And so with all of those thoughts and memories culminating in my mind, I smashed the iron so deep into the back of the bloody mess – that at one time had been the head of my friend – that it looked almost organic.

I finally let go of the weapon, letting it lay in the cesspool of Xavier's mangled remains, and wiped his blood away from my face.

"I'm sorry my friend," I whispered. And then my lunch from that day came back up into the trunk of the police cruiser.

71
Mindy

He actually did it!

That spineless, sniveling excuse of a man actually killed his fellow officer. With all of his talk about being innocent and how the Sheriff was just out to get him, I was almost certain that he would have flipped out and ruined the entire thing. He had altered the original plan a little, which I was not happy with to say the least. I had wanted to watch everything take place – I desired it almost as much as I longed to see the look on Clyde's face when I showed up in his bedroom in the middle of the night. So when Hank snuck up to the back of the patrol car and killed the big, black brute with the trunk lid obstructing my view, I was not too thrilled at all. But the deed was done and the results far outweighed the means of getting to the end.

When Hank finally got around to opening the door for me, he looked as if he had dipped his face into a vat of strawberry syrup. He was an abomination to look upon even though the color of the blood was something to revel in. That was why I shook off his hand as he tried to escort me into the free world once again. He was filthy, and just the sight of him made me long for a hot shower and two bars of Zest. Despite his repulsive appearance, I allowed Hank to free me from the handcuffs with the key he had snatched from the dead cop.

"How the hell did this go wrong?" I asked as I rubbed at my bare wrists. Freedom had never felt so good.

"What do you mean? He's dead and you're out. What part of this is wrong?"

I hurried back to Hank's car and found the red duffel bag in the backseat just as he had said. I hurriedly changed into the navy blue sweatshirt, the pair of jeans, the ski cap, and the gloves, then disappeared into the surrounding trees just in case anybody nearby had heard the crash and decided to investigate. I wanted nothing more than to run for Clyde's house, anxious to be with him once again. But the scarecrow had given me very specific orders that night in my cell. He had told me to get out of the mountains and then to wait — wait for the snow. I was to travel only at night and keep far away from any of the main roads. Rest by day, he had said, and it made sense the more I thought it through. The vastness of the fields during a massive snowstorm would keep me hidden from any of the rural homes that were scattered all throughout Bridgeton. So although I desired to be at Clyde's house by sunup, I had to make sure and follow the directions explicitly. The last time I had ignored the scarecrow's call, I had ended up in prison. So I had made a promise to him that I would see the mission through if he saw fit to grace me with a second chance. And he had, so I was not willing to blow it. I would get to Clyde when the time was right, and if that meant waiting for snow, than I was willing to wait. In the meantime, I had a few hours left of darkness to try and get myself out of the mountains and down into the valley.

Leaving the scene of the crash, I began by tracking north. For most of the ignorant townspeople, maneuvering throughout Bridgeton without being seen would have been difficult. But not for me. I had spent weeks in Bridgeton searching for Clyde, and had learned quite a bit about the layout of the town in that time. Therefore, I knew that traveling in any direction other than north would be my best way of getting myself caught. And I couldn't afford to disappoint the faceless scarecrow that way. I wanted to obey the orders I had been given. I wanted to find favor in the eyes of the one who had no eyes. As twisted of a thought as it was, I could not shake free of its white-knuckled hold; nor did I desire to do so.

A few hours of stumbling through the darkness finally brought me to the lip of a rocky, maze-like bypass. It must have been early Monday morning because I could feel the imminence of the dawning sun — a concept that made me sick to my stomach because the night was when true life was lived. The daylight was the time of the Takers, and therefore I despised it.

The bypass was a long and narrow corridor through the mountain, perfectly etched out of the mountain's side by the hands of nature. In most places, the footing was slick and steep – and that was in the dry, summer months. But as I stood at the entrance to the bypass, staring down into the haunting path as if I were staring a snake in the mouth, I saw nothing but a stairway of rock and ice stretching into the infinite darkness of night. I pushed forwards despite the stifling winds. The cold air bit at my face and hands; I was sorely underdressed for walking at night in such harsh conditions. Had it not been for the fires of revenge that burned deep inside of me, I might have died on top the mountain that night.

It took almost ninety minutes for me to track my way out of the mountain, being careful with each step that I took so as to ensure my safety. When I reached the bottom, the winding bypass emptied out into a large, undeveloped area of land. The miles of acreage had apparently been purchase by the local 'deep pockets' for the sole purpose of avoiding the aesthetic pollution of rural life from coming up out of New York City. For me though, the empty fields represented the first phase of success on my journey. The next step was to find a place to rest my cold and weary body; a new day would be dawning soon and I needed to go into hiding.

There was a gathering of large oaks at the foot of the mountain, but one of them in particular looked as if it had fallen down decades ago. The long shaft of the dead tree had been hollowed out by time, providing a dry and windless covering for me to crawl into in order to escape the snow that was beginning to gently fall. But it wouldn't stay that way for long, so I crawled into the gut of the old tree and handed myself into the hands of a restless and haunting sleep.

"You saved me," I whispered aloud before falling asleep, hoping that the scarecrow would hear my words. "I owe you my life."

snow-covered face, looking for anything with which to grip for support. Under the sheet of fresh snow however, there wasn't much in the way of support. I reached out for a large tree root that had broken through the hard earth, but my frozen fingers could not seem to wrap around the gnarled root with enough strength to lift my body weight. My hand slipped away and I immediately began to tumble back into the ditch. The pain in my legs shouted in agony as I rolled down the hill, kicking up a cloud of fresh snow as I fell. The misery within my lower body was intense, but the thought of failure hurt all the more.

The second attempt was far more successful than the first because I had chosen a different path to take up the hill. I snaked up the ravine like a wounded soldier on a field of battle, using all of my physical strength to lift me towards the top. Without the use of my legs, the task was overbearing and daunting, but I climbed on. I exerted all of my energy in the attempt to rescue myself from the ditch, but as I looked down to see how far I had traveled, I slipped against an icy portion of the hill. Gravity once again took hold of me and propelled me back into the ditch.

At the last second, before bouncing off the ground below, I was able to snag the tip of a thin gangly root with my left hand, keeping my feet from slamming into the frozen earth. The sudden stop jerked at my shoulder, lifting my body slightly away from the slope before smashing back down and kicking up a dusting of fresh powder. I grimaced in pain but refused to let go of the root. I was not going to fall back into the ditch. I refused to, but there was no way I could make it up the slope. Not of my own strength at least. If I was going to make it to the top, I was going to have to look beyond the ability of my own arms and legs. It was the only way.

"I believe," I whispered in prayer through panted breath as the wind kicked up fierce and frigid. "I can't do this alone, but I *can* do this."

With a sudden surge of strength, I began the climb again, keeping my eyes focused on the top the entire time. I refused to even consider defeat as an option. I was not going to return to the ditch. Not during the climb. Not during my life. And so I climbed steadily upwards, looking beyond the river of pain and the mounting fatigue. I kept my head turned up and my eyes looking within. Each strenuous yard was buffered by the remembrance of Spock's sacrifice. Every cold minute was veiled in the warmth of God's love that I had neglected for far too long. I might not have understood it completely, but I also didn't know how a crippled man was going to crawl home in the midst of a swarming blizzard. But I had hope. I believed.

After struggling up the ravine for a span of time that I could not remember, I finally reached the pinnacle of the climb. I slid my heavy body into safety and laid in the collection of snow, humbled by the accomplishment of my scramble. I had managed to make it out of the ditch, but my achievement could not fair in comparison to that of Spock's. His love was shown through both his life and death, and as I lay in the snow within a solitary moment of thanksgiving, I prayed that the remnants of my life could make the kind of impact on at least one other person, that Spock had done for me.

With the thought of my beautiful dog still freshly in my mind, I rolled onto my side and looked at the heart-wrenching sight before me. Spock's coat of blonde fur was hidden beneath two inches of snow; he would soon be covered completely. Covered, but never forgotten.

I turned my gaze away, and as I did, I noticed something in the snow that captured my attention. Imprinted in the winter-laden ground was a set of footprints that weaved through the bloody remains of Powe and his lackeys. Along side of every other print, was another indentation that I couldn't decipher at first. But after following the path of prints with my eyes and realizing where they led, I knew immediately what I was seeing. The footprints belonged to Flash; the other obscure marking was made by his walking stick. The set of prints led back out in the direction I had seen Flash come from in my dream. The old Walking Man had left me a trail to follow, but if I didn't move along quickly, the increasing snow would soon erase any signs of his presence.

Not only was the volume of snow beginning to increase – almost double – but the strength of the wind followed suit. Heavy gusts began to roll down out of the mountains, kicking up drifts of snow and freezing the exposed areas of my skin.

Visibility was steadily decreasing as well, especially since the sunrise was still a few hours away. Flash's path was there to follow for the time being, but contrary to the Rolling Stones, time was *not* on my side. So despite the excruciating pains flowing through my body, I began to crawl alongside of Flash's fading tracks, hoping and praying to make it to the barn before anything else could go wrong.

I trudged along on the ground, weaving in and out of haunting trees, as well as rising and falling with the uneven land at an out for sleep. The suffering was so intense, that I could feel its sting piercing into my head as if I had just strapped a dozen nine-volt batteries to the tip of my tongue. To this day, I do not recall crawling into the safety of the barn, nor do I remember opening or even unlocking the sliding glass door in order to do so. I only remember feeling the warmth of the heat as it circulated throughout the barn, pressing down upon me like a hot iron to a wrinkled shirt. Before closing my eyes however, I remember seeing the kind and smiling face of Gordon 'Flash' Hightower as he stood above me.

"Rest, Mr. Clyde," he said as the chasm between his voice and my ears grew wider. "You rest now. And when you're ready, you tell the world about true love. Do it for me, hoss. For me."

Then I slept.

* * * * * * * *

I must have slept for a few hours because when my eyes opened, the daylight outside was once again giving way to the darkness of night. I wouldn't have noticed the fade of day had I not been laying on the floor of the barn looking up at the ceiling. That was how I noticed that the bank of lights above was once again turned off, painting the inside of the barn with the gray pallor of a winter's evening. With the diminishing light, came an array of swarming questions, all of them leading my mind back to one common denominator...*Flash.*

Upon waking, my brain felt waterlogged with a monotonous hum, feeling as if my skull was being strained within the grips of a vice clamp. I could vaguely recall the journey back to the barn – remembering absolutely *none* of how I had actually gotten inside. I did remember seeing Flash however. Or at least I *thought* I had. Flash had been standing over me – I was almost sure of it – with the lights on and the heat thawing out my frozen body.

But had it really happened or was I just dreaming? There are no signs that he had been with me in the barn.

The lights and the heat were now shut off.

But it could have been the storm that knocked out the power.

What about the footprints on the deck? Or even the walking stick I had seen on the way inside?

Covered up by the snow, perhaps? There is nearly twelve inches collected already.

I tried searching for a reason to believe that Flash had been there – that he was indeed real and not just another manifestation from beyond the gate – but I couldn't find anything. The only thing I had to go on was my memory, and that was shaky at best. Regardless, I still clung to the words that I *thought* I remembered hearing Flash say.

"*You rest now,*" he had said to me, with a heaping of empathy choking back his tears. "*And when you're ready, you tell the world about true love. Do it for me, hoss. For me.*"

I forced myself to sit up and stare around the large room that was growing darker with each passing moment. It wouldn't be long before the remaining light was fully swallowed up by the night, and so I didn't allow the constant throbbing of pain to keep me down.

Being inside the old barn again felt very much like a déjà vu' experience. I hadn't been in the oversized, upper room since I had first moved into the Sugar Hill Farms Estate, but yet I couldn't shake free of the dream that had brought me almost to the very exact place. I remembered seeing Powe and his gang in the south corner of the room tearing into Flash the same way they had torn into Karla. But on that cold winter evening in November, the corner was filled with cardboard boxes instead of belligerent ruffians. In the dream world, the barn had been completely empty, save for my old typewriter and a stack of paper beneath a longneck desk lamp. As I looked around the room however, with nostalgia glazed over my eyes, it was clear to see that the barn was far from empty. My old office furniture and decorations were still stacked against the east-facing wall, lining the majority of the sixty-foot perimeter as if there was a clearance sale in an Office Depot warehouse.

The rest of the room was peppered with dunes of cardboard boxes, each of various shapes and sizes. Some of the boxes had even been stacked upon my old mahogany writing desk and the green-and-white striped sofa that I had spent many hours on, napping whenever inspiration had been in short supply. The room was cluttered with the boxes – the cardboard coffins of my Shadow Life – and as I looked upon them, I was suddenly inundated with the suffocating weight of guilt.

Staring at the boxes reminded me of the land beyond the gate. Although the gate had been closed and locked, the evilness that plastic covering around the outside, which acted as a sleeve for inserting paper or other thin decorative items such as index cards or photographs. The piece of paper that I had slipped into the clear pocket was almost completely blank, except for the one single word that I had typed in bold letters directly in the middle of the page: SEVER. With extreme hesitation, I opened the binder and began to flip through the pages of the last manuscript that I had ever written.

There were nearly three hundred typed pages that had rolled out of my typewriter and into the binder. It was the workings of a rough draft that had never been completed, but it was the book that I had been most excited about. The book SEVER was to have been my third novel, and I had felt that as an author, my writing style had matured enough to do justice to the story. But as I held the unfinished manuscript in my cold hands, the novel felt as unsound and evil as the barn did. Wrong and insidious.

The story of SEVER had been set in a small farming community, not unlike the town of Bridgeton. The main antagonist in the book was a seven-foot tall scarecrow with white gardening gloves for hands and a burlap sack stuffed with straw for a head. The character of the farmer who had set up the scarecrow in his cornfields had never given a face to the mannequin, only a large straw hat atop its head, an old red and black flannel shirt, a pair of faded blue jeans, and two dirt-covered boots for feet. THE FACELESS ONE was the name I had coined for such a creature. And for a few reasons. The obvious reason went without saying, but the truer meaning went far deeper. A face is what gives identity to a person; a face and a voice to be more precise, which were the two thorns that I had given the scarecrow within the story. Although THE FACELESS ONE did not have a face at all, he did possess a small fraction of a voice. The tone of the scarecrow upon speaking (although without a mouth) was raspy and off-key, almost akin to an untrained singer who is searching for the right note but hits all of the wrong ones instead.

What I had liked at the time about the character of THE FACELESS ONE – what had made him different from the other antagonists in my previous books – was that he never carried out the evilness that he so cunningly schemed. THE FACELESS ONE worked through the people of the town, stirring the melting pot of evilness within the community by persuading others to do his bidding on his behalf. What the character of the scarecrow had learned was that his face and voice could be found, not of his own accord, but through the validation of the people who carried out his work. Needless to say, the bloodshed that had occurred within the story was far greater than anything I had ever written before. The publisher would have loved it.

You might be wondering what the scarecrow's purpose had been in doing such things. It was simple. THE FACELESS ONE despised the concept of *love*. He *loathed* it. To the devious scarecrow, love was nothing more than an illusion, and anyone who believed in it was weak and dangerous. The infamous line that THE FACELESS ONE would have been known for – had I actually finished the novel, was the following:

> *"Several the eyes,*
> *that wear a disguise.*
> *So silence the lies,*
> *And sever the ties."*

The story of SEVER was about the disguise of love that people wear, and how ridding the world of such petulance was the only solution for the faceless scarecrow. Death was IT's goal. To sever was to kill, and IT's weapon of choice were mindless people. It was the outcome that had befallen both Karla and Spock.

As I flipped through the pages of the manuscript, the original outline of the story began to recycle within my mind. I was able to remember the first few chapters of the book as well as the last five or six that I had never written, nor would I ever. I could not – in right mind – continue on with a story that talked against everything that Spock had lived and died for. The other reason that I could not bring a story to fruition that spoke against love, was because I no longer felt that way in my life. Sure, love meant sacrifice, but just as Karla and Flash had once said while talking about 'the ways of the farmer': it was a beautiful sacrifice. *Beautiful indeed,* I thought.

I put the manuscript back into the box that I had taken it from, watching a cloud of dust kick up out of the box as it landed inside. My life would never truly change unless I became the change, so the third and final book had to be written. But SEVER would not be the final product.

With the first winter storm of the year brewing outside, trapping me within the confines of the barn with a flogging of snow, I felt a sudden urgency to begin writing the new book. The feeling within me was powerful – just as intense and focused as the strength that had lifted me out of the ditch had been. And time was not a luxury that I possessed. My supplies of food were limited to Pop-Tart crumbles, and with the electricity shut off, I had no way to keep warm. Even in the short time I had spent awake in the barn, I was able to notice the drop in temperature. There was also no telling how long the storm would keep me trapped inside the barn. I had barely been able to climb up the back steps, and that was when there had been only a few inches of snow. Now, there was already a foot of fresh powder on the deck, and by the looks of it there was going to be much more. With that said, descending the steps was not going to be a feasible solution for me. I was in far too much pain. Even the task of setting up my old typewriter on the top of the mahogany writing desk was almost unbearable, requiring me to rest for a few minutes before moving forward with the new project.

When I finally felt up to the task, I changed out the ink of the typewriter with a spare that I had found within one of the cardboard boxes. I grabbed a ream of paper from a different box and then carefully sunk down into the black, leather office chair. I stared at the typewriter in front of me (with the power out, I was suddenly glad that I had opted to use a typewriter and not a computer). I thought about the book that I needed to write, and immediately thought about Spock. From there, I thought about the example Karla had shown me also, coming to a quick understanding about an important fact.

Love was not about severing, as I had originally thought, it was about *serving* – about giving oneself completely to another individual without attaching any selfish motives. My best examples had been Spock and Karla. They never had a secret agenda for loving me, unlike Mindy and my parents (that was if their perverted ways of thinking could even be construed as love). They had just *loved me*, and it was that concept that I thought about as I slid the first piece of paper into the typewriter.

I aligned the paper carefully and then typed out the title page for the new book – a book that would teach about validating the things of truth and love rather than fear. With a single word etched into the paper, the title page was complete. I pulled the sheet of paper out of the roller and set it on the desk next to me. The third book was no longer to be called SEVER. Instead, the black ink on the page stared up at me with conviction. The new title was simple, and yet surrounded with a realm of complexities. I couldn't take credit for the title however. I had Wilma Parker and the dream that she penned into her journal to thank for the idea. She had delivered her message to me, and now it was time for me to put her wisdom into play. The new book was to be called SERVE.

73

Karla

The snow was miserable, and it wasn't common for me to say something like that. I had always been the kind of person to enjoy the New York winters. Snow was magical, purifying the earth after nine long months of heat and growth, not to mention the joy in making snow angles or curling up by a fire with a book and a blanket. But as the winds gusted down out of the mountain range, shoveling a heap of fresh snow all over the Hudson Valley, I couldn't enjoy a single moment of it.

Clyde was still on my mind. I took the Sheriff's advice and spent most of my stint in the hospital with my ear glued to a phone. Unfortunately, I had talked to no one and my patience with ringing phones diminished. The Sheriff, who had been a real sweetheart by picking me up out of the hospital the following day and taking me home, had even taken me to Clyde's house. Together we had rung on the doorbell while kicking up a ruckus on the front door. But Clyde never answered. I would have at least expected Spock to have responded in some way, but the house remained as silent as a graveyard – and that was the analogy that scared me the most.

When I woke up Monday morning I snatched up the phone and immediately tried calling Clyde – four times. But the results were never different. I had one other option at my disposal, and I had held off using it for fear that I was overreacting and that Clyde would pop-up out of nowhere and chastise me for it. After all, he had been very upset with me the last time we had talked, so perhaps he was doing nothing more than giving me the silent treatment. It was a juvenile idea, but it at least gave me some hope of his safety. However, after listening to Clyde's answering machine four more times that morning, I caved in and made the other call.

I was not surprised when I was forced to listen to four or five more telephone rings before yet another answering machine picked up the call. The voice on the other end belonged to Clyde's agent. I left him a very brief message of concern, yet making sure not to come across with excessive panic. I never mentioned to him that Clyde was missing because that wasn't something I felt comfortable leaving on an answering machine. So rather than being specific, I just told him that I had a situation that required his immediate attention. At that, I thanked him and disconnected the call.

The level of fear within me began to climb, starting in my heart and expanding to the nerve-endings all over my body. I hated being in the dark. I was helpless, and although Clyde and I had not parted on the most amicable of terms, I still cared deeply for him. Actually, if I'm being honest with myself, I was actually falling in love with him. Despite the argument. And regardless of Pastor Rob.

meal. As I wrote, I held onto the memory of that moment for support, not with the intention to tease myself with the remembrance of food, but because it had been the last meal that Spock and I had shared together. Had I known then what I did now, I would have cherished that time together, taking in every detail that I could about my beautiful dog: the way he would rest his head on my lap until I would share my breakfast with him, the look of contentment in his brown eyes just partaking in my company, and the constant wag in his tail like a pendulum counting the time of eternity. Those were the thoughts I held onto while I wrote, trying to avoid the idea of eating altogether.

Water was a different story for me, however. When the final bottle I had packed was at last empty, I scooped piles of fresh snow from the back deck into the empty container and brought it back into the barn with me. Once it melted, I had at least some form of water to keep me hydrated. It wasn't the best of situations, but I knew that sustaining life would be much easier without food as long as I kept some flow of water in me.

Tuesday came and went, but I continued working all through the night. Time was short and I didn't have the luxury of rest. I knew what the goal was. I pushed through, watching the pages roll out of my typewriter just as quickly as I rolled them in.

By Wednesday morning, the book was nearing completion. It wasn't as long as my usual horror novels, but it didn't have to be. It just had to be honest – like I had promised Flash – and it was.

The new book was about a dog named Spock who lived and died giving all of his love for others, serving them in any capacity that he could. I did not bog down the story by intertwining the information about Flash. As a matter of fact, I never even mentioned Flash's name in the story, but I didn't think he would mind. After all, the story wasn't about an old man walking around at night. The story was about the example of love that God had given me in my life, and that example had been Spock.

The only other person that I mentioned in the novel was Karla, and that was because she had been the fruit of Spock's laborious devotion. Had it not been for my dog's nudging, I never would have had the gusto to look at Karla as anything other than a hired hand. Even if my time with her had been short lived, Spock had still led me to that point of being able to enjoy the affection of another person once again.

"The ways of the farmer," I thought aloud. "What a beautiful sacrifice."

The sky outside on that Wednesday afternoon was unlike the previous four days. A cloudless and blue awning stretched from horizon to horizon. The brilliance of the sun shown down upon the undisturbed fields of snow, causing the ground to glisten like a vast array of diamonds. The sunlight streamed into the barn with tendrils of warmth, painting a hue of life back into the gray and sterile room.

Despite the pain, hunger, and cold that were chipping away at my resolve, the view outside sustained my focus. The droning sounds of the typewriter as it CLICKED and CLACKED seemed to take on a flowing rhythm as the daylight gave promise to a fleeting situation. The story was nearing its conclusion, and when it was done, I would finally be able to rest. Things were beginning to look up.

Or were they?

75

Mindy

I couldn't wait any longer. The damned sun was taking
forever to go down and every inch of my body was infested with
the cold, like termites to a house. Not to mention the pain in my
legs and back from having walked through four feet of snow. I
needed rest, and I was so close to Clyde's house. I could already
hear the incessant barking of that stupid dog in my head. So
waiting for the sun to go down wasn't just unbearable. It was
insane.

But I'm not insane! I'm NOT!

I cupped my hands over my frostbitten ears with hopes of
shutting up Clyde's damn mutt, and then raised myself out of the
ditch. My body shivered from heels to nape. My teeth clattered
together like castanets; I could not rid myself of the freezing
weather. My face was so frozen that I felt as if my cheeks had
overdosed on Botox injections. The sweatshirt and jeans that the
departed Hank had provided me with were board stiff; they did
nothing in the way of providing winter protection. I wasn't at all
surprised that the half-cocked cop had screwed me over, even from
beyond the grave, which made me glad that I had at least taken his
jacket. It had been the only silver lining of the entire damn mess.
Even his oversized boots had blistered my feet.

Not only was I wet and filthy, but the odor that I reeked with
was gut wrenching. Walking through the fields had been difficult
work, and of course had caused a profusion of sweat, but to keep
warm during the frigid nights, I had no choice but to urinate in my
jeans while walking. My pants were stained with frozen urine; the

audacity of the smell was almost too much for me to bear. This wasn't how things were supposed to have gone. Filth is for the Takers – the filth *is* the Takers – my daddy had taught me that.

"Don't tell the Takers about our love, princess," my daddy had said to me once. I never did, because we had a special love that nobody would have ever understood. And he was right. The Takers of the world tried to pollute our relationship. They lied about my daddy, and then they killed him, just like the Takers of old who killed off people like Gandhi, Martin Luther King, Jesus, and my daddy. The only difference however is that my old man was still alive. That special love of his still remained inside of me – inside of me and Clyde both – but if Clyde couldn't see it, then he wasn't worthy of the gift he had been given. He would have to die.

I set out through the fields on that Wednesday evening as the sky faded from a clear blue into a golden salmon color. As the sun began to recess behind the Cotaquins, the temperatures began to follow suit. The winds kicked up out of the north, catapulting my body into a frenzy of shivering convulsions. The cold air was definitely keeping my pace to a minimum, but after only an hour, I arrived at the destination.

Clyde's white farmhouse was dark and empty, standing tall within the winter wonderland. The sky above was a dark purple, with flaxen wisps feathered into the tapestry of the changing expanse. It was the ideal setting for reuniting with my brother – the completion of my father's love. It was a sign from the universe that the joining of our lives was putting right all the wrongs that the Takers had caused; the Takers with all of their ridiculous fears and carnal cravings. But that was not the life for me and Clyde. We shared a bond that ran far deeper than that of the Pretenders of the world. We had a past – THE RED – and as I stared into the brilliant colors of that evening sky with my tired eyes, I knew that the struggles of our separation would soon be over.

I jumped over the fence into the backyard and slunk towards the house. I peered inside through the lightless windows and, although the house appeared to be empty and deserted, I knew that I could not take a chance breaking in for fear of being seen, regardless of how warm and comfortable I imagined the inside to be. I had acted with haste the last time. I wasn't going to repeat the same mistake.

I turned my attention to the barn across the way, but immediately disregarded the notion. Walking to the barn would require another one hundred yards of snow marching, and I was too tired to consider that option – at least for the time being.

That left me with only one viable option. So as quietly as I could, I slunk over to the detached two-car garage. Surprisngly the side door that led into the garage through the backyard was unlocked.

"Finally," I whispered into the chilled wind. "A break."

The inside of the garage smelled like oil and grease and was cluttered with miscellaneous pieces of furniture and unpacked boxes. Without a moment's hesitation, I stripped a few of the packing blankets from some of the old bureaus and other furnishings, and laid myself down on the oily, concrete surface between stacks of boxes. After covering myself beneath a thrall of dusty blankets, I fell into an undisturbed sleep before the last trace of day could be erased by the night.

76
Sheriff Eckhart

It had been a long couple of days for me, so when four o'clock finally rolled around, I was glad to be getting out of the office early. The last forty-eight hours had been nothing but intense investigation and a bunch of assumptions that I couldn't put to the grind due to lack of evidence. Not to mention the incessant panicking from Karla about Clyde's absence.

The problems began when I sent out Officer Woodard with a transport on Sunday evening, hoping to bypass the storm and not aggravate the courts with a cancellation due to weather. Plus, I hated sending out officers when the roadways were sub par. It was bad enough that the men and women under me had to put their lives on the line everyday, so making someone traverse an icy road through the Bypass wasn't fair in my eyes. So I had figured that I would obtain upper hand by sending the transport a day early. But when the call came in from the courthouse asking why Miss Mindy Baker had never arrived for her sentencing, I felt as if my cotton-picken innards were being twisted in a vice clamp.

I immediately ordered for all hands on deck so we could begin to find out what had happened to the transport. No matter how I tried to spin the scenario in my headache-clad mind, there were no outcomes that I settled upon that offered me any reassurance. There had either been a severe accident…or worse. I hated thinking about one of my officers being injured, or even killed on my watch, but if there had not been a car accident, then it left only one other option: Mindy had escaped.

"I was hoping you wouldn't mind escorting me to the Wednesday night service at my church tonight? I would drive myself, but I still don't feel too comfortable behind the wheel. Not yet at least. I normally wouldn't ask this of you, but I've really been giving thought to what we talked about the other day and feel very strongly about being at the service tonight."

I inhaled a deep breath of the stuffy office air. "And there's nobody from the congregation who wouldn't mind carpooling with you?" A silence entered the conversation, and suddenly I felt guilty, not for having asked the question, but for the frustration that had come through in my voice *while* asking. "It's not that I don't want to help you Miss Turner, I just figured that you'd probably feel more comfortable going with someone who shares the same emotions as you do about that church. I don't know if I'm necessarily the best person for that job."

"That's actually why I'm asking you, Sheriff, because we share more of a like-mind than you might realize."

Confused, I said, "I don't understand."

"You will. So, what do you say, Sheriff? Would you mind doing me this small favor? I really could use your support tonight?"

After glancing at the clock one last time, realizing that I was about to catch a boatload of flack from my wife, I obliged.

"What time should I pick you up?"

77

Karla

The Crossroads Reformed Church was not a large building by any stretch of the imagination, but it was large enough for the Bridgeton population that frequented the pews every Sunday morning.

The attendance for the Wednesday night service was typically half of the usual Sunday crowd but on that night, as I graced the doors with the hefty-sized Sheriff by my side, the majority of the Sunday audience seemed to be in attendance, despite the icy roads. Holidays typically brought larger crowds – pastoral paydays as the Sheriff called them – and so the night before Thanksgiving was no exception to the rule. There also happened to be a lot of buzz in town about the disappearance of Kelly Summers, so fear was the other magnet that seemed to gather the flock into the church's pen that night.

The Sheriff escorted me into the sanctuary as the pianist softly repeated the chorus to "It Is Well". The lights had been turned low, leaving only dim candlelight to create the orange halo of light that surrounded the inner sanctum of the church. My first instinct was to look upon the crowded front pews, remembering vividly the conversation that had taken place with Clyde's sister. But all I could remember was the knife. I could almost feel the danger all over again, fighting the urge to look over my shoulder for fear that Mindy was standing behind me. But all I had to do was remind myself that Mindy was in prison and I was safe. I was with the town's Sheriff for crying out loud, what was there to be afraid of?

The front of the sanctuary was lined with a long, wooden dais with a freshly polished podium to match. The front of the podium had been engraved with a large wooden cross, inlaid with gold and set into a swatch of purple felt, cloth.

A large stain glass window depicting Jesus praying on his knees, hung behind the stage platform with its array of colored tiles facing east. During Sunday morning services, when the sun was bright and shining, a spill of majestic, colored light would envelop the platform where Pastor Rob would preach. It was Rob's favorite part about sunny church days.

The ceilings were obscenely tall for such a quaint building in a hole-in-the-wall town like Bridgeton. The cathedral styled roof narrowed in at the top, forming a dome-like canopy overhead. Wooden beams and planks framed the entire structure, giving the sanctuary a well-polished, rustic appearance. Everything seemed to be well polished in the church – polished on the outside at least.

Upon entering the building, I was immediately inundated with whispered stares and judgmental eyes. The scowling faces jumped out at me from all over the candlelit room like demonic daggers, piercing through my innocence in search of blood. It was so apparent, that even the Sheriff could observe the hostility that fell over the church like an oppressive fire blanket. I couldn't understand why such hostility was so prevalent amongst those who claimed holiness. What had I ever done that was so wrong?

"Are you okay?" he whispered into my ear as we took a seat in the back pew. But I remained quiet. There wasn't much I could think to say because I didn't fully know what to expect. It was one thing for Clyde's demented sister to attack me in the church – that could be reasoned – but to have the church do the attacking was another thing entirely.

I glanced at the Sheriff, and with a partial grin, thanked him for being there with me. I could tell from the look in his eyes that he knew what I meant to do – the reasoning behind my imperative visit to the mid-week service. If the sullen looks of disappointment from around the room – even from the parishioners – were any sign of the confrontation that I was going to encounter, then I was definitely glad he had accepted my invitation.

The service began as usual, with the singing of some of the traditional hymns. The congregation stood in song, with hands lifted and eyes closed – a sight that the Sheriff seemed to find ironic as we stood in the back without participating.

426

Pastor Rob was up front, keeping an eye on the congregation as they put on their clamoring show of song.

But Pastor Rob wasn't staring at the congregation as a whole. He was watching the Sheriff and I as we stood in the back pew like foreigners. He had been pleased when I had entered the sanctuary, but when he pinpointed the burly face of the Sheriff in my company, his defense mechanisms must have fired off flares of alarm within his head. Even as he sung, the weight of stress pulled at the manicured smile that he donned as the pastor; his glamorous appeal stretched thin like a child's tee-shirt on an overweight adult.

At the conclusion of the ending song, Pastor Rob sent the ushers through the aisles to take an offering as he went through some of the mid-week announcements, reminding the congregation to remember the family of Kelly Summers as they opened their wallets for the tithe.

"A little extra can go a long way," was the phrase he used to instruct his flock to give extra money.

From there, Rob went on to mention a few of the absent elders who had taken sick and needed prayer, as well as some of the members who had been healed during the week from illnesses and financial burdens. Not once however, did he mention the miracle of my recovery although he made sure to pinpoint me with his dark, warring eyes. The final announcement was punctuated with a prayer for the missing college girl, as well as for her family who would have to endure the Thanksgiving holiday without her.

With the announcements wrapped up, Rob moved the service into what he called the 'open mic' segment. It was the traditional portion of the service that allowed any member of the congregation a chance to relay a praise report or a prayer request to the rest of the church. Being as though that particular service was the eve of Thanksgiving Day, Pastor Rob urged people to give a brief report of something they were thankful for.

As soon as the floor was opened to the church, I rose from the pew – hands sweating and slightly trembling – and made my way to the front of the sanctuary. A tremor of whispers flowed in my wake. I ignored it as I took my place behind the microphone, next to the pastor who was forcing a tight smile.

"Hello, my name is Karla Turner, and for those of you who don't already know, I recently got out of the hospital after almost a month-long coma."

Eckhart shifted in his seat at the uncomfortable, quivering sound in my voice. Sadly enough, I did not feel like a member of a

78
Clyde

It was finished!

The new book, titled SERVE, was stacked in a pile of white typing paper on a dusty mahogany desk within an old horse barn.

"God sure does have a sense of humor," I thought to myself as I released a wheezing cough into cupped hands. A trickle of pain weaved throughout my chest as I expelled the hot burst of air from my lungs.

The temperature inside the barn had dropped as soon as the sun went down, resting just above the freezing point. My body shook from the fatigue of the work as well as from the cold, keeping a constant haze of pain trembling throughout. My lower extremities were ablaze with agony, lamenting with a consistent throb. No matter how I shifted my weight, I could not find comfort.

I rested my head against the back of the office chair, enjoying the sweet sense of relief – despite the pain – knowing that the book was complete. It was much different than anything I had ever written, and I doubted if the publishers would accept it. If not, I would self-publish – no big deal – but that was only if I made it out of the barn alive. There was no doubt that without food and warmth, nor without any way to communicate to the outside world, that death would come knocking on my door soon enough. There was no fear however – fear was a byproduct of my Shadow Life, and that life was gone. So as I rested in the dark, I found myself thinking of Spock and his playful ways, utilizing those memories as a focal point for my contentment.

"*Thank you, Spock*," was the whispered tribute that I sent into the darkness of the barn.

Time ceased to exist as I sat in the discomfort of the oppressive silence, waiting for the natural order of life to take its course. I watched as the moonlight streamed in through the door and windows like a flow of silver liquid, casting a trim of brilliance around the boxes and furniture as if they were aglow with an arcane fire. The site was one of odd beauty, but yet it was all I could do not to stare in wonder. They say that a picture is worth a thousand words, but as I studied the portrait before me, only one word came to mind.

FIRE.

My racing thoughts took me back to the items I had packed before setting out on the trip – two of them sticking out like a blood blister on the hand of an albino. Pushing the discomfort behind a revving engine of adrenaline, I wheeled the chair over to my backpack. Reaching inside I pulled out the last two items remaining: the canister of lighter fluid and the silver, Zippo lighter.

A spark of hope dawned.

The time had come to finally use the lighter. Wilma Parker's dream had been correct after all.

There was a large amount of the cardboard boxes near the sliding glass door – many of them containing copies of my first two published books as well as the original manuscripts. So there was plenty of material for burning there. What I needed however, was a container that would safely handle the fire without burning the barn down and killing myself in the process. I scanned the room, straining my eyes to find something in the darkness that would work. There were a few bins, but they would hold fire about as well as a colander holds water. There was a small, plastic garbage pale but that wouldn't work any better. I looked feverishly for something that would do the trick but my options were few, and quickly diminishing.

I hacked up another series of painful dry coughs as the glimmer of hope that had sparked in my head began to fizzle out...that was...until I saw something next to the desk that got me thinking. Pressed up against the side of the mahogany writing desk were two large file cabinets. As I stared at them, considering the cabinets for possible use, I thought back to the day I had ordered them. I had been in need of protecting my personal information from theft or damage (my O.C.D. thoughts had always gotten me carried away), so instead of ordering just any run of the mill file

79

Karla

Sheriff Eckhart held the door open for me as I slid into the passenger seat of the police cruiser. Once inside, he made his way around to the driver seat and let himself in. The interior was almost as cold as the world outside, but couldn't hold a flame to the frigidness that we had felt inside the church.

The Sheriff started the engine and immediately a blast of hot air began to pour out of the vents and into the vehicle. He looked over to me, knowing with his keen investigative prowess that I was hurting. And I was. I could feel it like a low-grade fever, burning inside me for relief.

"You are one brazen young woman, Miss Turner. I don't know too many people who could face that kind of firing squad with the bold composure you just displayed. For what it's worth, I'm glad I was here to see it."

I glanced back in the Sheriff's direction through a thin film of tears. "Thanks again for coming, Sheriff. God knew I was going to need at least one faithful person to turn to during all that."

Suddenly, there was a light rapping against my window, startling me something fierce. I turned and looked at the old woman standing outside in the cold, peering into the police cruiser with wide eyes. The lady was dark-skinned with a contrasting head of white hair. Her face showed the signs of a long and difficult life, yet her smile carried a sunny disposition. She was bundled in a heavy winter coat – the color of caramel – and a long thick scarf that bore the many brilliant colors of the rainbow.

"Can I help you?" the Sheriff asked as he motored down my window. Ignoring the question, the old lady reached in and gently took hold of my hand. When she spoke, her voice was jarring and coarse. Despite the edgy sound however, her words were seeped in genuine heart-felt emotion.

"I heard what happened to you in there, honey and I think it's just *awful* how they treated you. I just wanted a chance to talk to you before you left, to tell you not to lose heart over this."

"Thank you so much, ma'am," I replied, my grin widening into an appreciative smile.

"You have a good soul and a kind spirit. I know that God will hear the prayers of your heart – even for that man you was asking prayer for. I knew Clyde when he was just a little knee-biter. He was a good kid; just raised up amongst a bunch of weeds, poor thing."

"He still has a good heart," I added. "He just has to find himself."

"Oh he will, honey. Clyde just fell into the cage of fear that most of us do – especially when it came to his old man. I knew his daddy too. I knew both them parents, I kid you not. We's all grown up around the same time and they were always so happy; like termites in a lumberyard. Heck, I even remember the day the two of them kids met. I was working with the horses down at the farm and they came riding by at the same time. Once they locked eyes together; that was all it took. You know what they say: 'First comes love, then comes marriage'. The rest is written in history."

The Sheriff leaned forward, interjecting, "You were there when Clyde Baker's parents met?"

The old woman leaned down farther to be able to meet eyes with the Sheriff. "Oh, yes sir. I most definitely was."

"But you just said that you were working on a farm when they met. I was always under the impression that they had met down by the river."

The old woman chuckled heartily. "No, sir. I don't know where you happened upon your information from, but I remember that day as clear as crystal. It's as frozen in my brain as this snow is on God's earth."

The Sheriff grunted mildly under his breath as he sat back in his seat, deep thoughts racing through his head.

"Well, I had best leave you to your business. I just didn't want you leavin' this place tonight without knowing that the prayers of your good heart will be heard. So you make sure to keep the faith Miss Turner, and you can pass that along to Clyde for me as well."

With that said, the old woman straightened up, the sounds of her knees and back popping like bubble wrap. With one last smile, she began a slow saunter down the sidewalk. I rolled the window back up and glanced over at the Sheriff who was clearly in deep thought.

"That was sweet," I said, finally feeling confirmed of the actions that had taken place within the church.

"You don't by chance know who that woman is, do you?" the Sheriff asked.

"No, who?"

Speaking about the encouraging woman pulled my attention back to the sidewalk one last time – wanting to see her again as the Sheriff pondered his web of thoughts. But as I looked outside, I saw nothing but an empty sidewalk stretching long in either direction. The woman was nowhere to be seen.

"I've never seen her before. I was hoping you would have been able to tell me," he suggested.

"What's on your mind, Sheriff?"

"Clyde's on my mind."

"What about him?"

"If what that old woman just said was true, and Clyde's parents did indeed meet at a horse farm in Bridgeton, then that means I was looking for the body of his father in the wrong place all those years ago."

"But that was so long ago, Sheriff. What would it matter now?" I asked, slowly growing afraid of the answer I might get in response.

"Clyde's father was killed in the same place where he and his wife had met. But there has only been one horse farm in Bridgeton. *Ever*. And that would be the Sugar Hill Farms Estate."

A gasp of shock escaped my lips. I locked eyes with the Sheriff, finally piecing together the connection that he had already made.

"Wait. Are you saying that Clyde ended up renting the very property where his mother murdered his father?" I asked.

"It appears so," the Sheriff replied, nodding his head absent-mindedly. "But that's not even the worst of it I fear. Clyde's father was killed in the summer of eighty-five. Three months after he was killed, is when the murders started happening beyond the gate."

"You're scaring me, Sheriff. What are you trying to say exactly?" I watched the seasoned officer as he ran mental calculations in the silence of the car. After a moment, the Sheriff sat bolt upright and threw the cruiser into drive. He flipped on the blue lights, leaving the siren off, and then sped down Route Thirty-Three, heading west towards the mountain.

"Where are we going?" I asked. Confused.

"I think I might know where we can find Clyde," he said while racing through town. "I just hope it isn't too late."

80
Clyde

"Welcome to the barn, son," said the scarecrow, far enough out of the reach of the moon's silver bands to where I could not see more than a phantom silhouette.

The truth: I *wasn't* surprised. I had been expecting THE FACELESS ONE all along. I had sensed the increase of evil over the last three days but had ignored it for the sake of the book. Even within the cover of darkness – just out of reach of my sight – I could feel the thickness of the scarecrow's depravity. The thing that bothered me however, more so than knowing that the scarecrow had arrived, was the sound of IT's voice.

In the book SEVER, I had described the raspy voice of THE FACELESS ONE as being akin to the sound of sandpaper being filed against cement, but the voice that spoke from out of the shadows had a normalcy that made the hairs on the back of my neck stand up on end. Something about it wasn't right.

I spun around to face the menacing visitor, remaining seated on the floor as I did so. I rested my back against the file cabinet, making sure to conceal the bottle of lighter fluid and the Zippo behind me. I wasn't exactly sure how to handle the situation, but I knew that if my only two weapons were discovered, then I would have nothing to defend myself with.

Through a haze of pain that clouded my vision like a morning fog, I took a quick survey of the room, realizing that THE FACELESS ONE was still a good thirty-or-so feet away. I considered lighting the books behind me on fire, hoping that burning the manuscript for SEVER would eliminate the problem entirely. But I knew better.

The words had already been written – validated by my heart and mind – so burning the pages would have no affect other than to reveal my hidden weapons. So rather than acting rash, I carefully slipped the can of lighter fluid into the waistband at the back of my jeans, hiding it beneath my sweatshirt and jacket. As for the lighter, I kept it buried within the clenched fold of my left hand.

"I knew you would follow your destiny, Clyde. *I've been waiting for you.*"

With his last words being whispered, the seven foot tall scarecrow stepped towards me and into the moonlight. With fear and trembling I looked upon the abomination, not just because I had created such a devilish character, but because THE FACELESS ONE stood before me with a *face* of his own.

The scarecrow was the same as the character from the manuscript in every slight detail: red and black flannel shirt, white gardening gloves, dusty old brown work boots, and even the oversized straw hat that I had found to be particularly haunting when I had dreamt up the idea for the book's antagonist. *Everything* was as it should have been, except for his head. There was no straw-stuffed, burlap sack with an absent face. Instead, looming beneath the sagging brim of the large hat, was the face of Phillip Baker...my *father.*

My heart leapt into another world. I opened my dry mouth to speak but the words were siphoned out of me, replaced with a listless exhale. The shock of the moment flushed my mind of all thought. The pain in my body even seemed non-existent.

"Expecting someone else?" my father asked, ambling throughout the maze of boxes. A loud scraping noise seemed to follow behind him as he walked, sounding oddly like the dragging fetters of Jacob Marley's ghost.

At first, I was unable to answer, dumbfounded at the unearthly sight of my dead father's head melded with the body of a fictitious scarecrow. It was horrific to see, especially the grotesque scars that rallied around his face like a web of thick, bloated tracks.

"*Axe markings,*" I thought.

"It's been a long time, *son.* A little too long."

The temperature in the barn seemed to plummet without notice.

"What are *you* doing here?" I asked as soon as the words were finally able to formulate on my tongue.

A single tear traced the curve of my cheek, falling like sand in an hourglass. I remained in the seated position – hoping that I still possessed the strength to make the stand – while my father towered over me. The glow of moonlight cut into the room from behind his monstrous frame, eclipsing me in the darkness of his shadow.

"So then you began to write. You poured your hatred into those damn books of yours; you poured *me* into them. You spent your life following in my footsteps, Clyde: The hatred for your whore of a mother, the way you despised anyone who wore the illusion of love, and the way you wanted to *sever* all of them out of your life. Well, today you get the chance."

My father bent down, staring into me with his cold, dark eyes. Up close his skin was waxy and decaying; the scars seeming to hold his flesh together like patches of a rotten quilt. The stink of his breath was colder than the temperature in the barn and heavy with the malignant stench of death. I fought back the urge to gag, focusing on keeping my hand clenched tightly around the lighter.

"*Keep it with you,*" Wilma Parker had said in her dream. "*You'll know what to do with it.*"

I readied myself, seeking the opportune moment.

Surprisingly, my father held the axe out to me, dropping it on the ground next to my feeble legs. The metal handle rattled with an uncomfortable CLANK as it came to rest against the wooden floor. The large scarecrow backed away from where I sat, as if he could sense the danger of the fire in my hand. I looked back and forth between the axe and my father, confused as to what his intentions were for having given up his weapon. From the distant darkness, he began speaking again.

"It's time for us to take SEVER to a new level, Clyde; time for you to finally man-up and take your destiny by the horns. Unleash the hatred. Release the pain that has kept you from finishing the book – our *legacy.*"

"I'm not finishing the book! It's over!" I said into the darkness and the unknown horror beyond, waiting for an explosion of anger to rebuttal my words. However, there was no outburst of rage or blind-sided attack. There was only a chair; a chair that evolved from out of the darkness with the evil scarecrow-man standing behind it. The chair was my writing chair, but it was not empty. There was a person sitting in it; I could make out the human form although the inky darkness made it too difficult to determine any noticeable features. My first thought was Karla, or perhaps even Flash, but I just couldn't be sure.

"Have you not been listening to me you damned nipper! SEVER is more than just a book. You should know that more than anyone – you wrote the words."

My father hesitated his speech as he rolled the chair and its mysterious rider towards me.

"Several the eyes, that wear a disguise..."

The chair drew near and the body took form – it was a woman.

"So silence the lies..."

The woman was looking around with blank, wandering eyes; suddenly I knew why the axe had been given to me.

"...And *sever* the ties, Clyde."

The woman was my dead mother.

"Here she is, the woman who ruined your life; the whore who lured me to this very barn and did this to me." My father pointed to the lattice of scars across his face that gleamed like polished silver in the moonlight. "This is what that woman did! This was the reality of her love, Clyde! Too many people in this pathetic excuse of a life claim that same kind of love. It's the disguise they wear, hiding the true motives of their hearts; their motives to destroy and control others, to manipulate this world like it's their own pathetic game."

My eyes filled with immediate pools of tears as I stared at the woman in the chair. The folds of her paisley nightgown tightly traced the plump curves of her body. Her jet-black hair glimmered a sweaty blue within the hue of the moonlight. I knew in my mind that she was not real – that she was *dead* – but I could not help feel all of the repressed emotions and pain as they resurfaced within me, lodging inside my throat.

"Mom?" I said through a whispered shriek of heartache.

"Clyde? Is that you?" The woman in the chair said, her eyes still wandering in the darkness as if she was blind. But she was not blind, and I knew it. Instead, she was in her final stages of depression and insanity, just as she must have been in the moments before the bottled up pressure within sent her to her bathtub-coffin.

I stared at my mother through painful tears, remembering the hatred and the bitterness that I had harbored since I was fourteen years old. Her face was drained of color and vigor; seeing her that way replayed the movie of my past in the theater of my mind. But I remained silent – unable to speak.

"I know you're there, Clyde. I can smell you, son. I can smell the stink of your cowardice. You're not a man! You never

protected your mother, and I *needed* you. You left me all alone
with that whore of a sister. But when you get to hell someday, I'm
going to eat your face and pick my teeth clean with your bones.
I'm going to enjoy tasting your endless fear, son! You will become
what you fear the most. You will become the faceless one!"

As I listened to the hateful words of my mother, I found
myself groping around in the darkness for the handle of the axe. I
ran the fingers of my left hand over the handle without letting go
of the lighter. Before too long, both the Zippo and the axe were
being clutched tightly in the same hand. The weight of the axe was
surprisingly light, providing me with a sense of strength that I had
never been familiar with. I stood to my feet, using the axe as a
crutch, and hobbled over to where my mother sat in the chair.

"See what you made me do, Clyde! Look at what you
caused!" The hefty woman lifted her hands into my line of sight.
The whites of her palms were dripping with a murky-colored
substance that reflected the silver rays of moonlight. It looked as if
she had just dipped her hands into a vat of luminous chocolate.

Blood. Her hands were covered with the blood of my father.

The sight of such cruelty and madness unburied sobs of
repressed pain. I could feel the all-too familiar anger reaching up
from my broken heart and into my mind like a vine that had grown
out of control – a vine that had been choking the life out of me for
years.

"My fault?" I heard myself shout back through an ocean of
tears. "This isn't my fault, Mom! You chose this path! *You*
validated the demons of your past. Not me. And look what it's
done to you. Look what its made of you!"

I stood over my mother with the axe in hand, paying no
credence to the scarecrow version of my dead father that stood just
beyond, nor to the feelings of sharp pain that fired off throughout
my legs and back. A dichotomy of emotions battled within my
mind as I stood there sobbing, staring into the lifeless eyes of my
deranged mother.

"*Sever the ties, son,*" my father whispered like the voice of a
demonic conscience. "Right the wrongs that she caused you. Claim
your destiny tonight. *Sever.*"

With streams of cold tears flowing down my face, I leaned
forward towards my mother while tightening the white-knuckled
grip of my left hand. As I drew close, the reek of decayed flesh
satiated my nostrils. I thought of Spock and Karla one last time,

and then did exactly what had to be done – what I knew I should have done year's prior.

"I forgive you, mom," I sobbed, letting go of the axe. It dropped to the floor with an echoing THUNK. "I forgive you for what you did. I have no more hatred for you; for either of you. I forgive you both, but I'm done with it all. It's over."

A loud shriek of anger rose from behind the chair, sounding as if a cat was being burned alive.

I squeezed my left hand into a tight fist, making sure that I had not dropped the lighter. To my relief, the Zippo was still within my hand. I glanced up at the screeching fiend moments before his gloved hand swept across my line of sight and connected against my right cheek. I saw something in that moment that lifted my spirits despite the pain that only seconds later exploded in my jaw. The face of my father was no longer visible. It had been replaced with the faceless burlap sack that I had known all too well from my manuscript.

The backhand slap from the scarecrow pummeled the side of my face with an amazing feat of strength. A flash of brilliant pain starred my vision as I flew through the air, crashing against the file cabinet. My back struck the edge of the hollowed out locker, creating another burst of agonizing torture throughout my being. My body went numb and limp, the Zippo lighter slipping from my hand.

"You fool!" cried the scarecrow. His voice resounded once again with a raspy and detuned drawl, plagued with an over-saturation of evilness. The boom in his voice surged through the cold air with such a demonic force, that the body of my dead mother exploded into a heap of dust and ash. Her remains hung in the air momentarily, before evolving into the nothingness of the night.

The thudding sound of the scarecrow's boots echoed within the foggy haze of my mind as he drew near to me. He plucked the axe from the ground; I could hear the blade scrape against the floor like a sword being drawn from its sheath.

In the face of great pain, I sent my left hand searching the floor for the lost lighter. It could have bounced anywhere. Blindly I searched, watching as the straw-stuffed despot made his way towards me in a blazing trail of wrath. My hand felt nothing but the cold, carpeted floor; each empty search leaving me to drown in a growing sea of desperation.

about in the wind. At the sound of his whaling cries, the three windows blew out one-by-one in a succession of broken glass. The walls rattled at the deafening sound; the floor quivered like rippling water. The sliding glass door pulsated as if it contained a heartbeat all it's own, and then shattered out into a universe of diamond shards. The cold, outside air rushed into the barn, but was halted as the fire began to spread.

I hit the ground, landing instinctually on my right foot. A sudden throng of pain sliced through my casted leg. I could feel the broken bone shift under the weight of my body yet again. I fell to the ground beneath the intense heat of the jerking scarecrow, momentarily blinded by the nauseating pain.

THE FACELESS ONE, engulfed in a fireball of golden flames, rushed towards the mounds of snow that waited on the outside deck. A trail of fire whipped out behind him like exhaust from a rocket, spreading faster across his straw-stuffed body regardless of his agonizing, wraith-like shrieks. Consumed with madness and folly, the scarecrow ran headlong into the side of the file cabinet, falling into the pile of lighter fluid drenched books within.

A rush of stinging, hot air flowed overhead as a giant fireball shot towards the ceiling. The cabinet of books burst into a pit of fire as THE FACELESS ONE kicked and screamed within the inferno. The weight of his wriggling frame knocked the cabinet on end, spilling a blazing river onto the carpeted floor. The fire took to the carpet like a rioting crowd to the streets, eating away at the fibers with a crackle of purifying laughter.

The nearby cardboard boxes were the next to be consumed by the crawling flames. As the fire spread, the darkness that had horded the barn was replaced with a blaze of orange light. The temperature inside the upper room rose by leaps and bounds, becoming a suck oven more so than an old horse barn.

A cloud of dense smoke began to gather at the top of the ceiling, forcing out the breathable oxygen the way the scarecrow had tried to do to me. The only difference was that the collecting smoke was being more successful, despite the portholes of open air. Every breath I took filled my lungs with more ashen, carbon monoxide, causing a succession of whooping coughs to follow. The back deck was my nearest and only attempt at an escape, but THE FACELESS ONE – who was now nothing more than burning residue – had created a wall of fire in front of the door. The spiral staircase at the far end of the barn was the only other exit, but I did not have enough strength to make it there. And even if I did, there was no way I would have been able to descend the narrow, metal stairs.

I stared into the raging inferno, shielding my eyes from the intensity of the brightness. I felt confident that my death would not come in vain. I would die, knowing that the evil I had created – the wickedness I had harbored within – was finally dead.

"I'm coming, Spock," I whispered into the roar of flames.

Then I closed my eyes, waiting for death to take me.

81
Sheriff Eckhart

The driveway leading into the Sugar Hill Farms Estate branched out into two directions. The path to the left led to the old farmhouse where the Parker's had first dreamed of creating a legacy for the town of Bridgeton. The path to the right, opened into a large gravel parcel of land, which contained the old horse barn.

I brought the police cruiser to a speeding halt, stopping directly in the fork of the driveway as to create a single blockade for both exits. The flashing, blue lights atop the cruiser pierced the night while painting phantom, shadow dancers all throughout the property.

"Look, Sheriff!" Karla said with a burst of fearful excitement. "There's a fire in the barn!"

I followed Karla's pointing finger with my eyes. Through the three side windows I could definitely see the roaring fire within. There was a cloud of smoke escaping through the windows as well, although the majority of the plume seemed to be emitted from the rear of the barn. The flames lapped at the shingled roof like a dog's tongue licking at a bowl of water. With the imminent danger unfolding before us, I dialed the CB radio into the proper frequency, requesting for immediate emergency fire and medical backup.

When I was done calling in the order I turned to Karla, saying, "Stay here. If you see anything unusual, lay on the horn and don't stop until help arrives."

"What if I don't know if it's unusual?" she asked.

"You'll know, Miss Turner. Just keep your eyes open." I jumped out of the vehicle, grabbing a fire extinguisher from the trunk. I un-holstered my nine-millimeter weapon, but before leaving, I peaked my head into the cruiser one last time.

"And *now* would be a good time to keep those prayers going for Clyde, too."

I traipsed through the thigh-high snow leading to the large, sliding door that would allow entrance into the barn. Although the driveway had been plowed (an automatic perk that must have been in the lease when the property was rented), the gravel lot in front of the barn had not been, so I was forced to trudge swiftly through four feet of frozen snow.

I never would have expected that Clyde Baker's horse barn would have become the pinnacle of my career, but as I rushed towards the main entrance, I thought only about helping a life that was in need. Nothing else mattered. Nothing.

82
Mindy

The blue lights from the police cruiser spilled into the garage, catching my sleeping eyes with winks of colored flashes. Upon waking, I watched with bloodshot eyes as blue shadows hopped about on the ceiling above like an animated Rorschach Test. It didn't take long for me to conclude that the flashing blue lights spelled one of two conclusions: either the Sheriff had tracked me down, or it was time to carry out the assignment that had brought me to the cold, greasy garage in the first place.

I ripped away the dusty blankets and snuck to the porthole windows of the garage bay doors. Carefully I peeked outside with deprived eyes: deprived of sleep, deprived of satisfaction, but moreover, I suddenly found myself deprived of my right mind. Although Clyde was refusing to embrace THE RED, I was not. Nor would I ever. It was my only connection to my father, and if it meant giving control of my mind over as well, than so be it. My father was the only person who had ever looked at me as more than just a child. He had loved me – in that special kind of love we shared – and it was still alive and well within me. It burned within my heart and mind like a tormenting swarm of locusts stinging away at my conscience – eating away at my very soul.

After looking outside through the garage doors, I quickly discovered that the source of the blue lights was from only one police vehicle over at the barn. As I watched the Sheriff – *alone* – rush to the main barn door and shoot the lock free from the latch, I became overly elated.

"Kill the damn Takers," I whispered to myself within the lonely silence of the garage. "You saved my life; I kill the Takers for you!"

84
Clyde

The heat grew stronger, burning my skin with an intensity I had never felt before. The nearing flames lapped at my chest, causing me to writhe in agony as if my lungs were being infected by the inferno. The pain was beyond tremendous as the flames began to dance upon the front of my shirt, burning away at the last of my resolve. I blindly began to swat at my chest, forgetting about the stiffness of my broken wrist. As I did so, my right hand shrieked out in pain, pleading with me to stop. And so I did, not realizing that the suffocating heat was gnawing away at the flesh on my hand as well. With one last possible effort, I began to roll around on the carpeted floor until the front of my shirt was extinguished. But although the flames were gone, I could still feel the unrelenting seize of the heat, as if I were slow roasting in an oven.

As I waited for death's messenger, I prayed – not for safety – but for my third and final book to withstand the rigorous flames from within the fireproof cabinet where it had been stored away. I hoped and prayed that the words would fall into the hands of a desperate reader; someone who would cleave to the concepts of love taught by such an incredible dog named Spock. I did not want to see my only true work be ravaged by the same flames that would claim my life.

And so I prayed.

Suddenly there was a noise. A voice calling to me from the distance and nearly drowned out by the roar of the flames. My first thought was that the fire had won and that I was dying. But the voice was not calm and satiated with the angelic peace that I would have expected from a heavenly being. Instead, my name had been spoken with feverish alarm.

Next, there were footsteps – or at least something that resembled boots against wood – followed by an arcane explosion of sounds that caught my ear like an amplified bottle of hairspray. Bewildered by such noises within the raging fire, I forced my eyes to open regardless of the sting from the smoke. Through clouded and weary vision, I saw a sight that made my heart want to burst into joyful tears: Sheriff Eckhart stood beside me. How he had found me, I was unsure. But he did. And he was battling the nearing flames with a bright red fire extinguisher in hand.

The battle raged for a span of time that I could not recall. The hot, ashen air was potent and overpowering. I could feel my lungs spasm with each sweltering, inhaled breath, hoping that the Sheriff's rescue attempt would not prove to be in vain.

The white residue from the extinguisher began to cover the room like snow; the inside world beginning to resemble the world outside the barn. Slowly but surely, the fire began to retard, relinquishing its hold on the fuel it had been feeding on. As the Sheriff's efforts grew in success, the cold fresh air from the outside began to blow into the barn with an icy goodness that I had never been so thrilled to experience before.

The hissing song of a dead fire played throughout the barn; music to my ears it was. Eckhart ran to my side, rolling me carefully onto my back although a fresh batch of pain boiled within my body.

"What in the name of God's green earth happened here, Baker?" Eckhart asked. His voice was hard-hitting and emotionless, but the favoring smile across his soot-smudged face spoke much louder. Something in his eyes told me that he already knew more about the situation than I would have expected him too. "Are you able to walk?"

I shook my head NO, and then added, "Too much pain."

Despite the diminished fire, my breathing was still laborious and shallow which told Eckhart that we were not out of the woods just yet. But regardless of time, I reached up a shaky left hand and took hold of his.

"It's over," I said through a series of stale coughs. "It's finished." It was all I had to say because he was the one person who knew exactly what I meant.

From somewhere outside, a car horn honked once, then twice, and finally a third drawn out blast. Eckhart's attention shifted towards the spiral staircase.

"We've got to get you out of here," Eckhart said while attempting to stand back to his feet.

In one moment, I could see the overweight Sheriff stretching and straining to rise to his feet again. The next however, I watched as a bloody piece of his scalp came ripping off the side of his head due to a long metal object that struck him with a vengeful THUD. Eckhart's eyes rolled up into his skull as a painful grimace manifested upon his face. He looked as if he were trying to see the attacker behind him without actually turning around. A spatter of fresh blood soaked into the white of his thinning hair like wine into a carpet. He swayed on his feet before toppling to the floor. As he disappeared from my sight, Eckhart's assailant became visible.

Mindy!

As hard as it was for me to believe at first, my sister was once again standing before my eyes in the smoldering remains of the fire. The backdrop of night cloaked her filthy body in a rim of silver moonlight. She held a long crowbar in her hand; the tip of the weapon coated with a small, blood-soaked patch of flesh and hair. Her heart beat with an absurd quickness as she stood over the wounded Sheriff like a lion about to administer the killing blow to its prey. Her eyes were like the dead of night – cold and full of unspoken secrets. Although she stared me down in that moment, undoubtingly seeing the look of defeat splayed across my weary face, she paid no attention to me as if I weren't even there. Instead, she turned to face Eckhart, thrusting the tip of one of her shoes into the portly gut of the wounded man. A low groan escaped Eckhart's lips, but not before a second kick was planted into his side.

"Mindy! Stop it!" I cried out as best I could. But my rebuttal only seemed to fuel the assault.

"Shhhh," Mindy replied, hushing me as if I were an infant she was trying to cradle. "This will all be over soon, my Clyde. But we can never be together unless the Takers are removed from your life. It has to be done." With that said, she planted one final kick into the Sheriff's gut.

"He hasn't done anything to you. Leave him alone" I argued through a lungful of smoke and ash.

"Why?" moaned the Sheriff through an almost incoherent mumble. He had been saying something else as well, but the authoritative boom in his voice had been stripped so far down that I hadn't been able to make out any other words.

Turning to me, Mindy spoke in her soft mother-like voice again, "Why are you so worried about him, Clyde? Look at him. Can't you smell the fear all over him? The stink of it makes me sick, and it's making you sick too. These people are trying to take you away from me – from the life that we were always meant to have together. So yes, honey, this man is guilty of much, and he has to pay for his sins."

Mindy whacked the crowbar against the side of Eckhart's knee like a drummer crashing on a cymbal. The sound of a kneecap being smashed echoed in the barn. I cringed as Eckhart whaled loudly into the darkness of the night.

Mindy slowly paced to the other side of the blubbering Sheriff. She wielded the crowbar as if it were a sword and she were a knight. Victorious and valiant. Her eyes, although not blue as I had last remembered them to be, pithed my brain like a pair of demonic awls. The confusion that rushed over me was astounding. And so I screamed. I cried out with my diminishing strength. I screamed for her to stop; for the madness to be over with. But no good came from my fleeting efforts, as if Mindy hadn't even noticed me.

"Death comes to all, but only the Takers fear it." With another swing of the bloody crowbar, Mindy gave Eckhart a matching pair of shattered knees. "You're not afraid are you, Clyde?"

The Sheriff released a maddening cry into the darkness, rattling the walls and my ears alike. The sound pierced my heart with a helpless abandon because I was unable to do anything to stop the insanity. The sound of the Sheriff's whaling lament seemed to aggravate my twisted sister, because the soft demeanor with which she had been speaking, left immediately.

"Will you shut up with all your whining," she screamed while placing her hands to her head as if there was a much louder voice on the inside trying to escape. "It's inevitable Sheriff! It's just the way it has to be! Why can't anybody see that but me? Do you see what he's done to you Clyde? How he's polluted your mind with all of his damn noises and...and his..." Mindy began to stumble over her words and then trailed into a deafening yell as the madness overtook her completely. The fire that had moments ago been devouring the barn was now eating away at the last bit of sanity that she possessed.

was coming in for a kiss. However she stopped three inches away from my lips with a wicked lust burning through her golden eyes. Being so close to her again after a year was surreal to say the least, and as she drew near, the burning sensation on my chest and hand began to pulsate like a beating heart.

"But there was no way that I was going to allow our mother to escape my wrath. She tried alright, but the bottle of pills she downed wasn't a good enough sentence for her. That bitch slaughtered the one man that loved me. Her blood for his. It was the only way to find justice for what she did to our father. So when I found her slouched over in her own vomit, I carried her into the bathtub and cut her up real nice."

Mindy sat backward and began to laugh, especially after seeing the look of confusion peek through the pain in my face. "Don't look so surprised, brother. You were too busy getting settled in to your new college life to notice that I hopped on a plane one morning and flew back out here. It was a rush – really it was. I just wish we could have shared it together. But from now on, it's just you and me. No one else. No Takers."

"So you wrote her suicide letter?" I asked as my entire world began to spin in reverse.

"Don't be stupid. I wasn't going to be pinned to her murder that easily. I could have cared less what that whore's final words were. She just needed to bleed like the pig she was. She was half dead when I got there. I just wanted to make sure that she could look into my eyes one last time before diving headfirst into hell."

"But how did you know what she did to dad? It could have been anyone?" The more that we talked, the more my anger began to stir up against the demented murderer hovering over me.

"I could see it in that woman's eyes. Wasn't it obvious to you! She was a Taker – daddy had told me – and so she had to die. That's why you have to cleanse yourself Clyde! It's the only way that we can carry on daddy's legacy." She began to rub her hands over my chest, as if she were prepared to rip out my heart if I didn't offer it to her willingly. She then took the middle three fingers of her right hand and wiped at the beads of clotted blood that stained her face. She then held her hand out to me, showing me the palm that was now soiled with the innocent blood of a decent man.

"Can't you feel it deep inside of you, the connection we share? Don't deny our destiny Clyde, because together we can purify this stink hole of a planet from all the Takers like mom – all of those self-righteous pricks that couldn't understand the power of THE RED if they were choking on it. We can share the same kind of love that me and daddy did. It's what he would have wanted." Mindy leaned in even closer. She put her lips close to my ear and whispered something that pulled on my spine until it was as taut as the deadly crowbar: "The scarecrow told me so."

With those words fresh off her bloodstained lips, she traced her left palm against her face just as she had done with the right, until both of her palms were covered in the Sheriff's blood. She then began to rub her hands over her chest and torso, leaving red streaks against her body like a grotesque finger painting. Her head swiveled around on her neck as if the sadistic hand-painting gesture was somehow orgasmic for her. She was bathing in innocent blood and the sight and smell sickened me. The sister I had once hoped for had irrevocably been overrun by the demonic series our father had created – THE RED that he passed down into both Mindy and myself.

"What scarecrow?" I asked, trying to roll away from the brutality of the moment, crying all the more as I realized the fullness of the mess I had created with my books. But as I tried to move away, every inch of my body roared beneath the unrelenting hands of pain. My legs and back cried out for a dose of medication that I would never see again. My broken wrist throbbed as if it contained its own pulse, and my chest felt aflame with fire. My thoughts were clouded in the dusk of my mind, and my breathing was heavy and laborious within the smoke-filled barn. I longed for death yet I refused to let THE RED be my demise. My Shadow Life was over and done with. I was going to break the chain of wickedness that my parents had created, whether it meant my life or not. Spock had taught me that lesson, and if I had learned enough to write about his example, than I should have expected to live it.

"You will love the scarecrow, Clyde," Mindy said as she paused her blood bath long enough to act like she was ten years old all over again. She placed her hands on her knees and sat up straight as if she were at a slumber party talking about the cutest boys in her class. "He has no face, but his voice is magical. He helped me get out of prison and find you. You're going to just love him. You'll see."

An explosion of euphoric delight sent Mindy reveling about like a person who relives the memory of a first love in their mind. But her joy was short lived as I spoke up.

465

"He's dead." I was suddenly surprised to hear a resurgence of strength in my voice, so I repeated myself. And louder. "He's dead, Mindy! And I killed him!"

"No. You're lying," she mumbled as her sporadic movements stilled beneath the weight of my unsuspecting comment. Instead of looking down at me however, she stared straight ahead into the darkness of the barn. Her pupils twitched rapidly back and forth as if she were R.E.M. sleeping while being completely awake. "You're a damn liar."

"Look for yourself! He's right over there!" I pointed to the file cabinet that was lying on its side. Mindy rose to her feet and glanced down at the pile of charred books that had been coated with a thick layer of the fire retardant residue. The moment her eyes spotted the remainder of the straw hat that THE FACELESS ONE had worn, her countenance darkened as if by a storm cloud.

Mindy's head slowly turned – her golden eyes streaming with tears as she looked down at me with a contemptuous snarl.

"You killed him," she said in an unusually soft tone as she bent down and unfastened the gun from the holster on Eckhart's side. With the nine-millimeter in hand, she raised it to my face, my eyes staring down the endless chamber of the gun. "You're a damn Taker, just like mom was. Now you have to die."

BANG!

The sound of the gunshot rattled the old horse barn.

A discharge of blood exploded out of Mindy's chest, painting my face with the sticky clumps of her life source. My possessed sister did not fall however. She spun around, facing in the direction of the spiral stairs. She raised her weapon towards the marksman standing in the shadows, but a second bullet pierced through her body. Mindy dropped to her knees, and then finally to her death, facedown in Eckhart's pool of blood.

As she collapsed to the ground, the shooter rushed towards me. When my eyes finally focused, I began to believe that I had been the one shot and killed, because I was seeing the face of an angel hovering over me. The beautiful eyes of Karla Turner looked down into mine, ushering me into a deep sleep.

PART FOUR
the ways of the farmer

85
Clyde

Thanksgiving that year was spent at Saint Luke's Hospital, but it was the best holiday I had ever experienced.

I awoke sometime early Thursday morning; Karla's shining face was the first thing I saw. There was so much that I had wanted to tell her – so many questions I had for her as well – but before I was able to tap into that wellspring of information, I had to dive into the pool of humbleness. I laid out my apology to Karla with cold, bitter tears, relieved with her acceptance and awestruck by the apology she offered in return. We cried, holding each other within the small confines of that hospital room.

With the air finally cleared, we spent the next couple of hours rehashing the events of the past month, starting first with how she had managed to rescue me from Mindy. She explained how she had tried signaling to the Sheriff with the car horn when she saw Mindy running towards the snow-covered back deck, crowbar in hand. Seeing the woman who had been arrested for attempted murder, slinking towards the barn had sent her into a defense mechanism mode. So Karla had searched the police cruiser for any kind of weapon, happening to stumble upon Eckhart's spare gun in the glove box.

From there, we backtracked and discussed her stand at the church and the mysterious old woman who had given the missing clue they had been needing about the barn and the evilness that had been validated within it. It was the key that Eckhart had needed to make the proper connections.

that required McNamara to fix up the barn into pristine shape at the first sign of Spring. All I had to do was fund the project, which I gratefully agreed to do.

I had considered asking McNamara to fortify the gate and stonewall with much greater reinforcements, but I never thought to do so. Had I ever opted to walk out that way again, I would have learned that the fire that had been spreading within the barn that night had also symbolically spread across the land beyond the gate, purifying it from the evilness that had been so prevalent over the last twenty-five years. Nobody had ever been able to give me an answer as to why the barn and the gated land had possessed such a mystical connection, but the reasoning wasn't too important to me. I had learned what I had needed to from the place, and in the end, that was all that really mattered.

My agent, Jackson Slater made a visit out my way for the New Year. I had called him out, telling him that I had finished a third book, but that I wanted him in my presence while he read it. He had been confused – of that I had no doubt – but the elation of the news urged him to oblige my request. After reading through the book, his reaction was just as I had expected.

"Nothing like your other books, that's for sure," was the comment Slater repeated well into the New Year. I informed him that there would never be any other books like the first two, and that the publisher's would just have to understand. Slater didn't believe it would work, but as my agent – the man receiving a hefty payment to push my stories through to print – he agreed to give it a lick-and-a-promise.

By mid-January, the publisher's were still considering the idea of printing a book that was so out-of-the norm for me.

On February twenty-second, the phone call came in from Slater. He advised me that the publisher's agreed to send the book to print, but for only a limited amount of copies. They weren't willing to the throw their money into the fire because an author decided to 'find God', as they called it. The repercussions for pushing the book through to print were simple: there would be no renewal of contract for Clyde Baker. I was more than fine with that decision.

Other than that, the remainder of the winter was spent with Karla. As I had hoped, our friendship danced into a blossoming relationship. The air outside might have been cold during the lingering winter months, but the heat of our love grew by unstoppable leaps and bounds.

The Spring rains pushed into Bridgeton by early March. By the end of the same month, all residual snow was gone from the land. As promised by McNamara, the first week of April found the barn swarming with construction crews. The men worked long days, utilizing the comfort of the Spring air to kick their work into high gear. By the second week of May, the restoration of the Sugar Hill Farms horse barn was complete, punctuated by the package I received in the mail from Slater – the first two copies of my book SERVE. Hot off the press. Just as I had requested.

The following night, as I handed Karla her copy of SERVE, she found an engagement ring hidden within the carved out pages within. She received my offer with joyous tears and delight. We were married the following month.

The connection that Karla and I shared was just as magical as the bond that had linked the barn to the land beyond the gate – even more so. My love for her grew exponentially with each passing day and I vowed to myself that the ways of my Shadow Life would never enter the marriage. As I contemplated that thought, I stumbled upon a clever realization. For thirty years I had lived to please only myself; to fulfill every want and dream of mine that I could. But in light of my new life I began to think of ways to bring the joys of Karla's heart to fruition. Her love was where my heart resided and I sought to put her needs before my own. I remembered back to one of our very first conversations together, and how she had told me about her desire to live on the beach somewhere down south. So with that in mind, I began researching homes for us – and for the family that we would start together. In love. When I shared the idea with Karla, she was overcome with joy.

"Besides," she had said, "we're never going to make the impact that's needed without moving into something new. We're stagnant here. We have to push forward. We have to give SERVE a chance."

After some minor planning, Karla and I had decided that a fresh start for the both of us would be on the beaches of eastern Georgia. We also agreed that we would settle into the new home, and then immediately take to the road on a national book tour of our own. We knew that the publisher's were dropping the ball with the marketing of SERVE, and that the only way to get it in as many hands as possible would be to self-promote it. So we began to plan accordingly.

been too small for the both of them, which is why Maureen had opted to rent the old Sugar Hill Farms place.

The prospect of having such a large spread of land to adventure was appealing at first to young Emmy, but it didn't take long for the illusion of joy to be squashed by the reality of loneliness. Maureen would spend nearly twelve hours a day at work and the rest of her time at Jack's – the local two-steppin' country bar near the college – looking for Mr. Right, or at least a less-attractive stepson version who would be willing to put out and shut up. So needless to say, young Emmy found herself all alone. And the property that had once looked inviting quickly became suffocating. So afraid of spending her time all by herself, Emmy had asked her aunt for a dog, but Maureen adamantly refused.

"A dog would destroy the house and cost too much damn money," was the aunt's typical response, leaving Emmy to fend for herself in a loveless world.

As the fall season prepared for winter, Emmy stumbled upon quite a surprise while getting off the bus one blustery day after school. There was a small black puppy; cold and hungry in the Timothy grass near the old horse barn. The sound of the young dog's crying is what had snagged Emmy's heart and drawn her attention to him. The puppy was skittish at first, but after waiting patiently through the sniffing ritual that bonds a stray dog to its new friend, the two of them became inseparable.

"Are you lost little puppy?" Emmy would ask him. "Do you not have anyone to love you either?"

Emmy immediately had her craw set on keeping the dog, but she had to be clever if she was going to outwit her aunt. So rather than bringing the hungry and cold puppy – whom she had named Boo because of the dog's crying that had caught her attention – back to the house, she found refuge in the newly constructed barn. But as Emmy stepped into the upper level of the barn with Boo cradled in her arms, she stumbled upon a book that she found lying in the center of the great room. With immense curiosity, the young girl sat herself down in the middle of the barn and began to read from an odd-looking book called SERVE. She read it aloud to Boo as they cuddled away the afternoon.

Everyday Emmy would return to the barn with food and water for her newfound companion, reading a new chapter each visit. It didn't take her too long to finish the book, but when she was done, she found herself crying hysterically with cold bitter tears for the loneliness and loveless life that she endured. The next day, little

Emmy started the book all over again, finding the story within to be steeped in a reality that she had never known but had always hoped for. So as the days slipped away, both human and puppy who had not known love, learned to love each other with the greatest of zest while reading a thin paperback book in the arms of an old horse barn.

After reading through the book a handful of times, Emmy Freedman's outlook on life began to change. She realized that there was a true, genuine love that did *indeed* exist in life. Boo had been her Spock, and had loved her greatly, but little Emmy Freedman was determined to find the same kind of love within another person. A few months later, after more disappointing heartbreak and endless searching, the young, country girl found what she had been looking for – the true love she had been in need of. She found it within the love and forgiveness that only God could offer. It was a find that caused her much ridicule and scorn from her classmates at school, as well as from her aunt and her revolving door of boyfriends, but Emmy cleaved to the love that she and Boo had found, never wanting to let go of such an amazing gift.

Years later however, Emmy found that same kind of love from a young man at the college she attended. Soon after, they were wed and began a family of their own.

Her husband's name was Edmund Hightower. They had a son who went on to share the ways of love's beautiful sacrifice with thousands of people worldwide, launching one of the largest revolutions of faith and love in the twenty-first century. Despite the rough times that their son endured in his adolescent years, Edmund and Emmy Hightower were beyond proud of him.

Their son's name was Gordon.

His friends all called him Flash.

Afterthoughts

If you've reached this point in your reading, then let me begin with a great big "Thank you." As an author, I appreciate the dedication and commitment that a reader makes when embarking into a new book – an unfamiliar journey. And that is exactly what this novel has been. *A journey.* The story was written and crafted with that very purpose in mind, albeit not just a literary expedition, but rather an opportunity to allow the concepts of this story to venture into your heart and mind.

Beyond The Gate deals with many issues, many of them darker and edgier than what we normally allow into our personal comfort zones. But then again, life is uncomfortable as well. Unlike this book, we cannot close life and hide from it. We must face it head on, dealing with the highs-and-lows, the ins-and-outs. The choice we do have however, is whether or not we will allow the fears and trepidations of life to overtake and consume us, or if we will learn how to overcome and rise above it all. It is that dichotomy of life – the battle within our souls – that was created through the characters of Clyde and Mindy. Which path are you following? Which will you seek?

This novel cost two-and-a-half years of my life to put into words, and underwent many literary facelifts along the way. And it was well worth it. For you. *The reader.* But regardless of the edits and rewrites that took place, the concept of Flash's character remained a constant from the beginning. The story was forged from the idea of Flash – the notion of how exponentially amazing love can blossom if we seek out the needs of others in this life – even if we have never met the other individuals. Even if they haven't been born yet. If we look beyond our own selfish desires, we might just hear the broken heart of someone in need – a soul that is crying out in desperation. Perhaps from a loved one, a family member, a neighbor, a colleague, or a complete stranger that we've never met. If we allow love to shine on our path, we will bypass the pitfalls of this life and be able to reach out a hand to that burdened soul.

I, myself was that person crying out in need, seeking a love that I knew not from my youth – seeking a truth that I had blinded myself from for far too long. But I eventually discovered *that* love – I found it within the forgiveness and grace of my Lord, Jesus Christ – and it was that very love that allowed this novel to pour out of my heart and into yours. I have recently been honored and privileged to proof-read the forthcoming book by Christine Bowen titled "Be The Storm". I mention it here because it speaks of one's journey through life, searching for goodness. In the case of this novel, Flash's character needed Clyde to speak of such goodness. But what about in the case of your life's story? Is there someone waiting on you to reach a hand of help? Is there another person hidden by the shadows of your own fears?

All in all, I want to say thank you one last time. Having you come along on this journey with me has forged a relationship that I greatly admire and appreciate. More so than just a bond between author and reader, but rather a connection that goes so much deeper. It is found in the words between the lines, in the love behind the pages, and in the journey beyond the gate. God bless.

– DTA

About The Author

DANIEL T. ADAMS is a debut novelist, but is never in short supply of events with which to fill his time. He lives in Atlanta, Georgia and is the mohawk-wearing, bass guitarist for the rock band TRUE WITNESS (www.truewitness.com). When he's touring with the band, he finds quiet moments with which to sculpt his story ideas. You can visit him at www.danieltadams.com and sign up for the Daniel T. Adams Newsletter.

Made in the USA
Charleston, SC
12 March 2015